Shadow Summoner

Choronzon Chronicles Book One

Tess Adair

Cover designed by Ravven (www.ravven.com)
Formatting by Polgarus Studio (www.polgarusstudio.com)

Published in the United States by Tower Park Press
ISBN: 978-0-9977500-0-3

If you would like to get access to free content and be notified when Tess Adair's next novel is released, please sign up for her mailing list by going to her website at: https://www.tessadair.com/

Origins

My father always told me I was born with my eyes open. It was a story he liked to repeat from time to time, like a favorite party anecdote—only he couldn't relate it in company. This story was private. Creation myths, they're called.

He told me the myth because he thought I needed it. He thought I sensed that I was wrong somehow, and I needed an explanation. He used to bring out the photo albums that archived my early years—picture after picture of a small, oddly still child, dark eyes wide and unblinking. I'm never smiling in those pictures, either alone or in a group. Every few pages, the books are punctuated by entire class portraits. In every one, a girl with dark eyes and tied-back dark hair stands a little apart from the other children—or perhaps they stand apart from her—and stares with those wide eyes at the camera.

He need not have bothered with the myth. Every child thinks they're a little different—it's our earliest solipsistic impulse. It's so human. To feel lost is to feel alive; we're a species of solipsists. Big human brains are a mistake of evolution—too big to find satisfaction in small lonely lives.

And anyway, when I was that young, I never suspected a thing.

I just didn't like to get my picture taken. I found cameras innately suspicious. Why would anyone need an image of me? I quietly held the belief that their purposes were nefarious, and I expressed it by refusing to obey any photographer's request for a smile.

I never thought anything was wrong with me. He could have just told me the truth. I think about that sometimes. What would I have done differently, had I known?

When she was ten years old, they went on a road trip to see her aunt. Charles Logan loved road trips. He liked to think of himself as something of a nomad, even though they never moved anywhere. He'd called the estate his home base since before she was born, but they went on trips all the time. When she was ten, they went to see her aunt at Other Side, and they stopped at a gas station.

The rain was hard against the window, and the sky was so dark she could hardly tell it was day. Charles pulled to a stop near one of the pumps, set the brake, and turned to her.

"Do you need to go to the restroom?"

She shook her head, staring sullenly.

"All right. I'm going to go inside, and I might be a few minutes." He turned down the edges of his mouth, his best attempt at looking stern and imposing. "You will stay in the car. You will not wander off, under any circumstances."

She didn't nod this time. She only stared. Charles sighed and went inside.

Years later, when she tried to recall the memory in full, the only thing she could be sure of was the sound of the rain. She remembered, vaguely, reading a book about another world, but she couldn't remember the book or the world. And she remembered thinking she could see something, about thirty feet ahead of her. Something out in the rain.

Did she see something? It was gone so fast.

She had to wait in the car. She looked over at the store inside the gas station, checking for her father's outline. He would know what to do, if anything was to be done—he was good at that. As she watched, he disappeared behind the bathroom door.

Then, all of a sudden, the rain seemed to get quieter, almost silent. She glanced out the windshield ahead of her, but it looked as heavy as ever. It was only the sound that had changed.

She told herself to ignore it. To go back to her book. Back to her second world.

But then, again, she saw something. Just for a moment, just a flash. Something flashed in front of her.

The rain was definitely quieter now. In fact, she could barely hear it. She could barely hear anything. It was almost as though someone had shut a door somewhere, and it had sealed her off from the auditory world.

Then, at the back of her brain, she felt the slightest suggestion.

Come find me.

It was similar to hearing a voice, only she heard nothing. Instead she *felt* it. She could feel, in the back of her mind, a presence trying to speak to her.

She also felt, somehow, that she wasn't supposed to know it was there. She could feel the voice, but the voice didn't know that. The voice thought it left no trace.

She was supposed to come outside. She was not supposed to know that someone had whispered it to her first.

Come find me.

The sound of the rain came back. She glanced back inside the gas station, but her father hadn't come out yet. When she looked down, she found that her hand already hovered over the door handle. She pulled it back, to make sure she could. Then she pressed down on it and stepped outside.

Even zipped up in her rain coat with the hood fully secured over her head, she felt the force of the wet cold outside. She closed her door audibly and walked forward, absolutely certain that if she only went far enough, she would see what she had already seen—the brief flash in the storm.

After a moment, she realized she was coming up on the broad side of an eighteen wheeler truck. The rain was so thick she hadn't seen it before. Now she could make out the outline, the edges, and the wavering shadow on the side.

The shadow? What shadow? There was no shadow.

Only there was. She blinked, and it was gone. Had never been. She blinked again and it returned. She stopped walking, closed her eyes with purpose, and took on a stern tone inside her own head.

The shadow is real. You see the shadow.

She opened her eyes again.

She could see the shadow. Only it wasn't a shadow—it looked like a man. An old, pale, shriveled man, shoulders slumped forward and curling inward inside a tattered trench coat. She couldn't quite make out his face, but what she could see of it looked crumpled somehow. The longer she looked, the more pronounced his deformity became.

When he grinned, his mouth revealed a deep black hole. No light escaped. As she gazed at it, a thought came to her like something unbidden, like it had been planted there by someone else: *nothing escapes.*

The grinning hole tilted slowly to the side.

Come find me.

She looked it straight on, but she sensed that it didn't quite look back at her—its eyes moved in her direction, but only took in her form. It never fixated on her face.

It didn't know yet that she could see it, too.

Come find me.

She knew she was supposed to keep walking. It wanted her to. She was more vulnerable if she kept walking. Harder to help.

She planted her feet. She allowed her gaze to go slack, to drift aimlessly around ahead of her, keeping it in her sights but not pinning it down. She couldn't let it know that she knew.

Come find me!

Impatience seeped through the voice now. The misshapen man took a step forward, and the hairs on the back of her neck stood up.

How quickly could it move? It took another slow step, halting and awkward. Was it still finding its footing? Or was its hesitance some new kind of trick?

Come find me.

How limited was its coercion? How broad?

Come find me.

It took two more halting steps, and she tensed invisibly. She was ready.

With another flash, the misshapen man closed all the space between them, launching himself at her in full attack.

Years after this moment, she would remember that she raised

her crossed arms over her face and launched herself right back at him.

Apart from that, she wouldn't be able to remember much. Her father came outside and screamed some nonsense words into the air, and she saw the gray sky turn red with fire, and then the fire was gone. And so was the misshapen man.

She bore no signs of an attack. No bruises, no abrasions, no broken skin. Her father turned her arms over in his hands, checking to make sure when she told him she wasn't hurt. Then he told her to get back in the car.

"What was that?" she asked.

Charles Logan said nothing. He turned the key over, and the engine came to life. Did he think if he ignored her, she would forget?

"What *was* that?"

"It wasn't much," he answered gruffly. "If this rain doesn't let up, we're going to be late getting into Other Side."

She stared at him in disbelief. He ignored her and drove.

She turned her arms over, trying to see them on all sides.

How could she be unhurt?

She remembered throwing up her arms, and she remembered feeling something, some kind of incredible pain bursting through her forearms, from her wrists to her elbows. Had he struck her? What else could it have been? But her arms looked perfect now—completely unmarred. Had she imagined it all?

Later that night, she dreamed of monsters. Or, at least, she thought she did. She dreamed that she walked through a crowd of hooded creatures, each one facing away from her. The closer she got to any one, the more certain she became that it was a monster. But when she reached it, she spun it around to face her.

And instead of a monster's face, she saw her own.

The whole thing was quite enough to make her question her solipsism.

Chapter 1
Pest Control

H. C. Logan opened her eyes onto a room she didn't recognize. It wasn't the first time. Rolling over to her side, she swung her arm over the edge of the bed until she found the nearest phone. One button click—10:47am. She felt a stab of confusion, followed immediately by annoyance. Hadn't she set an alarm the night before?

Then she heard it. The faintest sound, a little *meep*. Barely audible. She pushed herself to standing and followed it over to the far end of the room. There, on the floor, a little light blinked through the fabric of her pants. She reached down and clicked her phone off, irritated but not surprised to see that her battery was almost depleted: the alarm had been going off for over three hours.

With a sigh, she pulled her pants back on, then started a search for her shirt. A solid black bra hung draped over a lamp in the corner of the room—had she thrown it? She walked over and grabbed it, watching the straps slide over the unnatural-looking markings on her arms. Only the inscription inside her left elbow was actually artificial, but fortunately for her, that was the one most people asked about. She made one more sweep of the room and finally located her shirt, then slipped it on and covered up most of the markings entirely. She glanced back at the bed—her companion slept soundly. As her gaze briefly lingered, his body shifted, causing the blanket to slide softly off his chest. For a moment, she contemplated what it might be like to rouse him for another round. But she quickly dismissed the thought. She had other things to do.

Once she'd checked her fully clothed appearance in the mirror to make sure she looked roughly civilized, she slid out and relocked the door, then scampered down the stairs.

At the bottom, she clicked her phone on and redialed the last number called, hoping her battery would hold out. She listened to it ring twice, then heard a female voice answer.

"Hi, Miss Humphrey? This is Logan. Yes, the private contractor. Listen, I'm calling to let you know that due to unforeseeable circumstances, I'm going to be about an hour late. Oh no, I'm fine. I, uh…to be honest, I took the wrong exit. Well, I figured it out eventually, and I'm on the right path now. Yes, I will see you then. Ciao."

With that out of the way, she took a sweeping survey of the street around her, trying to get her bearings. She remembered that she'd left her bike at the bar because her companion the previous evening only lived a few blocks away. After a moment, it clicked into place. She headed south.

There, about a block and a half down, she found the bar. At the far end of the miniscule parking lot, she spotted her neon green Kawasaki Ninja. Good. At least no one had stolen it. Clearly the thieves in Ohio didn't appreciate a good bike when they saw one.

She crossed the lot and fished her keys out of her pocket, then pushed the small one into a lock just underneath the back end of the seat. The seat swung up, revealing a hidden storage compartment, and her messenger bag. Propelled by a sudden stab of suspicion, she pulled open the bag to check on the contents—and found her sealed cedar case of tools right where she'd left it. She closed the bag again. Glancing up, she scanned the street before her for a sign of coffee. She didn't have to look far. Making sure to close the compartment until it clicked shut, she took her bag and strode across the street, where a small café was in full swing.

She needed to make sure she looked presentable and clean, and she needed caffeine. After that, she had a job to do.

The sun still shone a little brighter than she liked when she exited the café twenty minutes later, having downed three espressos in quick succession while her phone charged underneath a table. She couldn't explain why, but for some reason sunny days had always made her nervous. She preferred a slate-gray sky—the kind that endlessly promised rain but never delivered. Sunny days were too complacent, too cheerful. Sunny days allowed people to lie.

She returned to her Ninja, put her bag back in its hole, slipped on her jacket, and unstrapped her helmet from the back. When she'd first started riding, she hadn't liked the helmets. She'd found them cumbersome, uncomfortable, and a little dorky. But the more she rode, the fonder she became of them. The helmet afforded her something that nothing else ever had—anonymity. Inside it, she became unrecognizable and undifferentiated. It helped, of course, that her thick leather jacket happened to disguise most curves in her body, and to exaggerate her shoulders ever so slightly. In the jacket and helmet, speeding down an open road, she felt more like an extension of the motorcycle than a separate organic being.

Aside from that, she'd once been thrown from the bike and over a nearby fence. She liked the helmet a lot more after that.

Just as she swung her leg over the side, the phone in her pocket emitted a shrill ring. She pulled it out to check the screen. *Knatt.* She sighed and started the engine, debating setting her phone to silent and ignoring him for a while. But the ring of the phone felt far more pressing in her hand than it had in the jacket. If only she hadn't pulled it out at all.

"Good morning," she said as she answered the phone, trying to sound like a happier, more prepared version of herself. Trying to sound cheerful, like the sun wanted her to be.

His response fell short of cheerful.

"You're late, aren't you?" His clipped British accent lent an extra note of condescension to his restrained annoyance.

"What makes you say that?"

"The fact that it is currently 11:20am in your time zone, and yet you are not currently located at the private residence of Miss Adelaide Humphrey, our client."

"And how do you know that I'm not currently located at the private residence of Miss Adelaide Humphrey, our client?"

"I gave her a call two minutes ago to ask her, and she informed me that you were not there."

"Well, it hurts to know that you don't trust me, Knatt. I thought we were closer than that."

"I can hardly be expected to trust you, Miss Logan, if every time I look to find where you are, I discover that you are not where you are supposed to be."

Logan let out a quiet huff, which she hoped he couldn't hear. Half the reason she always showed up late to these things was that she didn't want to do them in the first place. Taking money from wealthy clients had been her father's way of doing things. If she had her choice, she would have forgone the mundanities of paranormal nuisance in favor of bigger challenges. But Knatt had been her father's partner, so he was used to her father's business strategy. He expected it. He expected it of her. When she'd taken over, he'd been completely incapable of accepting any change.

And Logan had to get used to that.

"All right. Yes, I am not with the client yet. But I informed her ahead of time that I was going to be late, and it's only because I got a little lost on the way to her place. She didn't have a problem with it, and she knows when to expect me. Okay?"

Knatt was silent for a long moment. She wondered if perhaps, at last, she'd performed acceptably. But when he spoke and she heard the tone of his voice, she knew immediately that she hoped for too much.

"Henrietta Logan. I have known you since you were an infant. When you were four years old, your father forgot you at a park two miles away from the estate. By the time he realized his mistake, you'd already found your way back. In your entire life, you have never once *gotten lost*."

Now it was Logan's turn for silence. She remembered the story, but it meant something entirely different to her. To Knatt, it was an example of her ability and her competence—proof that when she made a mistake, it was not out of ineptitude but carelessness, the more dire sin in his eyes. But to her, it told the story of her entire childhood—always forgotten by her father, always left alone to find her own way. If she was good at it now, it was only because she'd had no other choice. And Knatt knew it.

"Fine," she answered, her tone blank. "What matters is that I've already informed the client. The rest is my own business. I'll see you when I get home."

She hung up without waiting for his response and slid her phone back into her pocket. This time, she set the ringer to silent.

Miss Adelaide Humphrey's estate was about 30 miles out of town. Logan maneuvered carefully past the small suburban stretch, then took off, racing down the lonely backroad far above the speed limit. All too quickly, she arrived at the dense line of trees demarcating the entrance onto the hundred acre property. As she passed through them, she forced herself to slow down. The drive up to the house was lined with security cameras.

Just as the land before her started to curve upward, she found her way obstructed by a gate. She pulled over to the right and pressed the buzzer. After a moment, the gate clicked and swung wide open. She and her Ninja sailed on through, and it swung shut again behind her.

She hated places like this. It all felt so ostentatious— ostentatious, and paranoid. In fact, those two words described the majority of her father's clients. And underneath the shallow grab to impress with material wealth, she always felt something rotten lurking. Places like this had bad histories. They had ghosts.

A small mansion loomed before her, waiting at the top of the hill. It looked like something in a movie, like it had been ripped out of the past and transplanted to this spot, right in front of her. The drive curved in front of the door, then continued around, making a circle around the building. She pulled up to the huge oak front doors, where a young, white, blonde-haired woman stood with a straight back, silently watching her.

She swung off the Ninja and removed her helmet in one smooth motion.

"Good morning, Miss Humphrey." She projected that voice again—the happy morning-person voice.

Her face impassive, the young woman glanced down at her gold-banded watch.

"I suppose it is still morning, yes. Are you Henrietta?"

"Actually, I prefer Logan. Henrietta is my father's name."

A mixture of confusion and mild distaste took over the young woman's features. She couldn't tell if this was a joke or not, and she didn't seem to approve of the ambiguity.

"Very well. You may call me Adelaide. Please come along inside, I'd like us to get started as soon as possible." Just as she was about to disappear into the house, she paused to glance back at Logan once more. "Oh. I realize I never mentioned this to Mr. Knatt, but you'll be meeting Richard inside as well. Hope that's not a problem."

Logan's features froze in her placating smile, and she used all her concentration to keep from rolling her eyes. She knew for a fact that Knatt had relayed the necessity of clearing the house of all other occupants. Adelaide appeared to be ignoring this directive without shame. She barely even paused long enough to let Logan know before striding forth into her foyer.

With a sigh, Logan got her bag from its compartment and clipped her helmet to the back once more, then followed Adelaide in. Unlike her client, she was in no particular rush to get started. She knew that starting earlier didn't mean ending earlier—these kinds of things worked on their own schedule, not the one you set for them. But it was always impossible to tell the client that.

When she passed under the doorway, she felt an electric shiver shoot up her spine. Out of habit, she glanced around, but the cause was not immediately visible. This surprised her none.

The house looked exactly like she had suspected it would. They came into a tall, wide entryway with a marble staircase in the center, curving upward. The ceilings were high, and the walls were adorned with massive paintings in thick, heavy frames. She followed Adelaide back into the house, until they passed through double French doors into a large dining room with a long stone table running through the middle. A white, brown-haired man, presumably the aforementioned Richard, stood at the back of the room, leaning against the window and staring out onto the grounds. He didn't look back at them when they entered.

"So how does this work?" the young woman asked with a certain sharpness to her voice. She entered last, and shut the French doors behind her as she did.

Logan restrained the rush of frustration. Some clients were a little *too* eager to get to the point of it all. The sooner they learned to follow her lead, the better.

"We will certainly get to that." She hiked her bag a little higher on her shoulder, surveying the room to decide the best place to set down. "But before we do, can you tell me if there's anybody else in the house?"

Adelaide paused, her pale, pinched brow furrowing ever so slightly.

"The house is empty. We dismissed the help for the day, just as Mr. Knatt requested."

"Good. It makes everything easier to clear the property as much as possible." She glanced over at Richard by the window, but didn't mention that she wished he had been cleared out for the day as well. There was little she could do about it now.

"So, what do we do?"

Logan had reached the mid-point of the table, which looked to be approximately the center of the room as well. She set her bag down on the stone top and pulled out a few tapered candles.

"Tell me your story," she said, now pulling out a high-backed chair and sitting in it.

"Pardon?"

Logan leaned back and gave her a well-practiced smile.

"I want you to tell me everything that's happened so far. You know, your version of events. Your, I suppose you'd call it, *experience* here. Why did you decide to call Mr. Knatt in the first place?"

"Ah, yes." Adelaide glanced over at the man by the window, who still hadn't turned around. When she turned back to Logan, she looked uncertain. "Didn't, ah, didn't Mr. Knatt tell you…what we told him?"

Knatt's precise words had been, "It sounds like a standard

summoning gone wrong, but it's difficult to say how long ago it happened. Either Miss Adelaide Humphrey has no knowledge of the original event, or she has chosen to withhold that information, for reasons which remain her own."

But her client didn't need to know about any of that, so Logan just turned on a new smile.

"He did, but I find that some stories lose a certain flavor in the retelling. So I'd like to hear it directly from you. How did this all start?"

Almost like an unbreakable habit, Adelaide's gaze flicked back over to the man in the corner before settling on Logan once more. Then she pulled out the seat across from her and perched on the edge of it. "Well, ridiculous as it sounds…it would seem we're being…haunted."

She paused, possibly for dramatic effect, and glanced over at Logan like she was waiting for a reaction. Logan nodded blandly and motioned for her to continue.

"Well, it's the house, really. The house is haunted. We always thought—well, my father had a bit of a penchant for traveling to foreign lands and bringing back, you know, *exotic* artifacts. They all had these stories attached to them—this item was cursed, this one belonged to a ghost, that sort of thing. Of course I never believed any of it, until…until things started happening a-again. And, you know, I remembered that Father used to talk about these men he knew from a long time ago—a Mr. Logan and his partner, the paranormal contractors. We were to call them if we ever came across anything *out of the ordinary*, he used to say. The number we had on file still worked, so…here you are."

"You said things started happening *again*," said Logan

without missing a beat. "When did they happen before?"

"Well, the house has always been strange," said Adelaide. Already, her demeanor relaxed, her voice taking on a warmer tone. So keen to tell her story, she forgot to maintain her veneer of disapproval. Logan was unsurprised of course; people loved telling their own stories, and they loved it best when they suspected that the story made them in any way more interesting than they otherwise would be. "Ever since I was a little girl, there have been…signs. Nothing ever seemed to stay in the right place, you know? It always started small—you put your glass down on a table, then you turn around and it's on the counter instead. Or sometimes, you'd be across the room and a glass would topple to the floor and shatter, even though no one was around. But then it got bigger—paintings jumping off the walls, tables flipping over by themselves. I thought it had stopped sometime after I went away to college. My parents certainly claimed it had. But…it seems to have started up again. A few months ago, the chandelier fell down from the ceiling of its own accord, nearly killing one of the staff. And with that, everything flared right back up again."

Logan tapped her fingers on the table in front of her, considering her phrasing carefully. "You said your father used to collect…extraordinary artifacts?"

"Oh yes," said Adelaide, nodding enthusiastically. "He used to call himself, uh, a *connoisseur of the mystical and bizarre.* Why do you ask?"

Logan's smile drew taut. "The more information, the better. Do you know if your father ever *used* anything he collected? Did he simply store them somewhere, or did you ever see him take them out and do anything with any of them?"

Adelaide appeared uncertain. She flicked yet another glance over at the man in the corner. "Well, yes, occasionally. One item in particular he'd gone to some lengths to get, so I think he felt rather proud of it. I saw him bring it into his office from time to time. Why? Does that matter?"

Logan braced herself for the blowback that was likely to follow. "As a matter of fact, it does. You see, while the events you've described could possibly qualify as a *haunting*, so to speak, that's actually rather unlikely. If by 'haunting' you mean the deceased and angry spirit of a human being trying to make its presence known, of course."

Adelaide folded her arms over her chest, looking petulant. It occurred to Logan that her client didn't like to be told she was wrong.

"I don't understand. What else could it be?"

"Well, it's not a definite, but it's much more likely that we're looking at a demon, probably trapped just beyond the veil, so to speak. Most hauntings, as you think of them, are more about the *occurrence* than the entity. A being of some kind is trapped between worlds, or between states, and whatever it's doing inside that in-between state is reverberating through to this side. Portraits falling, objects moving—those are reverberations."

"But, if it's a demon instead of a ghost—then how did it get there?"

Logan clicked her tongue, considering again. There was no way to answer that without at least implying an accusation. Of course, she could choose to be indirect about it. "If a demon's there, then that means someone summoned it—or, actually, that they tried to summon it, but they either couldn't finish the job, or they chose not to. So, with the ritual started but not completed…the demon gets trapped."

That mixture of confusion and disdain crossed Adelaide's face again, but she quickly shook it off.

"I see," she said. "Well, I still think ours is a ghost. We've seen—oh, what do they call it? Ah, yes—*spectral phenomena*. Haven't we, Richard?"

At long last, Richard, still standing silently at the window, noticed the presence of the women in the room. He turned to face them, revealing his pale, pinched demeanor—which was not entirely dissimilar to Adelaide's. He huffed at the sight of them, and placed his hands delicately in his pockets.

"We have," he answered, surveying Logan closely. "Are you the person she hired? The expert exterminator, or whatever?"

Logan's practiced smile unfurled.

"The private contractor. Yes."

"Private contractor. Right. Professional ghost chaser."

Her smile held tight. Despite his proximity to their conversation, he'd clearly absorbed only select pieces of it—and apparently none of those pieces included anything Logan had said. Still, she'd heard far worse.

"If you like. Now, could you please detail for me what kind of phenomena you've witnessed?"

Adelaide jumped back in, bouncing a little in her seat as she spoke again.

"You see, that's how I'm sure it's a ghost. Every time we've seen it, it's looked exactly like a little girl. She's either got a little doll or a little ball, and she throws it at you. Or sometimes she runs at you. But she always disappears before she gets to you. Just like a ghost."

Logan nodded patiently at Adelaide before glancing back to Richard.

"Is that what you've seen, too? You've seen a little girl?"

Richard's mouth pushed into a thin line. "I've seen what she's describing."

The answer struck her wrong, its careful avoidance sticking out immediately. Logan could feel her patience running out. "Have you seen a little girl?"

"Well, no." He glanced briefly over at Adelaide before dropping his gaze to the floor. "When I see it, it's a little boy. But everything else is the same."

Logan looked back at Adelaide, who wore an expression of shocked betrayal on her face. But she soon seemed to pull herself together with a small shake, and spoke again.

"Okay, so, what—it's a ghost that changes genders?"

Some people really took to an idea and held to it.

"Like I was saying, it's unlikely that it's a ghost. There's a chance it didn't even originate in this reality. Most likely someone tried to summon it here, although it may have tried to break through on its own. And then it got stuck. Now, it's trying to get itself unstuck."

Of course, the barriers between this world and every other could get complicated, as could the ways a demon might find itself stuck between them, but the likelihood of it being anything other than a summoning gone wrong was so remote, Logan found no point in bringing it up. Besides, she had learned that the simpler the explanation, the likelier the client was to understand it.

"Unstuck?" Adelaide asked, eyebrows raised. "How does it do that?"

"By breaking through into the world it was called to in the first place."

Logan reached into her bag and pulled out a few more candles, planning to place them strategically along the table. Luckily for her, she didn't need much light to see by, but most people needed a bit more help.

"So you're going to stop it?" Adelaide nervously fingered her crystal encrusted watch.

"No, I'm not. I'm going to help it." She pulled out her lighter and picked up one of the long tapered candles, then flicked on the flame and held the base of the candle over it until it began to soften and melt. Holding it firmly, she pressed it hard into the stone before her and held it down until it could stand on its own. Then she picked up the second candle and did the same.

"But why on earth would you help it? We don't want it here!"

"Of course you don't; neither do I. But you do want it to stop, don't you? The spectral phenomena, the *haunting*? You want it to go away."

"Well—yes, of course."

"If there was another way to do it, I would. But there isn't. Either we can let the phenomena continue indefinitely, or I can finish the summoning. Which means I'll be bringing the demon right here."

For a moment, Adelaide sat before her, a stunned and disbelieving look on her face. Logan observed her silently, wondering where her thoughts might take her.

Finally she spoke again.

"So…it's definitely not the ghost of a little girl? Or a little boy?"

Logan shrugged. "You each saw what, on some level, you expected to see. In essence, you saw a reflection of your own mind superimposed over the reality of the situation. Happens a lot more often than you'd think."

For a brief moment, Logan couldn't help thinking that her entire life could be explained in those two sentences.

"Right," said Adelaide, sounding defeated.

Logan took a brief moment to mentally fortify herself. There was no doubt about what she had to do next: try to convince Adelaide and Richard to leave the house, for their own safety.

"So, now that we've established all that, it's time to discuss a point of procedure." She glanced over at the corner. "This goes for you, too. The thing is, once I summon the demon…you both need to be gone from here."

"What are you saying?" That look was back—the combination of confusion and disgust. Logan got the feeling that their whole conversation was a bit too much for Adelaide to absorb.

"It would just be better in the long run, safer, if you both vacated the premises for a little while. You don't have to be gone long—I'd suggest leaving a little before sunset, and not coming back until the sun is up again. If it gives you peace of mind, I've got a few cameras we can set up so you can be sure I don't take the good silver. Does that sound acceptable to you?"

Adelaide's outraged expression spoke the answer before her words could.

"Absolutely not!"

Of course it wasn't.

"Miss Humphrey—Adelaide—I'm not sure you fully comprehend the danger you'll be putting yourself in if you stay here tonight." She glanced back and forth between the two of them, wondering what the best tack to take would be. She also wondered, passingly, what Richard's relationship to Adelaide was. Were they siblings? Were they lovers? She couldn't tell. Her gaze settled on Adelaide when she spoke. "Have you ever seen a demon? Apart from your recent experiences, have you ever seen anything paranormal before at all?"

Like, maybe, your "connoisseur" father trying and failing to summon a demon, she thought but didn't say.

"Well," said Adelaide slowly, apparently gathering her thoughts, "if you're asking if I've ever seen something that's difficult to explain—"

Behind her, Richard scoffed. "Of course she hasn't. Adelaide's got an active imagination, but she's not insane."

Logan kept her expression bland and neutral, and offered them a shrug.

"Then you really don't have any idea how dangerous it will be here tonight. I highly recommend that you both go into town and find a hotel for the evening, then come back in the morning. I should be finished by then, unless something goes wrong. Of course, there is a very real possibility that something *will* go wrong, which is one of the many reasons the two of you should vacate now."

"I'm not leaving my home," said Adelaide, pulling her spine straighter, as if to emphasize her point. "Richard, you can go if you want."

Richard huffed, his chest puffing up like an echo of her. "I will not leave you here alone."

Logan felt certain that spending too much time with either one of these people would drive her insane. Her left hand traveled up to her face to pinch the bridge of her nose, as if that action stood any chance of alleviating the headache she felt coming on.

"I want you both to understand something," she said slowly, taking a deep breath to keep herself calm. "Tonight, in this room, I am going to summon this demon and bring it into fully realized existence. While I don't yet know what kind of demon it will be, please believe me when I tell you that I have never once met a demon that was peaceful and nonthreatening. In general, demons are violent and bloodthirsty, and ten times more powerful than a human being. When this demon comes through, it's going to do what demons do. By which I mean it will try its best to kill and eat you both."

Adelaide and Richard both stared at her, neither one moving. Logan sighed.

"Okay. It's your house, you are certainly free to stay." She reached down into her bag and pulled out a folder, then produced two stapled stacks of paper and handed them over. "I'll need you to sign these waivers acknowledging that I told you that you might die, so you and your family have no right to sue me if you do. Understand?"

The pinched-face twins took their papers from her and looked them over. Logan had read through the document before, so she knew how extensive it was—there were sections on beheading, disembowelment, getting eaten alive, general loss of limb. The draft of it had expanded over time, as her father and Knatt had encountered ever more new scenarios deemed waiver-necessary.

Adelaide signed hers first and passed it back.

"So," she said, looking pleased with herself, "what happens now? Are you going to walk through the house with a little EMF device or something?"

"Why would I do that?"

"To detect its presence, or whatever people like you do."

People like you. Logan took a second to try and figure out what Adelaide's impression of people like her might be. She considered Adelaide's insistence that her "haunting" was a ghost, recalled her use of the term *spectral phenomena*. Then it clicked.

"Adelaide," she tried to sound neutral, not patronizing. "Do you happen to watch a lot of ghost-hunting TV shows?"

Richard laughed. "She can't get enough of them."

"I understand they're very popular," Logan said, restraining a sigh. "But it's really best to treat them as entertainment only. They're not exactly educational. And no, I'm not going to go around with an EMF detector. That wouldn't tell me anything, except maybe that you've got a power line nearby."

"Fine," said Adelaide with a huff. "Do we do anything now?"

Logan reached into her bag once more and pulled out a bundle of sage. "I'm going to smudge the room with this. Then we wait."

For a blissful moment, neither client spoke. Logan stood from her chair and pulled a lighter from her pocket to get the sage started. Barely thirty seconds had passed when Adelaide impatiently broke the silence.

"How *long* do we wait?" Her voice was like the whine of a small child.

"Until sundown."

"Sundown?"

"At the earliest." She turned the sage over in her hands, making sure to light it evenly, then blowing on the edges until it smoldered. "Feel free to go get yourselves some lunch."

She started toward the corner of the room, then paused.

"Let me know if you make any coffee, will you?"

She couldn't help but enjoy the affronted shock that settled over Adelaide's face.

To Logan's delight, her clients grew bored of waiting after only an hour. They left her alone and disappeared off to some distant corner of their castle to entertain themselves. Once they were gone, Logan pulled out her chair and knelt down on the ground with a piece of chalk to draw a symbol she'd learned a long time ago—a graphic tree, with the roots and branches stretching and curving outward, forming a circle. The tree symbol was a standard representation of knowledge and truth, and Knatt had taught her how to use it when she was a child. Strictly speaking, she knew she wouldn't need it, but its unnecessary protection gave her a sense of comfort anyway.

"Today, I'm going to teach you about letha summoning," he'd told her. As he spoke, he used black ink to sketch out the tree on a large piece of paper. "Letha summoning can be used for one of two potential purposes, but both types of casting require the same ingredients. First, one must use either an imbued object or a powerful symbol to help concentrate one's cast. Next, an herb with magical properties to strengthen the cast; technically herbs are optional, but if you don't wish to exhaust yourself entirely, I do recommend them. Finally, the caster must speak a spell word or two, then spill fresh blood for a catalyst. Some may choose to sacrifice an animal for this, but many casters prefer to use their own blood. After all, for most summonings, you will only need a little."

After he'd shown her the symbol of the tree with interwoven roots, and made her copy it out over and over again until he was satisfied she'd be able to draw it on her own later, he showed her how to activate it. He took out a metal device that looked like a small hammer with a lever in the handle. Holding it just below his left wrist near the outer bone, he flicked the lever in one quick motion, setting off the device, and a tiny drop of blood flew from the skin of his wrist and onto the image before them. Much later on, he explained that the small hammer was actually a modified medical device for diabetes patients. He called it the blood-letter.

She did now as he had done then. With one quick motion, she produced the tiny amount of blood needed to activate her simple protection summon, and she let it fly onto the chalk. The symbol blazed with light as if it had caught on fire, but only for a moment. Then it was motionless once more, as though nothing had happened at all.

As she briefly surveyed her work on the symbol, she got a flash of what her aunt might say about it at Other Side. *All this letha nonsense, and for what?* Not that her aunt never added a performative aspect to her casting—it was just that, at Other Side, the performance was for show only. Their magic needed no medium. Still, when the occasion called for it, they did love to pull out all the pomp and circumstance they could. *I love a good ritual*, her aunt would say.

With the knowledge that she'd done her due diligence, Logan

sat down again and leaned back in her chair, now pulling a small book out of her bag. There would be nothing else to do for several more hours. Most contracts she took with Knatt left her with large chunks of time to kill between the set up and the actual work. Knatt always insisted she show up on site sometime in the morning, even though they almost always dealt with phenomena that resisted showing themselves until nighttime. Since her second job with him, she'd made sure to bring a book or two wherever she went.

Another hour into her wait time, her cell phone—charging silently in a corner—buzzed on the floor. Logan put her book down to go check it.

First, she read the name *Matthew*. Then she read the message.

Any chance you're still in town and looking for something to do tonight?

To her chagrin, she couldn't immediately place the name Matthew with a face. Then it clicked—her companion from the unfamiliar room that morning. Good to know she'd gotten his name at some point.

She took a moment to remember the previous evening's events so she could gauge what kind of a response he warranted. As far as she could recall, he'd been pretty good company. He might be well worth another go.

She wrote him back: *I have to work tonight, but I could be free tomorrow.*

She started to put her phone down to go back to her chair, assuming that he'd take a few hours to get back to her. To her surprise, her phone lit up before she could let it go.

That's perfect. I can meet you at the bar again if you want.

As a rule, she preferred city boys, and city girls. But every once in a while, she didn't mind the sweetness, and the promptness, of a small town native.

Sounds good.

Then she went back to her chair and her book. She still had hours left to wait.

The pinched-face twins came back into the room just as the sun started to slip behind the trees. Without a word, they walked to the other side of the table and seated themselves directly across from Logan. While Adelaide smoothed the ends of her hair with her fingers, Richard cleared his throat and straightened his spine.

"Will it...start soon?" he asked, waving his hand around vaguely in the air.

"Yes," said Logan. She lit the candles anew.

Ever so slowly, the sun dipped lower. Shadows pooled at the edges of the room and grew outward, stretching toward them. The night was coming on.

As the sun finally disappeared, Logan felt the same unexplainable shiver she'd felt when she'd first walked in. Her spine automatically straightened as her body began to anticipate the imminent fight.

Good, she thought. *It's close.*

She didn't say anything to them, of course. Scaring people tended to make them act like idiots. And these two didn't need any help with that.

A muffled crashing sound came to them from another room. Richard's head whipped wildly to the left, in exactly the opposite direction from where the sound was actually coming.

"Did anyone else hear that?" he asked. His tone sounded almost conspiratorial.

"Of course we did," Adelaide snapped.

Richard turned a sulky glare on her.

"It doesn't hurt for me to ask, you know," he said.

"You always think you need to insert yourself into everything."

"Well, sometimes when I don't insert myself, you end up backed into a corner by Rodney the tennis instructor—"

"That was one time, and I'm perfectly capable of—"

"Hey!" Logan held up both hands, one for each of them. They fell momentarily silent. She wished they had never come back into the room. More than that, she wished that Knatt would let her turn down jobs, especially if they wouldn't meet her terms. "Does everyone remember my speech about how dangerous all of this would be?"

They nodded.

"Okay," she paused, and let the rest of her words come out slowly, so she could be sure they would be understood. "So now, I want you both to shut the hell up as if your lives depended on it. Unless, of course, one of you was really keen on spending the next week cleaning the other's guts and brains off the ceiling." With her mouth pushed forcibly into a thin line, she added, "I want you both to take a good look at my face right now, so you can understand that I'm not *in any way* joking."

They both stared at her in horror, which unfortunately made it hard not to laugh.

Silence descended again. The twins kept their mouths shut, and apparently the "ghost" decided to follow their lead. They heard no more crashing from the next room.

Logan allowed the silence to stretch. In fact, she allowed it to stretch for a good half hour—primarily to make sure her clients could actually keep it up that long. When she was satisfied with their patience, and her own petty revenge, she reached down into her open bag and pulled out the blood-letter and a sachet of powdered herbs.

Holding the device delicately in one hand, she concentrated on the space between worlds, between existence and nothingness, held in her mind like water cupped in a palm. That was where the beast was, trapped and likely impatient. She imagined herself reaching out to it, tempting it. She raised both hands, still holding tight to the concept of the in-between. Then she spoke.

"*Invoco pecum.*"

As she said the words, she flipped the lever on the blood-letter, holding it down longer than she had before to let out a larger drop of blood. Her blood splashed on the table, along with a small sprinkling of powder, which lit up for a brief moment as it fell through the air, but stopped as it scattered on the stone. For a moment, the room seemed to rumble, like it was vibrating in anticipation, but then that, too, stopped.

Within seconds of the magic's burnout, they heard another sound from a farther room. This one wasn't a crash—in fact, it sounded like a wail. Hearing its siren call, Logan's blood began to race.

The lights above them flickered. As if on cue, rain began to fall heavily outside the window. The lights flashed again, twice, then went out. Immediately, Richard got up to stand.

"I'll check the breaker box."

"Wouldn't help," said Logan. "They'll only go out again."

Richard sat back down.

"Are we just supposed to sit here in the dark?" Adelaide's voice was a terrified whisper. With the gloom hiding her face, Logan couldn't help but smile. *So naïve, these rich kids*, she thought.

"If the dark worries you, it's not too late for you to leave. I certainly wouldn't blame you."

"No," said Adelaide immediately, apparently affronted at the thought. "No, I'll be fine. We'll both be fine."

She shot Richard a look, as though daring him to disagree. Though his expression looked stricken, he merely shrugged in response.

"Suit yourselves." With no further comment, she pulled the lighter out of her back pocket and lit up the rest of the candles that she'd set up along one edge of the table. They might not last much longer than the electric lights, but they'd be a help while they did.

After a moment, Logan realized the room had gotten quieter. Glancing to her left, she could see that the rain had not let up—they just couldn't hear it anymore. One look back across the table told her that her clients hadn't noticed yet.

As she looked out at the rain again, she heard something behind her—a kind of clicking sound, almost like an insect. Slowly her head turned back to the right, toward the sound.

Just like Adelaide, she saw a little girl. And just like Richard, she saw a little boy.

The figure standing beyond the table faded in and out, its shape in flux, never quite taking hold. The entity stood before her, but not fully—a thin veil of reality lay between them. Of course, it wouldn't look that way to most untrained eyes. Logan had figured out over time that most people interpreted the ambiguous one way or the other so quickly that they didn't even realize what they had done, and accepted their own ideas as truth, without question.

Adelaide had seen a girl. Richard had seen a boy. Neither of them had seen any such thing.

The creature, such as it was, reached a hand—possibly a claw—upward, then pushed it forward. Logan guessed that this was the motion Adelaide had interpreted as the little girl throwing a ball. In reality, the creature was trying to free itself from its caged state, stuck between worlds.

"Well," said Logan, "no time like the present."

She tightened her grip on the blood-letter in her right hand and pressed it to the skin just below the outer bone of her wrist until she drew a thicker line of blood. Then she hovered her wrist over one candle's flame.

"*Invoco*," she whispered. The flame grew larger and brighter, nearly engulfing her hand. "*Invoco pecum.*"

A bright flash filled the space, originating from the point of the flame. For a moment, it seemed like nothing else would happen. Then Logan heard a growl from the far end of the room. The veil was broken; the beast had come through. Hurriedly, she slipped the device back inside its protective box in the bag.

As Logan let her head turn slowly to the sound, she clocked her clients' frozen, terrified expressions. So they'd noticed the growling, if nothing else.

Finally, her gaze found the other end of the stone table. There it stood—only about three or four feet tall, its small gray head peering at them over the edge. Before Logan could consider her next move, it crouched down and jumped up, landing on the solid stone. Gray scales covered its entire body, from the hunched back to the elongated forearms—forearms which ended in curved claws that dragged along the table when it moved. Perhaps it was the wrong reaction, but a sudden surge of excitement moved through her body, and in an instant, she was ready.

With instinct as automatic as breath, Logan leapt onto the table as well. As she pulled the 8-inch dagger from the back of her belt, she cursed herself for eschewing any larger weapons from her home arsenal. She just had to travel light, didn't she? The beast, of course, didn't need to bring anything to fight her. She listened to the light scratch of its claws on stone.

The beast paused at the sight of her and looked her up and down, like it was evaluating her. Slowly, its jaws opened wide, and it made a loud clicking sound. Then it lunged at her.

Several things happened at once. Out of the corner of her eye, she saw Adelaide jump back from the table while Richard gave a scream but remained frozen in place. She threw her right forearm up in front of her face while she thrust the small dagger forward. The monster tried to pull back from her, but its swinging arm connected with her blade. As dark blue blood splashed on the stone, it roared and stumbled backward. Within moments, it turned around and disappeared through the far doorway.

"Well, fuck," Logan muttered as it skittered off. How was she supposed to track the damn thing and keep her fearful clients safe at the same time?

She turned to look at them. Adelaide stood near the wall,

gazing at the now-empty doorway, while Richard whimpered in his chair.

"That's not a little girl," Adelaide managed, her voice small and quiet.

"Observant, aren't you?" Logan slid the dagger back into the sheath attached to her belt.

Between them, Richard gurgled.

"Why did it run away?"

"Out of shock, I think. It's probably a little disoriented from its trip through the veil."

Adelaide cocked her head to the side, not entirely dissimilar to what the beast had done as it sized Logan up. "You make it sound like a lost animal," she said.

Logan shrugged. "That's what it is, in a way."

"Hmph. It's not like any animal I've ever seen."

"Of all animals that have ever walked or crawled, you've only seen a tiny fraction." Logan turned back to the chair she'd abandoned earlier and used it to jump down off the table. "When you deal with other dimensions, it's best not to assume your past experience means anything."

She surveyed them again, wondering how best to proceed. Despite what she told her clients, the truth was that past experience was her primary guide. That experience told her that the beast would hide to nurse its wounds before returning to the hunt—before returning to them. But how long would it take?

"So what do we do now?" Adelaide asked her.

"That depends on you," Logan replied. "And how you feel about taking a little risk."

Logan was full of terrible ideas, and this was one. She hunched in a linen closet at the end of a long hallway, catatonic Richard shivering in a crouch behind her. They had allowed the door to open the tiniest crack, giving her a view of the moonlight spreading slim pools on the dark carpet, the rain still beating against the tall windows.

As she watched, Adelaide walked into her field of vision, pacing slowly. Logan could only hope she remembered her whole part; it would be a shame to lose a client just as she'd started to like her.

Adelaide paused near the window and glanced around her, looking for a sign of the monster. She'd been pacing for a few minutes already, but the beast hadn't yet shown. It was time for step two. With a sigh that was audible all the way from the closet, she put her arm out in front of her and dragged a blade across the skin, drawing blood.

They were hoping the smell would draw it in. Logan's nose crinkled automatically as it wafted over to her, notes of copper stinging sweetly. For a few moments, everything was quiet but the rain. Then a long low scratching noise came from the end of the hall, and Adelaide froze.

Logan still couldn't see it, but she knew the beast had arrived. She listened to it stalking slowly closer, narrowing in on Adelaide. Then it broke into a run. As soon as its gray form flashed into her narrow view, Logan launched herself out toward it, knocking it to the ground before it reached its intended prey. To her relief, Adelaide immediately ran back to the closet with Richard and closed them both in.

The beast extricated itself from her grasp and started toward the door, likely still following the smell. Logan took easy advantage of its distraction and tackled it again, this time driving the dagger deep into its back. She'd hoped to hit its heart, or at least something vital, but even after the blade was in up to the hilt, the creature only roared and reared back, throwing her off.

It was perfectly possible, even likely, that her wild guess at the location of its cardiac muscle was wrong. It was also possible, even likely, that hitting its heart wouldn't kill it at all.

There were a lot of things the beast might be able to survive. But in Logan's experience, precious few creatures could live without a head. Again, she cursed her past self for leaving all her broadswords and axes at home.

As she scrambled back to her feet, the beast came for her. This time, it knocked her to the ground, pinning her underneath its unexpected weight. She managed to wedge her left arm under its chin, holding its gnashing jaws away from her neck, while her right hand groped frantically over its back, searching for the hilt of her dagger. Finally, her fingers made contact and closed firmly around it before pulling upwards, hard.

The beast roared and reared, and with a show of power, lunged down at her, burying its teeth in her shoulder.

Her body's response was automatic. Without any conscious bidding from her, four spiked ridges shot out from under her skin along the bottoms of both forearms. As the pain of their appearance spread through her body, she felt an accompanying burst of strength surge through her like a wildfire.

When the spikes came out, her left arm had still been trapped beneath the beast's collarbone, so her ridges had ripped right through its skin and wedged into something hard, like bone. Its teeth lost their grip in the process, giving her a new edge. She bent her knees and planted her feet on the ground, then used the leverage to push, rolling the writhing beast onto its back. Gritting through the pain of it, she forced her left arm down toward its chest, her ridges tearing flesh in their wake.

While the animal gasped and swiped weakly at her, she brought her right hand up to its neck and forced the almost inadequate blade down, sawing at skin and sinew. It was rough, slow work. She felt the monster grow weaker with every ragged breath, but it didn't give up the fight completely until her dagger cut through the final inch, and its head rolled slowly off to the side.

Before she checked for any other damage, she tugged her left arm forcibly free and closed her eyes. Taking a breath, she gave both arms a small shake, retracting the spikes back into her body. She chanced a look up at the closet door and saw that it was still closed tight. So, fortunately for her, Richard and Adelaide hadn't seen a thing.

She allowed herself to fall back on her heels, surveying the corpse before her in a crouch. It was hard to predict how paranormal bodies would decompose, and even harder if she couldn't be sure of their origin. Maybe the beast would disappear. Or maybe it wouldn't.

"You can come out now," she called toward the closet. "It's safe."

For a moment, the door in front of her remained perfectly still. Then, ever so slowly, the handle turned, and it swung forward. Adelaide stepped gingerly from her hiding space, though Richard remained huddled behind her in shadow.

"Well," she said, stopping short of the disconnected head and gazing down at it, disgust wrinkling her nose. "It's really dead, isn't it? It's not going to grow a new head or something?"

Logan glanced down at the oozing blue wounds. "Unlikely. Not entirely impossible, but unlikely."

"How can we tell for sure?"

In truth, they couldn't. But Adelaide probably didn't want to hear that.

"We can burn it."

They had to get Richard situated first. Adelaide took him by the hand and led him to their sitting room, where she had him sit in an overstuffed chair with an antique look to it, and threw a heavy blanket around him. She handed him a glass of Scotch, presumably aged and expensive, and pressed a few buttons in a clear-screened panel near the door until Chopin flooded the room. Richard slowly closed his eyes, apparently mollified.

That task complete, they headed back to the corpse. Logan took hold of the torso while Adelaide took the feet, and they marched it downstairs and through a door leading to the back of the house. Fortunately for them, the rain had let up.

"It's heavier than I would have thought," Adelaide commented as they descended a short staircase to the lawn.

Logan said nothing. Adelaide didn't need to know that she had taken on most of the weight herself, nor that she could have carried it without Adelaide's help at all. For as long as she could remember, her impulse had been to withhold any information about herself that wasn't strictly necessary to disclose. So she did. She rarely lied, of course; she merely self-censored.

They dropped the body near a stone fire pit. While Adelaide went to pull firewood from their porch, Logan ran back inside to get the head. She saw that blue ooze had settled into the carpet and shrugged. Her contract, which both clients had already signed, stated she wasn't liable for property damage.

Adelaide already had a small fire started by the time Logan came back to her. Once it was big enough, she put the head on first.

"I don't suppose you've got an axe anywhere, do you?"

Her client surveyed the body once more before meeting Logan's gaze.

"So you can chop it up?"

"Yeah. Easier that way."

Adelaide nodded and tucked a piece of hair behind her ear. The shallow wound on her palm left a streak of drying blood in her straw-colored strands.

"I'll get it for you."

As she walked back to the house, Logan couldn't help but smile admiringly after her. For a spoiled rich kid, maybe Adelaide wasn't so bad.

Logan remained with her clients through the night, primarily for the sake of their peace of mind. She was sure they would experience no more paranormal phenomena—or at least, not unless one of them attempted and botched a summoning at some point—but she also knew they were bound to be a little shaken up. It never hurt to ease a client's frazzled nerves by standing guard, even after the danger had passed.

Once the sun had risen, she decided to take her leave.

Abandoning Richard, now asleep, in his overstuffed chair, Adelaide walked her to the door.

"I've already wired our payment to your partner. I, uh...I added a little bonus. You know, for the overtime."

"Ah." Logan smiled, finding herself pleasantly surprised by the gesture. "Uh, thank you. Well, I'm sure everything will be fine now, but you know how to reach us if you run into any more trouble."

"Yes, I do."

Something passed over Adelaide's face. Logan couldn't quite tell what it was. With one foot hovering over the last stair, she paused and held her gaze.

"Is everything all right?"

At first, Adelaide nodded, her expression still distant and strange. Then, slowly, her nod turned into a shake.

"It's just...it's just...it's all so alien. Everything that happened last night—it was all so...so *not normal*. You know?"

Logan reached up hesitantly to pat her on the arm, in what she hoped was a comforting gesture. Keeping her voice gentle and soft, she asked, "What exactly were you expecting?"

Adelaide met her gaze and locked onto it, her eyes wide with uncertainty.

"I don't know."

To Adelaide's obvious shock, Logan broke into a grin.

"Good! That means you're learning."

After a moment, Adelaide shook her head. Though her expression remained bewildered, she let out a short laugh.

"All right," said Logan as she let her hand drop away. "Well, it was nice meeting you. I'll be off now."

She turned her sights on her Kawasaki once more. Her next order of business was to find herself a hotel room, so she could recharge for a while. After all, she had a date to keep.

Chapter 2
Coming of Age for the Cursed

He said he wanted to practice sword fighting. I should have known better, but I was so pleased that he asked me. He didn't run off to find another boy to play with him—he asked me. Like I was worthy.

And I wanted to do it. There were so many swords around the estate, but I was never supposed to play with them. Not that that stopped me—every time I was left alone there, I saw it as a chance to explore everything I'd been forbidden to touch. And I had a lot of chances.

But with Damien, it was different. Damien got lessons. When Damien picked up a sword, it wasn't playing. It was practicing.

To this day, I don't remember exactly why we were there. Charles Logan had business to do, and I was along for the ride. But Knatt hadn't come with us. Knatt always came with us. Or was that later?

We had to sneak into his practice room to take the swords, so I knew we weren't supposed to be playing with them. We took them outside. I think we had an idea about plausible deniability.

It went okay at first. I held my own for a few minutes, mostly by swinging wildly.

Then I tripped over a rock, lost my balance and my edge. He pulled some fancy trick I didn't understand and forced me backward, then swung his sword up high and brought it down.

I threw my arm up, and something about the movement triggered a memory. Hadn't I thrown my arm up before?

With a jolt of shock, I felt a searing pain explode along my skin. Had he really struck me? But he hadn't—I heard his sword hit the ground beside him, hard. He'd never hit me at all.

So why did I hurt?

I let my arm drop, twisting it around so I could see.

Four spiked ridges that looked like bone poked out through my bare skin, angled back, threatening. Each one was red with blood.

What was happening? What was wrong with me?

Why hadn't anyone ever told me?

Logan ran a hand through freshly laundered hair, tucking one of the longer pieces behind her ear. She always kept her hair in a short straight bob, usually falling just short of her chin. It was easier that way. When you regularly wrestled with beasts and did at least half of your showering in hotel rooms, it helped to have a little less hair.

Of course, that morning, she hadn't had to use a hotel shower. Matthew had offered his willingly, on the condition that she notify him if she ever rumbled into town again. That was unlikely, of course, unless Adelaide and Richard had more going on than she knew about.

She took another drink from her coffee, purchased at the same café she'd visited the day before. By her estimation, the primary downside to motorcycle riding, compared to other forms of transport, was the lack of a cup holder.

Finally, she was down to the dregs. With one last sip, she tossed her empty in the receptacle by the door and went outside to her bike.

In a perfect echo of the previous day, her phone rang just as she reached for her helmet. Knatt again. She answered.

"Hi," she said, this time with no attempt to inject cheerfulness into her tone.

"Good morning." Knatt, on the other hand, sounded considerably more upbeat than he had before. "You should be pleased to know that Miss Adelaide has posted a new review on our website, and it was *quite* favorable."

He paused to give her time for a response.

"I'm chuffed," she managed.

"Congratulations on a job well done."

"You sound surprised."

"I am."

Logan took a moment to soak up the insult.

"Right," she said.

"Anyway," Knatt bulldozed on, "the reason I called was to let you know we've got another job lined up. It's nothing pressing, just more pest control. In fact, I'd say you've got a little bit of time on your hands, if you want to take it. Time you might use to, for instance, visit you father."

Logan didn't respond immediately. She tried to remind herself that Knatt's heart was in the right place. It wouldn't be fair for her to hold him responsible for any of her father's sins. In truth, when she was growing up, Knatt had filled in for her father in a million unnamable ways. He wasn't the one who deserved her early-morning ire.

"It's also time I could use for just about anything else." She was channeling the sun's cheerfulness again, but with a different effect.

"Miss Logan," Knatt's voice dropped into a serious tone. "You ought to make more of an effort to visit your father. You haven't been to see him in months." He paused, likely to imbue the importance of his message. "He's all alone up there, you know."

Up there. A euphemism if ever she'd heard one.

"I'll think about it on the drive, okay?" She didn't want to talk about her father anymore.

"That's all I ask."

"I'm gonna hit the road now," she said.

"All right. Be safe."

She snapped off her phone and stowed it in her pocket before slipping her helmet on. Despite the fact that her time here had gone better than she would have expected, she was anxious to get going. Staying too long in small towns made her antsy, almost twitchy. She swung up onto her bike and thrilled at the roar of her engine as she kicked off.

Select few things in life never lost their flavor. Riding a motorcycle was one. Within moments of picking up a little speed, she felt her irritation and her guilt start to slip away.

The air was crisp and cool, but she could feel the spring, and the earliest signs of summer. Once the open road stretched before her, she pressed even faster. Much of the middle part of America looked the same as the rest, but she had to admit there was a certain charm to it. She felt at peace out here. She felt centered.

She couldn't say exactly how far she got before she was

interrupted. Based on her own perception, she might have been riding for hours. Or maybe only minutes.

The first warning sign was a sudden dizziness. Her head felt light and off-balance, and she briefly lost control of the bike, swerving suddenly to the side before she righted herself. Immediately, she understood what was about to happen, and she willed herself not to panic. Any time she'd had an episode in a precarious position, it hadn't ended well.

She'd never had one on the bike before. It wasn't a milestone she'd particularly wanted to hit.

With a quick glance behind her, she confirmed that the road around her was empty of other vehicles, and she forced the bike to drop speed as quickly as she could.

Not a moment too soon—the first prickle of the burn started up in her back, right in the middle of her spine. Within seconds, her eyes started to blur. Pressing the brake ever harder, she tilted off to the right, forcing the bike into the grass.

Then her back exploded in pain, and she tilted sideways, skidding hard in the dirt. Her right leg and torso collided with the ground, wrenching her from the bike, which kept on sliding away from her. Shock kept her from feeling the impact, and she forced herself onto her back to try and keep from breathing in too much dust.

Somewhere far above her head, she heard a car whizzing by on the road. She had just enough time to appreciate the fact that she wasn't dead before her world went black.

I worship…

Logan lost her sense of herself as she was pulled headlong into someone else. Inside another person's body, she could see a long, thin match catching the flame of a candle on an altar. Different shapes had been drawn on the walls in chalk, but the light was too low to make them out. Another flame lit up, but the shapes remained elusive.

The scene shifted. She walked in this alien body through bright white halls flooded with fluorescent lighting, blinking in her surroundings. She saw undifferentiated tile and white walls and a row of...blue lockers. School. She was in a school somewhere. The body she wore was filled with fear and paranoia, and just a hint of rage. It turned a corner and the rage seemed to rise.

Then that world went black again. In another moment, the altar appeared again. The anger inside her host's body had swelled to a fever pitch.

Somewhere nearby, a frightened animal made a noise. A hand—perhaps her own—grasped a butcher's knife, raised it up, brought it down. The animal fell silent. Blood spilled onto the altar, and she felt someone else's excitement as their summon began to work...

I worship...

Then she felt herself shift into someone new. Someone who was running. Was it someone? No, some thing. *It ran, and it panted, and it smelled. It smelled blood. It smelled a heartbeat. Logan could smell the heartbeat, too.*

It needed the heart. It hungered for the heart.

It ran through the woods, chasing the smell of that heartbeat. The woods grew loud with human voices and pungent with human scents. The beast knew its prey was close.

I worship...

So many smells, but it knew exactly which one. The heart it craved was drawing closer, drifting away from the other human smells. The beast waited, letting it come. Letting it walk into shadow.

Then it attacked.

It was all over so quick. Jaws and teeth and kill.

Nobody even noticed that anything was wrong.

I worship…the wolf.

Sight came back to her through a cloud of confusion. Every time she came down from a Choronzon Key vision, she suffered a few moments of debilitating disorientation as she grappled with the sudden appearance and disappearance of another person's psyche inside her head. She took a breath and collected her thoughts. As practicality set in once more, she ran a hand over her head, just to make sure she hadn't hit it on her way down. No obvious bumps or cuts, so that was good.

As she made her way to standing, she couldn't feel any other obvious injuries. Her legs and arms seemed intact and capable of their usual ranges of motion. She no longer felt dizzy, though her thoughts came to her at half their usual speed. And the mark on her back still stung smartly, like someone had held a branding iron to it. But that pain, at least, was par for the course.

The memory of the vision tugged at her brain, begging to be considered. She pushed it away, if only temporarily.

The bike had rolled a few feet farther than she had. For a moment, she had to struggle to set it upright—which was something of a novel experience for her. Though the bike weighed roughly 500 pounds, she'd never once had trouble lifting it. But it wasn't unusual for the Key's messages to sap her of her considerable strength for a brief time. Still, eventually she got it up and rolled it back over to the road. Then she was riding again, this time with an eye out for the nearest rest stop.

As she rode, she let her mind fall back into the vision.

What could she see? A lot of darkness and shadows and vague shapes. She could see evidence of magic, but she couldn't tell what kind or what it was meant to do. She could see a sacrifice—what kind of animal? Filtering out everything else, she focused on the sound of it—screaming, squawking—a chicken. Unfortunately, that didn't tell her much. Among letha casters who chose to use animal blood for their spells, chickens tended to be popular, likely because they were cheap, easy to acquire, and easy to kill.

So what about the rest? The vision had pulled her into two minds—the mind of a person and the mind of the beast. What could she tell about the person? He or she spent time in a school, and while they were at that school, they felt afraid and angry—so, probably a teenager. She couldn't say with absolute certainty, of course, but it seemed like a reasonable guess. And what about the beast? She returned to that, trying to let its instincts and senses fill her. What had it seen? Focusing in on the moment right before its kill, she forced herself to inhabit the beast in all its unseemly glory. The experience was aggressively unpleasant. She could feel its bloodlust, its hunger for violence, its rage.

But she could also see. She could see its victim—a teenage girl, maybe 17 or 18 years old, white, with dark hair and wide, terrified eyes. Wide eyes and flushed skin and young blood, rushing just beneath the surface—the smell of it—the need for more—

With a shake, Logan tore herself loose from the monster's psyche once more, but she made sure to hold the image of the girl in her mind. That girl, young as she had been, was dead now. She had to hold onto that fact. No matter what else happened, she had to remember her.

And what about the other part of the vision?

I worship the wolf.

What the hell did that mean? Logan grimaced as she realized she had research looming in her future.

To her right, she saw a sign alerting travelers to an upcoming rest stop, and she went for it. Her bike slowed as she passed along the drive through a copse of trees. The stop appeared deserted; hers was the only vehicle around.

After throwing down the kickstand and leaving her helmet haphazardly on the seat, she went straight for the bathroom and located a mirror on the wall. Shrugging off her jacket, she pulled up her shirt and craned her neck as far as she could over her shoulder.

There it was: the Choronzon Key. At one point in time, it had been a separate physical entity; she could have held it in her hand. But not anymore. Now it was permanently adhered to her skin, a tattoo she'd never chosen, and at the moment, it was a bright, burning red.

It was a labyrinth, or it took the form of one, at least. A large teardrop spread between her shoulder blades and down her spine, intricately curving lines inside it, outlining a pathway that led to the center—though there was nothing there. It had looked about the same before it adhered itself to her. Only then, it had been made of bronze.

If anyone had ever asked her, she couldn't have explained how she knew what to call it. The first time she'd ever seen it, the words had tumbled from her mouth before she could stop them. *Choronzon Key.* That was its name. That had been its name before it ever found her, and it would remain long after she was gone. She was almost certain that if she ever suffered some accident and lost all her memory, she would still know those two words. They had their own existence, independent of her. Independent of everything.

As far as she could tell from her research, nobody else in the world knew for sure that the Key existed. Well, that was no longer strictly true—Knatt knew, because she'd told him. But no one beyond that. Interestingly, when she went far enough back, she could find plenty of legend and rumor that referenced it, often recounted by dubious-to-incredulous sources. Most of it contained nothing helpful—the Key was rumored to be everything from a curse sent by the gods to a herald signifying the next savior. If anything, Logan might be inclined to believe the former; certainly nothing good had ever come to her because of it. But even if it was, what did that mean? What was the curse for?

Of course, Knatt didn't think it was a curse, and he didn't like to hear her talk about it like that. He believed it gave her a purpose—that it was a gift, a calling.

So he couldn't begrudge her for answering the call, could he?

She let her shirt slide down and pulled her jacket back on, then walked back out to her bike while she pressed the button to call him.

"Yes, Miss Logan?"

"Looks like the family reunion's going to have to wait," she informed him. "I just got tapped for something else."

"You had a vision?" She could tell from the sound of his voice that Knatt was intrigued. He always seemed to show a little more interest in her when the Key was involved.

"A vision, an episode, an epileptic fit. Whatever you want to call it. Happened while I was riding, so, you know, I crashed and nearly died. Not that that matters."

"Do you know where it wants to send you?"

"That's your first question? You're not even going to pretend you care about my well-being?"

"Sorry. Are you injured?"

"Nah, I'm fine."

"Good." He paused. "Do you need me to ask a follow-up?"

"No, we're good. Thanks."

"Wonderful. So, what was the vision about?"

"Well, a lot of it was pretty vague. You know, creepy voices, creepy animal sacrifice. And then something attacked a teenage girl."

"I see. Do you know where you need to go?"

He couldn't see her, so she let herself grimace. She could have figured that out first, instead of rushing to call him.

"Uh, just give me a second."

She closed her eyes, still holding the phone to her ear. With an ease derived from years of practice, she cleared her mind of conscious thought and focused on the labyrinth, inviting it to lead her where it would.

North. North and west. She could see an image of herself on the bike, speeding ahead, following the feeling.

"Montana," she said.

"Montana. Is that all? Montana's a big state."

The bike raced onward, until it passed a *Welcome* sign.

"Well. That's a bit of a coincidence. Or it might be, anyway. Looks like I'm going to a town called Wolf Creek."

"Wolf Creek? Why should that be a coincidence?"

"I'll tell you when I get there."

When she finally passed it, the sign looked just like it had in her mind. It stood solitary on the side of a deserted stretch of highway, and she saw the earliest rays of sunlight illuminate what looked like a 20-year-old paint job, complete with a dated picturesque scene of a young couple having a 1950s-style picnic in the woods. The sign marked a dip in the surrounding mountains that allowed just enough passage for the highway, steep inclines climbing toward the sky on either side. As Logan passed, she almost got the sense that she was entering another world.

She arrived early on a Monday morning, having ridden through most of the night. It wasn't a large town; she zeroed in on the first breakfast place she could find and parked right in front of it. On her way in, she grabbed a newspaper.

When she entered, she took in the old-diner feel of the place and seated herself at the counter. To her left stood a glass-encased cake stand piled high with donuts. To her right, the same stand, but holding only a single massive cinnamon roll. In her bleary, almost delirious state, it looked far too appealing.

The waitress came over and gave her a nod.

"I'll have a coffee please." As her stomach grumbled, she

glanced over at the top few items on the menu. "Uh, and the huevos rancheros. Thank you."

The coffee sat before her in less than a minute, for which she was deeply grateful. As she added a little cream, she spread the newspaper out in front of her.

She didn't have to look far. The headline she wanted was right at the top: *Town in Shock over Brutally Slain Teen*. She scanned the article, looking for the kind of details she needed, but they weren't forthcoming. All she could tell at first was that the death had been violent, and it was currently suspected to be a murder. At least now she had the victim's name—Violet Buchanan. They'd attached the girl's school picture, so Logan knew it was her. Towards the bottom, she noticed one final important detail—all inquiries were to be directed toward the sheriff's office. Since this town wasn't quite big enough for a full morgue, she guessed that was likely where they were keeping the body.

She flipped through the rest of the paper to see if there was any other mention of the story, but she found nothing. When she finally set it aside, the waitress placed a heaping plate of food in front of her. She reached over for the hot sauce, but paused when she heard a tut-tutting noise.

"You might want to try it first," the waitress warned her.

"Oh. Duly noted. Thanks." She took a mental note of the waitress's description in case she decided to come to this place again. *White, mid 30s, average height.*

She scooped a healthy mound up with her fork and bit down. The spikey sting of heat hit her tongue, and she smiled in utter satisfaction. Perfect. She had a feeling she'd already found her new favorite haunt for the duration of her stay here.

Once she was finished, she paid in cash and left a generous tip. Before heading out, she flagged the waitress down once more and asked her where she might find accommodations for a few nights.

Fortunately for her, Logan had long since accustomed herself to the sights and sounds of cheap motels. This one was right on the edge of town, backed in by thick woods on one side, with a small horse ranch on the other. Logan took her key and parked her bike right in front of the green metal door to her rented room.

She had hours yet until sundown. She planned to use it to get a little sleep.

When she woke up after dark, she felt certain that every dream she'd had during her rest had been a rehash of her vision. Violet Buchanan's terrified eyes were haunting her.

Before she'd faded out, she'd asked Knatt to get her the address for the sheriff's department. He'd complied, and with a town map from the motel's tiny front desk, she'd figured out its location in relation to her. Of course, she had tried to use GPS first, but the map refused to load, and eventually the application failed completely. There were a few possible explanations for this, and at least one was magical. It wasn't the first time she'd seen technology fail in a place recently subject to letha casting— the greater the summon, the more pervasive the effect tended to be.

She couldn't take her bike on this one; it attracted too much attention. Fortunately for her, the town was small enough, and her legs fast enough, that she could travel on foot. She took the main road into the center of town, then slipped into the plentiful trees once she hit the populated areas.

The sheriff's department was a small brick one-story building, lights blazing from windows high in the walls. She circled around behind, pressing deeper into the woods when she heard human voices passing by in the street. For a brief moment, with her back to the woods, she felt a chill up her spine. Unlike the chill she'd felt upon entering Adelaide and Richard's home, this one didn't strike her as magical so much as instinctual. She glanced back into the trees despite herself, and found nothing but the expected darkness there to greet her. The voices from the street faded, so she shook off her disquiet and crept forward through the underbrush.

The windows were higher than she liked but not impossible; the real question was how regularly the deputies locked them. She edged around to the back until she found a sizable window with no light streaming through it. Then, taking a second to gauge the distance, she crouched down and jumped.

The ledge wasn't quite wide enough to hold her, but she threw her arms out to the side and clapped her hands to the walls, using sheer muscle strain to wedge herself in. One push on the window told her it was, indeed, locked. With a sigh, she flattened her hand against the frame and gave a hard push, her extraordinary strength eventually splintering the wood. She swung the glass up and shifted her hips to dangle her legs inside, then lowered herself until she hung from her hands. And she dropped.

A few cardboard boxes were disturbed by her fall, but they

didn't make much noise. If she had to guess, she'd say she was in some kind of storage closet. She went over to the door and placed her ear against it, listening for voices. Nothing. With a slow and quiet turn of the handle, she pressed the door open and slipped out.

Her current hallway was dark, but the one beyond it blazed with light. Once she was halfway down the hall, she could hear the light clicking of keyboard keys. Someone was stationed at the front desk.

Then the part that repulsed her. She'd gotten used to it over time, but she never found it pleasant. She shut her eyes and took a deep breath through her nose. She was searching for the smell of chemicals and decomposition.

She found it, though not without a fight. The body had to be in a freezer, a sealed door muffling its odors. She drifted farther down the hallway and confirmed her growing suspicion: she'd have to get around the person at the desk to reach her target. It was a task that might have been easier if she had someone on hand to distract them; too bad her partner preferred to operate remotely.

Well, only one thing to be done about it, she thought.

She edged closer and peered around the corner. The deputy at the desk was a young white man with snacks arranged all around him on the desk. She peered a little closer and saw the he was typing in a chat window, and up behind it, he had a video playing. All the better for her.

With one deep breath, she cleared her mind of unnecessary noise. She could picture the trees outside, beyond the walls, and the space between them—the shadows, the darkness. She could feel the pull of that darkness, the way it called to her—and she pulled back at it. With a sudden rush, she felt it come.

It was a trick she'd mastered long ago—one of a handful of eira tricks she could perform at will. A single wave of her hand told her it had worked: as her hand moved in front of her face, she found her eyes unwilling to look at it, unwilling to see it. She had summoned shadows to her, and now she was shrouded in them. The trick didn't make her invisible, exactly—it just made her difficult to look at. It was as close to invisible as she had ever needed to be.

She didn't even bother to duck, just walked quietly behind him. She reached the other side without incident.

Following the smell, she went to the end of the other hall. Briefly she pressed her ear up to the door, confirmed there was no one inside, and opened it. The room was dark, but her eyes adjusted. On the left wall stood the walk-in freezer, held shut with a simple bike lock. Just as she was about to walk over and break it open, she noticed the key rack just above it.

I love it when it's easy.

She opened the lock and replaced the key, then pulled the door open. There she was—Violet Buchanan. Under a sheet, of course. Logan wheeled her table out, locked the wheels in place, and pulled back the sheet.

The first thing she saw was her face. It was almost exactly the same as the face she'd seen during her episode, only paler and more still, the eyes now shut.

The second thing she saw was her chest. It had been ripped open. She leaned over to peer inside. She was no medical expert, but it looked to her like something was missing: her heart. Logan pulled the sheet all the way back to give the rest of her body a once-over, but nothing else stood out to her. Nothing else needed to.

She pulled out her phone. Knatt didn't always take to technology well, but with some coaxing from her, he'd finally gotten the hang of texting. She sent him a short message.

Heart torn out. Case confirmed.

Then she covered Violet up again and rolled her back into the freezer. Just as she shut the lock once more, she heard voices in the hallway, coming closer. With a quick glance around, she located a high window and crossed over to it.

She could hear the deputies entering the room as she dropped to the ground, letting the window swing shut. Knowing there was no way they'd missed the sound, she hurtled herself into the trees at top speed and flattened herself behind a ridge of rocks and bush.

"Hey! Hey you kids, get out of here! Idiots."

The window slammed shut again. They hadn't seen her, and from the sound of it, their suspicions lay with youthful indiscretion.

Jumping to standing again, she brushed herself off and started her trek back to her hotel. For a moment, she considered going into town—there was bound to be a bar, bound to be one or two available people in it. But she decided against it. She was tired, and she'd had her fill of the small town social scene for a while yet.

Besides, there was no telling what Knatt would want her to do in the morning.

I worship the wolf.

The sound of knocking came to her through the haze of sleep.

Once again, the vision from the Key had infused her dreams. She couldn't help but wonder if there was something from the vision that she was missing, possibly something that could explain the only clear words she'd heard. But she had no more ideas now than when she'd first experienced it.

The knocking came again, but it sounded strange somehow. She rolled onto her feet without even opening her eyes and headed toward the door, but as she reached for the handle, she realized the sound originated somewhere behind her. Was she only imagining it? She turned around, back to the center of the room.

There, near the foot of her bed, unattached to any wall, stood a door.

Oh, lord. Of course.

She walked over and opened it, and found herself face-to-face with Hugh Knatt. *Well, who else would it be?* He wore an impeccably clean and crisp tan-colored suit, which complimented his dark skin nicely. His graying hair was clipped neatly close, and his expression, as usual, was one of mild distaste. With his hands held behind his back, he stepped carefully through the door and around her and began to inspect the room.

Logan couldn't help but feel like a kid again, waiting for Knatt's judgment, waiting to see if, for once, her room might pass muster.

"Up to your usual standards, I see," he said, letting his gaze rise up to the ceiling before rounding on her. "Have you made friends with all the cockroaches?"

I should really give up hoping that someday he'll see the value of my thrift.

"Oh, only the loud-mouthed ones. The shy ones won't talk to me." She felt her eyebrow arch of its own accord, perhaps more out of defensiveness than curiosity. "Why are you here?"

"Ah. Yes, we should be efficient. Follow me."

He walked back through the unmoored door. Bracing herself with a grimace, she followed him.

On the other side of the door stood a chamber far larger than her dingy motel room. She recognized it immediately—it was the travelling room on the ground floor of the estate. Once upon a time, her father had tried to get them to refer to it as the *wanderers' room*, but both she and Knatt refused to call it that. It looked as cold and uninviting as ever.

She stepped through the doorway onto echoing marble floors. Far above her stood a domed ceiling, covered in intricate patterns. A layperson might have assumed the patterns were paint, but Logan knew better. The last time Knatt had refreshed the spells on the room, she'd made the mixture herself. It was made of blood, ash, and ground up wolfsbane. The columns all around the room were painted with it, too. If she hadn't grown up around that kind of stuff, she imagined the truth might have creeped her out.

Knatt stood near the center of the room, right next to a rolling clothes rack. Glancing behind her, she could see the doorway she'd just come through, unmoored on this side as well. Her rented room was still perfectly visible on the other side, waiting for her to return.

"You'll be needing these," said Knatt.

She turned back to him, and he pushed the clothes rack a little closer to her. She stared at it in disbelief and confusion.

"Why would I ever need any of that?"

"Isn't it obvious? You'll have to look presentable before the impressionable young minds, of course."

Her eyebrow arched ever higher. She doubted it would come down again.

"What impressionable minds?"

"Well, we know you need to be able to investigate the young woman's untimely death, don't we? And if you're going to investigate, you'll need to be able to interview her friends, her peers. People her age."

Realization dawned unpleasantly on her.

"You got me a job at the fucking high school, didn't you?"

"Language, Miss Logan. Remember the impressionable young minds."

If she thought he was capable of lighthearted fun, she would have sworn he was enjoying this. She eyed the wardrobe he'd picked out with suspicion, though she had to admit he did have a sense for her style. Sure, everything was nicely pressed button-downs and dress pants, but he'd kept to dark and neutral colors, and she didn't see any skirts—skirts didn't function well with motorcycles. With a sigh, she admitted to herself—though not to him—that she could make this work. After all, she couldn't see that she had much choice. What better way to investigate high school students than to infiltrate the high school?

"So what am I supposed to teach them? Alternative History? Demon Physiology?"

"Don't be ridiculous. You're going to be installed as a temporary grief counselor, to help the students process their recent trauma."

She felt her mouth drop open as she stared.

"Right. Teacher is ridiculous, but therapist—*that* makes sense. Look, I know I can fool a few clients into finding me charming, but I'm not sure you can really call me a people-person. You know?"

Knatt stared right back at her. If he were the type to shrug, she imagined that's what he'd be doing right now.

"You need to be able to ask questions without arousing suspicion. Can you think of a better idea than this?"

With a huff of frustration, she brought a hand up to pinch the bridge of her nose, hoping to head off her growing migraine at the pass. Of course, he was right. As a counselor, she'd be able to ask probing, personal questions, and nobody would bat an eye. *Goddamnit.*

"Fine," she said, nodding finally. "So. How'd you manage it?"

Immediately Knatt's face broke into a smile of radiant self-satisfaction.

"A few suggestions to the right people, of course. That's all it ever takes. You'll need to be at the high school today at 4:00pm, to speak to a Mrs. Wendell, the administrator who will process your paperwork, and a Mr. Johnston, the school principal." He pointed to a bag swinging off the end of the clothes rack. "You'll find your paperwork in there. I've also included a guidebook that ought to give you a few ideas on how to communicate with the children." He gave her a pointed look. "With sensitivity, that is."

"Wonderful."

"Now," he turned to her, "we have one more thing to cover. I cannot in good conscience allow you to conduct another mission armed with nothing but that little butter knife. Let's get you some weapons, shall we?"

Finally. Something she would actually enjoy.

After she and Knatt had rolled the clothes rack and her new mini arsenal into the rented room, and the door to the travelling room had disappeared, she still had several hours to herself with nothing set for her to do. So she took up her usual workout routine, or at least the one she had on the road: a short three mile run over whatever rough terrain she could find, fifty one-armed pushups on each side, a few sets of ab ladders and boxer abs, rotating rock-climbers, one hundred squats carrying her heavy mace, twenty fingertip pull-ups over the bathroom doorway, and a final one mile run. She killed almost three hours with that, then moved on to sword practice.

She remembered the first time she'd ever really pushed herself, physically. As a kid, she'd never particularly stood out in her gym classes—she was usually right at the middle of the pack. Now, when she thought about it, she couldn't say exactly why that was. Maybe her strength hadn't kicked in yet. Maybe she'd felt an unconscious need to hide. Maybe she just never thought to try a little harder. Or maybe it was something else entirely.

But after the incident with Damien, she'd started to wonder.

He must have been the son of one of their clients; to this day, she couldn't remember for sure. After he'd dropped his sword, he'd run inside to tell their parents what had happened. But as soon as he'd turned his back, the ridges had slipped back inside of their own accord, and the briefly torn flesh had healed. When the adults came back outside, they saw no evidence of her transformation and dismissed it as childish fantasy. She'd wanted to come to Damien's defense, but one look from her father had silenced her.

She'd thought that he would explain it all to her later, convinced herself he knew and he would tell her. He didn't. He told her she had made it up, and that she ought to feel ashamed for dragging the boy into her fantasy. If she ever brought it up again, he said, she'd be grounded and she'd never get to go on another visit to Other Side. She couldn't stand the thought of never seeing her aunt again, so despite her fury, she'd kept her mouth shut.

After they got home, her father left within a day to go on another contract job. She couldn't have been more pleased. Knatt stayed home with her that time, but for the most part, he left her to her own devices. So she was free to experiment.

She went almost to the edge of their property line, until she was mostly hidden by the trees. A path wove deep into the woods, circled around a small pond, and came back around; its total length was four miles. So she clocked the exact time and started running.

Everything felt normal at first—she ran at a brisk pace, but it didn't seem like anything she hadn't done in class before. But after a minute, she realized she wasn't out of breath and her heart rate seemed normal—in fact, she hardly felt any different than if she'd been walking at a leisurely pace. Had it always been this way? She pushed harder against the ground, propelling herself a little further with each step—and she felt her body moving faster. The trees whipped past her, blurry even if she focused on them. *Is this running or is it flying?* she'd thought.

Then the path bent suddenly to the left, and, unprepared for the change, she tumbled head-first into a bush.

As she jumped up to get going again, she noticed a few long scratches on her arms, and felt at least one on her cheek. They didn't hurt too badly, so she gave herself a small shake and took off again. When she saw the next curve approaching, she decided to try the speed skater approach. She bent lower to the ground and leaned into it, even letting her hand brush the dirt as she moved. It worked okay—she skidded a bit but remained mostly upright, able to keep going.

Finally, she was back to the start of the trail, where she'd taken off from. She checked her time—about twelve minutes, give or take. So, a little less than three minutes per mile. She tried to remember the fastest mile she'd ever seen at school—maybe six minutes? Maybe five? And what might the world record be? And how far could she push herself if she trained?

She raised her hand to brush her cheek—and found her skin clean, unblemished. When her hand came back down, she assessed her arm—small red marks lined her skin where there had been open cuts only minutes before. And those marks were shrinking.

As she gazed down at her miraculously healing arm, she couldn't help but think about those ridges. She bent her arm at the elbow and ran her fingers along the bone—her ulna, she figured out later. Whatever her father said, she knew the spikes were in there. But how could she make them come out? She tried tapping her arm, moving up and down to see if there might be some specific pressure point. Nothing. She closed her left hand into a fist and slammed it down along the bone; that hurt but it produced no results. Knowing she would only heal if she truly injured herself, she walked over to the nearest tree and tried slamming her arm against it. Still nothing.

All right, she thought to herself. *What am I missing?*

What had led up to the appearance of the ridges in the first place? She'd been play fighting with Damien, and she'd been winning until she stumbled. Then she panicked and threw her arm over her face. So she tried that again now—closing her eyes, tossing her arm up.

Nothing. So it wasn't about the motion, then.

As she stood there, frozen temporarily in place, she had that nagging feeling again, like there was something she couldn't quite remember. *I've done this before.*

But when?

She moved her arm through the motion, backward and forward. The memory was there, just under the surface; she could feel it but she couldn't bring it forth. It was almost like someone had put it in a box somehow. The more she probed at it, the stranger she felt—how could her brain hold onto a memory but allow her no access to it? And yet she was sure. She was sure it was there.

She moved her arm again, but this time, she tried to remember exactly what she'd felt before. She'd stumbled and lost her footing, and she'd felt something she very rarely felt: *afraid.* What did it feel like, to be afraid?

That was it. Fear.

She felt that telltale pain in her arm, and when she opened her eyes, four spikes of bone were pushing through her skin. She angled her arm to get a better view, then reached out to touch them. Just before she reached the end, however, she realized how sharp the outer edges were—sharp as blades. So she touched the sides instead, marveling at their perfect smoothness.

A thought came to her then, unbidden—what would happen if something hit one of the spikes and it broke off? Would it grow back? She felt the reckless urge to give it a try but held back. Now that she'd finally discovered this part of herself, she didn't want to lose it so quickly.

As she touched the smooth bone one more time, she saw a sudden flash of memory—rain, and a quietness that didn't fit. Quietness, and rain, and a voice that was not a voice, tugging at her mind.

Then, all at once, it came to her. That day on their way to Other Side, when they'd stopped at the gas station and she'd seen something out in the rain, felt a force compelling her. She'd known, somehow, that the force didn't have the power over her that it expected to have—that it *should* have had. She pushed into the memory, but she couldn't quite remember how it had ended.

But that had only been a few months ago. Why hadn't she been able to remember it? What had happened to her memory?

The answer was obvious, but she hadn't wanted to see it.

Her father had hidden the memory from her. Using some kind of magic she didn't yet know about, her father had reached into her mind and manipulated it so she couldn't access a part of her own memory.

As the realization dawned on her young self, she felt sick. If he could do that to her, what else could he do? What else had he hidden? What else didn't she know?

In her rented motel room with a broadsword in her hand, Logan felt just as sick about it as she ever had. She'd never gotten a full answer out of him. In fact, when her father had come home, she'd confronted him about it—and he'd done another spell to hide it from her all over again. She hadn't gotten back the memories of that day until she was sixteen years old. That time, she knew not to tell her father what she'd recovered.

So she'd run away instead.

She glanced over at the clock on the small bedside table: almost 2:30pm. She decided to head over to the school a bit early, on the off-chance that observing the kids at the end of the day might yield some kind of information she wouldn't otherwise see.

That, or maybe she just needed a little distraction from memory.

If there was one thing Logan could remember with perfect clarity, it was this: high school was a horror. She parked the bike at the edge of the lot, hoping it would be far enough away from the rushing masses that it would avoid injury. She couldn't help but feel a little apprehension as she looked over at the school. Still, she had no choice. She straightened her jacket and made her way inside, marveling at how similar most high schools and most prisons looked. Or perhaps that was only her perception.

She passed in front of a waiting yellow bus and surmised that classes were about to let out. *Good.* She'd have a chance to witness a microcosm of the day.

Just as she walked through the double front doors, the class bell went off like a nuclear warning. She located the nearest painted cement column and stood on the far side of it, hoping to save herself from the jostling of the crowd.

The mad rush poured out all around her. In truth, her memories of public school were scattered and sporadic. The older she got, the more often Charles brought her along on contract jobs—even though, much of the time, he ignored her while she was there, and even forgot her from time to time. When she was thirteen, she'd tested into skipping a few grades and entered high school early, only to miss so many classes in the semester that they threatened to hold her back. That was when Charles transferred her to a private school that cared more about tuition than truancy.

She'd hated the public school, and she'd hated the private school, too. Part of it was the structure; it had always been hard for her to follow someone else's timeline. But she'd wondered more than once if she might have adapted to it a little better had her father let her attend for more than two or three days at a time.

Looking around her now, it was hard to say if she'd really missed out on anything. She could almost smell the misery on the air, or so it seemed to her. It was possible she'd find out for sure tomorrow.

The swarm of students rushed past her, but she could barely discern separate people, let alone single out who among them might be a murderer. She watched passively as the crowd swelled and then dispersed. Within a few minutes, only a handful of students were left.

She watched a group of girls gather near a doorway before marching as one down the hall and disappearing, and she wondered if they were on a team together. She wondered, too, if any of them had known the victim. Now that the halls were emptier, she detached herself from her post and ambled about, surveying her surroundings.

Near the bottom of the stairs, a table had been set up with a heart-shaped wreath on it, framing a blown-up portrait of Violet Buchanan. The students had already created a memorial to her, complete with candles and stuffed animals and hundreds of cards. She watched two students, a boy and a girl, stop in front of it and place their own tokens. By the sounds of it, at least one of them was crying. Perhaps it was an unusual thought process to entertain, but somehow it comforted her to think that at least some of the other students were grieving. Violet Buchanan was remembered, and she was missed.

As she turned away from them, she noticed an awkward-looking boy fumbling with something near his locker. To her eye, of course, every teenager seemed awkward and out of place, but she had to admit that something about him spoke to an even greater level of discomfort. He was white, pale, gangly, and slouched, with hair somewhere between brown and blonde. He must have felt her gaze on him, because he looked up. His eyes, for the moment they held hers, looked desperate and pleading. She offered him a smile, but his gaze turned hard in return—resentful and defiant. Then he turned away. Perhaps she'd embarrassed him; the thought had her regretting the smile.

She couldn't help but watch him a moment more—he looked so out of his depth. He walked down the hallway a bit, toward a pretty dark-haired girl in a brightly colored outfit, still standing at her locker, typing away furiously on her phone. When he reached her, he made some kind of noise that Logan couldn't quite make out, and the girl looked up. He shoved something into her hands before turning around and walking away with a noticeably duck-footed gait, right out the front door.

Logan switched her attention to the girl, who looked completely dumbfounded by whatever had just happened. She lifted the object in her hands—an envelope—and began to open it.

At that moment, a shockingly loud bang echoed through the hallway around her. She turned to the source—another student had slammed her locker door shut, and as Logan watched, she proceeded to kick it, hard, several times. Based on the force alone, Logan would have been surprised if it didn't make a dent. As she observed the scene before her, Logan couldn't help but notice the way the girl was dressed—pants so loose they might fall off, an oversized gray sweatshirt, and a baseball cap pulled low over her eyes. She looked like she was doing her best to become invisible. The only part of her that seemed to shine through was her hair, which hung in a long heavy braid down her back. Much like the pretty girl before her, this girl was staring at her phone screen. But unlike that girl, she wasn't typing happily away. What was visible of the expression on her face looked like rage and fire. Logan was almost afraid of it.

And yet a part of her immediately empathized with this obvious oddball of a girl. She recognized a piece of herself in her. She remembered what it felt like to know that nobody ever saw you, that nobody wanted to see you. And to wish you could just give up and vanish like they wanted.

Logan let herself look too long. The girl glanced up and met her eyes, and her nose wrinkled in disgusted fury. Then she gathered her books to herself and rushed out the door in a huff.

As she left, a dark thought crossed Logan's mind. Every kid she'd just seen was a suspect. She had to stop looking at them as projections of her younger self, and start looking at them as potential killers.

Maybe it wouldn't be too hard to do both.

Logan killed an hour walking around the school, cementing the layout in her mind and spying on a few afterschool activities. Then she made her way to the administration office at the front of the building for her meeting with Mrs. Wendell and Mr. Johnston.

The principal was curt, perfunctory, and nondescript. Mrs. Wendell waved him over when he walked by. Even after she'd explained who Logan was, he looked mildly confused and completely disinterested. He gave her a sorry excuse for a polite smile, shook her hand so briefly she could barely say for sure it had happened, and walked off again.

"Sorry about him," said Mrs. Wendell, before Logan was even completely sure he was out of earshot. "He doesn't really like talking to…well, people. Any people."

"So school principal was a great career choice," Logan blurted out, then grimaced. Magic or no, she should at least try to act professional.

But Mrs. Wendell loved it.

"I know, right?" she laughed. "He's an odd fish, that one." She leaned forward conspiratorially. "You didn't hear this from me, but let's just say I wouldn't be *surprised* if somebody someday caught him with pictures he shouldn't have. You know, of the students." Logan nodded. She'd understood the implication. "Oh, I know I shouldn't talk that way, but you just never know, do you?"

"That you do not," answered Logan noncommittally.

Mrs. Wendell was a short woman, white and in her forties, with plain, shoulder-length brown hair held back with a pin, and blunt brown fringe resting over her square glasses. She gave Logan a knowing smile as she appraised her.

"Oh, I can tell I'm going to like you. How long did you say you'd be in town for?"

Logan pursed her lips, wondering if Knatt had provided a specific timeline. Then she took a stab at a vagary of an answer.

"It really depends on the students. I'll stay until I'm not needed."

"That makes sense," said Wendell, nodding in self-assured agreement.

"So," said Logan, hoping to press the advantage of Mrs. Wendell's favor, "what can you tell me about Violet? It'll help if I can get at least a little background information, so I'll know more about where the students are coming from when I speak to them."

"Well, I'm sure you've seen the pictures," she motioned toward the front of the building, where the students' memorial lay just beyond the far wall. "Violet was beautiful. Oh, and she was popular, too." Mrs. Wendell's voice took on a forced wistful quality. "She was perfect, you know? She was a cheerleader, and a member of the prom committee, and she was almost homecoming queen."

"Almost?"

"Yeah, she lost to Missy Vreeland." Mrs. Wendell glanced around the office, checking to see if anyone was listening to them, then leaned in even closer to continue. "But I heard that was also the night that Missy's boyfriend, Jason Reed, tried to dump Missy so he could get together with Violet. But Violet was already dating Derek James, only they hadn't told anybody yet. So she turned Jason down, and he had to go back to Missy and pretend that he hadn't tried to hook up with Violet at all. And, you know, Violet and Missy are *best friends*." Mrs. Wendell's delighted expression suddenly faltered, and her face fell. "Were. They were best friends. Well, that's a funny thing, isn't it?" Her eyes drifted off to the left, like her mind was somewhere far away. "It's so stupid, really. Why were those kids even out in the woods in the first place? We should never have let them play out in the woods."

Logan felt a surge of pity for this strange woman. She reached out a tentative hand and patted her on the arm, in what she hoped was a comforting gesture.

"You didn't *let* them do anything," she said gently. "They made their choices. It's not your fault."

With curiously blank eyes, Mrs. Wendell let her gaze drift back to Logan's face, though she seemed to have a hard time focusing on it.

"She was so beautiful. You never think…" her words drifted off, her gaze sliding to the left again. After a moment, she shook herself. "But you're not here to listen to an old woman prattle on, are you? Let me get you some of the pertinent files, then I'll take you to the office you'll be using while you're here. Well, it's more of an empty classroom than an office." She walked into the room extending behind her desk and came back with a crate full of files, which she pushed into Logan's hands. "At the front, you'll find Violet's file. The rest belong to the students who have so far been signed up to talk to you. You might get other walk-ins, of course. Just take their names and I'll get their files to you."

Logan nodded, suppressing a smile. She had to admit Knatt had done his part seamlessly. She never would have guessed it could be so easy. Of course, the obvious downside was that she still had to spend the next few days talking to teenagers.

"Follow me," said Mrs. Wendell, walking toward the door. Logan complied.

She led her past the memorial, and Logan couldn't help but notice that when they passed it, Wendell's gaze jumped conspicuously around the room, looking everywhere else. They walked up the main staircase and down the hall to the right, then into a small out-of-use classroom with big windows. A few desks and chairs had been stacked against the back wall, leaving the floor mostly empty. At the front of the room stood a bigger teacher's desk with a swivel chair behind it.

"You can rearrange the room however you like," Mrs. Wendell said as Logan put the box down on the desk. "If you need anything, just let me know. Different chairs, a particular kind of coffee—just give me a ring!" She pointed at the old land-line phone stationed near the door. "If you press *pound one*, that gets you to the front office. Just say who you are and ask for me!"

"Thank you, that's very kind," said Logan. A part of her recklessly wished she could tell this woman why she was here—that she planned to find out what happened to Violet and to give her whatever justice she could. But, apart from all the other reasons that would be a bad idea, she suspected that discovering the existence of the supernatural world would traumatize Mrs. Wendell even more than she already had been. So she settled for something else. Reaching out to place a light hand on Mrs. Wendell's shoulder, she said, "You know, while I'm primarily here for the kids, my services aren't exclusive. If you ever need someone to talk to, feel free to drop by. You don't need to make an appointment."

Mrs. Wendell's eyes went wide and round in touched surprise; it was almost as though no one had offered her a sympathetic ear before. "That's so sweet," she said. Then her face fell into a sad smile. "You'd better watch that, or these kids will eat you alive." She gestured around her, as though the ghosts of high school students were all around them.

"I can hold my own," Logan assured her.

"I'll bet you can," said Mrs. Wendell, chuckling. Then she reached into her pocket and pulled out a set of keys, pointing to each one while she described its function. "This will let you lock the door to this room, this one will get you into the building after or before hours through the side door, and this one will get you into the teacher lounge. Speaking of, let me go ahead and show you where that is. Follow me!"

She marched out the door, and Logan hurried to lock up behind her—she didn't want anyone getting a look at those files who shouldn't. As she walked away from the door, she remembered the oncoming mass of students as they rushed away. She didn't want to have the thought, but it came anyway.

It could have been any one of them.

After she showed her the staff lounge, Mrs. Wendell excused herself so she could head home for the day. Logan trudged back up the stairs to her new office, hoping to get more of a sense for who Violet was before the next day began. She locked herself into the room and pulled the first few files out of the box, then spread them out on the desk before taking her seat.

She opened Violet Buchanan's file. The first page featured her school portrait and a summary of her academics. Violet had been an excellent student; her grades never hovered below a B+, and she'd followed her school's advanced track every step of the way. She was involved in cheerleading and the prom committee, yes, but she was also on the debate team. One of her teachers had mentioned in her notes about her that Violet wanted to be a lawyer.

The page after that took a turn away from academics. It was a bullying complaint against Violet by another girl, followed by how she'd been disciplined for it. The girl claimed Violet had gotten her friends to mutter "pig" every time she walked by. They would snigger behind their hands if she acted like she heard them. Violet claimed she'd done no such thing, and that she couldn't be held responsible for what other people said. Nevertheless, the teacher involved had required her to hand in a 500-word statement on the effects of bullying. Logan scanned the paper, and guessed that Violet had spent half an hour copying internet articles and tweaking the language to sound less formal or stilted. She ended the paper with the line: *Everyone should always be nice to each other, no matter what.*

Logan checked the date. The incident was from Violet's freshman year. Logan flipped through the next few files: four individual girls had registered bullying complaints against Violet, each one with little enough evidence that Violet had managed to feign ignorance one way or another. Each time, she was "punished" with the paltry task of single 500-word statement, explaining why one thing or the other was evil or wrong.

The fifth incident in her file, however, looked a little different. It started with a citation against two other students, Judith Li and Suzanne Grubb, who were charged with "inappropriate behavior and inciting mischief," for, apparently, streaking in front of the school. The next page, however, rescinded the citation. The page after that was another complaint against Violet—that she herself had made.

By Violet's account, the two girls disciplined for streaking were considered a running joke among some of their peers. In Violet's words, Judith Li was "a dyke-y Asian nerd with no life," while Suzanne Grubb was frequently referred to as "Grubby the fatty." Both girls were on the soccer team, which occasionally held their practices at the same time as the cheerleaders. Violet explained that she'd decided to prank them, so she'd gotten a few of her friends to wait with her in the locker room for the two girls to take a shower after practice. While Judith and Suzanne were occupied, they had stolen their clothes and taken them to the courtyard in front of the school, pinned them to the flagpole, and raised them up in the air.

Violet spared no details in her account. She wrote: *We went back to the locker room so we could see the looks on their faces when they came back and figured it out. Missy said she "couldn't wait to see that fatty lose her shit." They came back to their lockers and they saw us standing there, and we could tell they didn't know what was going on. Then Judith looked in her locker, and she turned to us and asked what we did with her clothes. Suzanne freaked out and looked in her locker, too. She didn't even ask us anything, she just burst into tears on the spot. She was trying to hold her towel up, but I guess it was a school towel, so it didn't really fit her all the way around. She had to use both hands to hold it together. Most teams don't want you to use your own towel, you can only use the school one. The more she cried, the harder it was for her to keep her towel up. That was when I realized what I'd gotten us all to do. Missy just started laughing, and so did the other girls. They thought it was funny. They all think I'm really cool now. They probably won't tell you that it was my idea, but it was. So that's why Judith and Suzanne shouldn't have detention. They weren't streaking, they were just trying to get their clothes back. It's my fault.*

A teacher's account of the incident followed.

On September 17th, students Suzanne Grubb and Judith Li were apprehended for streaking. Miss Grubb was found near the front door of the school, crouching behind a pillar wearing nothing but a towel. Miss Li was discovered in the front courtyard near the flag pole, wearing nothing at all. She claimed that her towel fell off while she was retrieving Miss Grubb's and her belongings, which she claimed had been strung up from the pole. Disciplinary actions against the two students were dismissed when Violet Buchanan corroborated their account. Miss Buchanan has been suspended from the cheerleading and debate teams pending a disciplinary hearing.

In the end, Violet had gotten two weeks' worth of detentions, then full reinstatement of all her previous privileges. For a moment, Logan felt a certain indignation over the light punishment, but as she flipped through the rest of Violet's file, she realized something: the complaints against her had ceased. Logan glanced through Violet's account of the incident again. It was difficult to gauge in her writing, but she had to think there was remorse in those words. After all, she'd turned herself in. She hadn't wanted them to get in trouble for something that she'd done to them. It was small, but it was something.

There were two more incidents logged in Violet's file, but these were logged by her and not against her. First, she'd filed a straight-up sexual harassment claim against Jason Reed. She alleged that despite her repeated rejections, he continued to proposition her in overtly sexual terms, often on school grounds. She also claimed that he'd started multiple rumors that he had already engaged in sexual acts with her, which caused his cohorts to harass and catcall her in the halls. Mr. Reed's defense of himself had been to state, "She should take it as a compliment. Any other girl in this school would be happy to get with me." He denied that he'd started the rumors, but one of his buddies had outed him, stating, "Yeah, Reed totally banged that slut!" Both boys had been temporarily removed from the football team and received in-school suspensions, which resulted in the need for them to take summer classes.

Logan checked the dates. That particular bout of harassment had occurred the year before, yet if she remembered Mrs. Wendell's story correctly, Jason Reed had continued his dogged pursuit of Violet through Homecoming of this year.

Violet had learned better. Jason had not.

Logan sighed, realizing that every name in Violet's file was a viable and likely suspect. She turned to the last incident, which was a little vague. Violet reported that she suspected someone might be following her. She'd found a note taped to her locker after cheerleading practice, and discovered a hand-drawn picture of herself inside it, with the words "my beloved" written underneath. She'd also seen someone standing in her yard at night, but she couldn't tell who. An unknown number called her phone but all she heard was breathing when she answered. She found another note on her locker, which read: *Nobody understands you but me.*

She thought it might be Jason, but she wasn't sure. The reports went nowhere. Teachers barely believed her, and Violet herself had conceded it might be a prank pulled by one of her friends.

Logan made a quick list of everyone in the files, everyone who might have wanted to hurt Violet. She put Jason at the top.

By now, the sun was disappearing behind the line of trees outside her window, past the short expanse of the soccer field below. She put Violet's file back in the box, and that box in the bottom drawer of the desk. The list she folded up and slipped into her back pocket. Then she left the room and locked it back up behind her. She planned to get some takeout from the diner she'd found the previous morning, then head back to the motel for mindless television and sleep.

An unsettled feeling creeped over her as she crossed the parking lot to her Ninja. Even though she couldn't sense anything but her own shadow, she couldn't shake the feeling, somehow, that someone was watching her.

Chapter 3
Elimination Rounds

I'd been on my own for over a year the first time I saw it. It was beautiful—shining and shimmering, like a mirage, full of light and promise. Just seeing it made me warm, made me hopeful. It was almost like its very presence melted away the outside world.

I'd been on my own for a year. At first, I stayed with my aunt at Other Side. I begged her not to tell my father where I was, but she could only hold to that promise for so long. In the end, all she'd told him was that I was safe, but that had been enough. He was there within the day, but I'd known him well enough to get gone long before that.

I made my way to an unfamiliar city, getting by like the rest of the homeless do. After that I spent some time drifting between the spare beds and spare couches that friendly acquaintances from Other Side could make available to me. When nobody had any room anymore, I started camping. I'd left home with just enough borrowed gear to make long-term camping semi-tenable, although food occasionally became an issue.

When I saw it for the first time, I'd been out of touch with real civilization for weeks. I was trekking west through the Cascades, and the last town I'd seen was long behind me. I'd made camp in a small enclave of trees, which offered weak protection against the snow. I'd finally drifted off at some point in the night, huddled in the bottom of my sleeping bag beside a slowly dying fire.

I'm not sure what stirred me. Maybe a sound, maybe just a feeling. But I woke up, and I could see a light somewhere above my head, spilling onto me in patches through the gap at the top of the sleeping bag.

I wriggled my way out into the open, and though the fire had gone cold, the air around me felt warm. No snow fell on my skin, but I could still see it coming down in the trees around me. I looked for the source of the light; it seemed to be some 10 feet ahead of me in the woods.

To this day, I'm not sure what I was thinking as I walked forward. Maybe I wasn't thinking anything. Maybe I moved on primordial instinct.

As I placed a hand on a nearby trunk and sidestepped it, I looked around, sure that I must be right on top of the light source by now. I was correct.

On the ground ahead of me lay a glowing bronze artifact. When my eyes found it, I fell completely still, briefly mesmerized. Then, suddenly, without a single conscious decision, I was on my knees before it, brushing away the leaves so I could see it in full.

It was an image similar to a labyrinth, like the kind I'd walked for meditation at Other Side—but different. Unlike a labyrinth, it wasn't perfectly round, but rather came to a point at the top—like a teardrop. And the design inside was different, too—the path of lines created a vortex at the top, just above but not connected to the landing point at the center. And of course, this artifact was much *smaller than a meditation labyrinth—only about two feet in diameter, far too small for someone to walk on.*

When I'd fallen asleep, I'd been thinking about how angry I was at my father—and how absolutely perfect it was that he finally cared about my whereabouts now that I wanted nothing further to do with him. I'd been wondering if anyone in the world missed me while I'd been off the grid. And I'd started laying pessimistic odds on my own survival in the mountains.

But all of that worry and anguish melted away as I gazed at the strange bronze labyrinth before me. I felt so warm. I felt right, *somehow, though I couldn't say why.*

The Choronzon Key.

Its name came to me before I ever thought to ask. And I knew, without a doubt, that it was right.

I gazed at it a while, letting myself feel that soft, sweet quiet. I felt compelled to touch it, so I did. It was so warm to the touch it almost burned, but not quite. I felt its warmth travel through my body.

And then, all of a sudden, it was gone.

The cold returned immediately, like the Key had never been. I ran back to my sleeping bag and hurried inside. I had no idea what had just happened, but somehow, I still felt better than I had before. I fell asleep again with no trouble, an alien and unfamiliar content settled over me.

I wouldn't see the Key again for almost a year after that. I don't know what it was doing all that time, but I harbor the sneaking suspicion that it was evaluating me.

I suppose I must have passed.

Logan woke in her small rented room. The Key stung slightly on the skin of her back, but she ignored it. It was prone to bother her for the duration of the missions she undertook for it. Was *missions* the word? Should she call them *quests*? *Does it matter?*

As she slowly lifted her head, a thin piece of paper gently unstuck itself from her face—she'd fallen asleep on the book Knatt had given her on how to talk to teenagers. Setting it aside, she pushed herself from the bed and showered quickly. When she stepped out of the stall to grab a towel, she couldn't help but catch a glimpse of herself in the mirror. Anyone who didn't know better might guess all her markings were tattoos; more than a few people had before. The Key certainly had the appearance of a tattoo, but by now, it wasn't the only unusual permanent mark on her skin.

The first ones she'd noticed had shown up on her forearms, right over the very spots where her ridges slid out. Four dark grey diamonds marked the skin over her ulna, each with a thin red line in the center where her skin always broke. She'd noticed them a few days after her twentieth birthday; they just appeared there one morning when she woke up. A year or so after that, she'd gotten what seemed to be identical rashes on the upper parts of her shoulders, near her collar bone...only unlike most rashes, these were purple. Within a few days, one of the alien rashes started to itch, the skin peeling. When she scratched at it, a thin layer came painlessly away. The skin underneath was a purplish black, and the pattern was more defined.

It looked almost like leopard spots, only a little too unfamiliar. It was like she was slowly turning into an alien.

A day later, the other side came away, too. Every year, the

two patches seemed to stretch a little farther. She didn't know what they meant or when they would stop growing. By now, they ran halfway down her upper arms. To a layperson, they looked like tattoos, so she let everyone who asked about them think they were.

As she examined them briefly in the mirror, she wondered if they looked bigger than they had the day before. Then she let her gaze fall lower, to the shiny three inch scar on her lower abdomen. With habit so ingrained it felt like instinct, she reached her right hand over to her left elbow, the inner skin revealing the only intentional mark she bore. It read *The Field Only Reveals*. Soothed as if by a security blanket or an old friend, she took a deep breath and turned away from the mirror.

She'd packed her messenger bag the night before with a few weapons and an old lore book, as well as a paper bag full of fruit-based snacks for the day. Once she'd dressed herself in a white collared shirt and tight black pants tucked into motorcycle boots, she picked up her jacket, helmet, and bag and headed out the door.

Her ride was pretty short now that she knew the route. Deciding that her strategy the day before to keep her bike safe from traffic had likely been optimal, she parked at the far end of the lot again. As soon as she jumped off and threw down the kickstand, she shrugged out of her jacket and carried it with her. Summer encroached on the last vestiges of spring; even without the jacket, she grew uncomfortably warm as she walked. Fortunately for her, she already knew the insides of the building would be crisp and cool, pumped full of artificial freeze.

Once inside, she headed for the teachers' lounge first. She had no intention of trying her hand at the day without the aid of a decent amount of coffee. She found the biggest mug the cabinet offered and filled it, adding a little cream on top when she was done. Then she headed toward the door so she could find her way back to the classroom that was her office.

"Excuse me!" a female voice called to her. She turned to the noise. An almost impossibly tiny woman was running at her—white, with curly gray hair piled in a loose lump atop her head. She smiled warmly at Logan as she approached. "You're the grief counselor, aren't you?"

Inwardly, Logan cringed. She'd been hoping to avoid any and all unnecessary conversation, with either students or teachers. But there was no backing out now, it seemed.

"Yep, that's me," said Logan. She used a voice that she hoped sounded counselor-worthy.

"Wonderful!" She struck out a hand, which Logan shook. "Esmerelda Swinson, lovely to meet you."

"H. C. Logan," Logan answered. "I usually go by Logan."

"I'm so pleased you're here," Esmerelda Swinson said, adjusting her hair-pile with a light pat. "And, frankly, shocked that anyone in admin bothered to send for someone like you. I'll be sending a number of students your way today, hope you don't mind. They might not all have much to say, of course, and that's perfectly all right. I'm just hoping to give the children all a chance to make their peace with what's happened, however they need to. But I'm sure you understand that."

"Of course," Logan answered, nodding automatically. She supposed it was a good thing that the teacher wanted to look out for her students, though she couldn't help but selfishly wonder if this woman was placing unnecessary work onto her plate. On the other hand, it was fully possible the killer never had a direct connection to Violet, so casting a wide net might prove the better option in the long run. "Feel free to send anyone my way that you think could benefit from it. We're all here for the students, after all, aren't we?"

"How right you are!" the tiny woman exclaimed, clapping her hands together with a look of delight on her face. "Well, it's just fantastic having you on the team, Miss Logan. I'll be seeing you around, I'm sure."

And with that, she tottered off again. Logan gave a small sigh of relief. If she could only get through all her interactions with so little effort, maybe this wouldn't be so bad. Maybe.

When Logan reached her makeshift office, she saw that a sign-up sheet had been posted on the door, and the first page of open slots had already been filled. She tore off the page and took it inside with her. Inside, she placed the list and her coffee on the desk, then arranged two chairs in front of it, facing each other. The part of her that remembered being a teenager didn't think she'd get too many answers out of people sitting behind that overbearing slab. On a sudden thought, she hopped over to the supply closet in the corner of the room and pulled out a box of tissues to place on the desk as well.

There. It was almost like she knew something about being a grief counselor. Almost.

The time was 7:45am. Only five minutes until the first class, which was also about the time her first student should show up, according to Mrs. Wendell. She pulled out the same book she'd brought with her to Miss Adelaide Humphrey's estate and propped it open. At the moment, she didn't have any particular interest in reading it, but she didn't want to look too expectant to the first student who walked in.

She needn't have bothered, of course. As soon as she cracked the spine, she heard a knock on her open door. Making sure to catch a quick glimpse of her sheet first, she turned to see her first potential suspect.

The slim girl with the downward slanting mouth who stood before her didn't look too much like a threat. Inwardly Logan braced herself, remembering the advice she'd pored over in the guidebook the night before. *Don't treat them like monsters*, she told herself. *It's counterproductive.*

"Hello," Logan offered with a welcoming smile. "Are you Ashley?"

The girl nodded without speaking, anxiously twisting the hem of her T-shirt.

"Come on in," said Logan, gesturing toward a seat in front of the desk. As the girl crossed over, Logan left the swivel chair to come sit on the other side with her patient like a good ersatz therapist. She got the sense that this one didn't need any help feeling intimidated. Once they were both seated, Logan took a stab at getting them started. The first direction from the book ran through her mind: *Stay open and make no assumptions.* "My name is Logan. I know your teachers may have instructed you to call me *Miss* Logan, but I don't think that's necessary. I usually just go by Logan. Do you like to be called Ashley, or is there something else you would prefer?"

The student paused before answering. Logan almost worried she'd overtaxed her already.

"Ashley's fine," she muttered.

"Excellent. And do you prefer female pronouns?" *We live in a world of increasing diversity*, the book had said. *Not every student will identify with the gender of their birth. Here are a few questions to help you avoid some awkwardness...*

Confusion took hold of Ashley's face but then disappeared again.

"Yeah, I'm a girl."

"Good to know. Thank you, Ashley. So, how about you tell me how your week has been?"

Ashley was quiet, still twisting the edge of her shirt, and now worrying her bottom lip between her teeth. Logan let the silence stretch almost a minute before breaking it.

"All right. We don't have to start there. We can talk about whatever you want. If you like, you can spend the hour telling me about your favorite TV show, or a book you read once, or whatever celebrities you think are cute. Or we can talk about how you're feeling now. Or, of course, we can sit here in perfect silence, too. It's entirely up to you."

The girl nodded slowly, her lower lip quivering dangerously. Both her hands now pulled at the white cotton fabric. Finally, she spoke.

"I was in...I had Spanish and Pre-Calc with Violet. I had... we...we used to ride the bus together, back in middle school." Her voice wavered and she shook her head furiously, like somehow that would keep her from crying.

It didn't. Seconds later, she burst into tears.

The rest of Logan's first hour was something of a roller coaster. Once the girl started crying, Logan hopped up to shut the door as quickly as possible, immediately angry with herself that she hadn't thought to do that as soon as the girl came in. She knew better now, at least. Then she spent the next few minutes assuring the girl that crying was not only natural and normal, it was even good.

"As awful as everything seems right now," she said in soft soothing tones, "it's better to let it all come to the surface instead of pushing it down."

She started by giving the girl a new tissue every time she needed one, but eventually she just grabbed the box and held it in front of her, so Ashley wouldn't need a middle man anymore. Slowly the sobbing subsided, and Ashley related her entire history with Violet, which didn't amount to much. When pressed to consider what affected her so deeply about Violet's death, she admitted her sense of trauma had more to do with the idea of death itself than with her actual relationship to Violet. After that, she and Logan ended up chatting for a while about the nature of death, why it scared people, the subtle and strange ways its presence shaped the world around them. All in all, Logan felt this was a pretty solid start to her morning.

In the end, when Logan got up to open the door for her, Ashley asked if she could get a hug before she left. A little bemused, Logan obliged.

"Everybody thinks she was so mean," Ashley said as she left. "But she was nice, too. She let me borrow her pink flower shirt one time. She didn't need to do that."

"That's true," Logan nodded.

Ashley's eyes rounded a little as she looked at Logan. Possibly in admiration, or something similar.

"It was cool talking to you," she said. Her hands no longer twisted at her hem. "Do you think I could come by again sometime if I need to? I mean, just if you have the time."

Huh. Well, that's...new. And, I guess... good. It's good. Blending in as a fake grief counselor. Cool?

"Of course," said Logan. "As long as I'm here, you are free to come back whenever you need to."

"Thank you." For a moment, Ashley's eyes got even rounder. Logan wondered if she was going to hug her again. Then she blurted out, "I gotta go. Bye!" And she ran off.

Logan immediately crossed Ashley off the mental list of possible suspects. She'd never even made it to the physical list. *If that girl is guilty,* Logan thought to herself, *she's too good an actor to catch.*

She crossed back over to the desk to see who was up next.

Missy Vreeland. Perfect. Missy was already on the list, so one way or the other, this interview was bound to tell her something. Logan wondered what the odds were that Missy would turn out to be as sweet and sensitive as Ashley.

Right off the bat, Missy wasn't quite as prompt as Ashley had been, but Logan chose not to hold it against it. She had an occasional habit of tardiness herself from time to time, if her last job weren't perfect evidence of that. When Missy rolled in about a minute after the bell rang, Logan gave her a quick smile and a wave and pointed her at the far chair, taking a quick mental note of her basic description as she did. *White, 5'5 or 5'6, brown hair. Distinctly a teenager.*

Choosing to learn from her mistakes, Logan closed the door right after her, before coming to sit on the chair across from her.

"Hello Missy," said Logan. "I'm Logan. Do you prefer female pronouns?"

Missy scoffed and cast her gaze down to her nails, which were meticulously painted in bubblegum pink. "Obviously."

"Hm. Fair enough," said Logan. She could feel the well-practiced smile she turned on for clients slipping into place. It was the kind of smile that humored without letting on. *I guess if the whole day is one-on-one, I can just treat each one of them like a client. A small and hormonal client.* "Tell me, what would you like to talk about, Missy?"

"God," Missy huffed. "I can't believe I even have to do this. I'm not some psycho basket case, you know."

Makes one of us, I guess. With years of practice behind her, Logan could be reasonably sure her sarcastic thought process wouldn't show through on her face.

"I never thought you were," said Logan. "Did somebody say that you were?"

"Of course not," said Missy. "I just meant—with all this." She waved her hand in the air around her, eyes up on the ceiling. Missy didn't seem overly fond of eye contact.

You're lucky I'm not supposed to assume you're being defensive, kid. The book taught me better than that. Knatt would be so pleased.

"It's my understanding that you and Violet were close friends. Were you not?"

"I guess so," she shrugged. "Does it matter?"

"I like to think that friendship matters quite a bit, actually. It's good to have friends. Sometimes friends can make you a better person." *Might not apply in your case, sweetheart, but I'm not supposed to say that out loud.* With considerable effort, Logan pressed pause on her own thoughts. *It's not even ten and I'm already getting salty.* She needed to pace herself if she was going to get through the day without exhausting herself. She took a breath and refocused on her attempt at playing the counselor. "And it's hard to lose them, especially if it's unexpected. When someone close to you dies, there's nothing unusual about talking to someone about it. It certainly doesn't make you a *psycho basket case.*"

Missy shrugged and shifted in her seat. A twitch of irritation came over Logan, but she brushed it aside.

"You don't have to talk to me, of course. We can sit here quietly. It's up to you."

Missy glanced down at her nails again, then let her eyes drift up to the ceiling. With a huff she said, "Yeah, I was friends with Violet. I guess. I never really knew if I could trust her." She clicked her tongue. "You can't trust some people."

So worldly, this one.

"Why is that?"

"Some people are just shady and jealous." She pursed her lips and deigned to glance at Logan. "Everyone's jealous of the pretty girls. And the pretty girls are jealous of each other, most of the time. Somebody's always out there trying to one up you so they can take what's yours." The hint of a smirk played at her face, curling up the farthest corner of her mouth. "Don't you remember that from when you were in school? Like, 30 years ago, or whenever?"

Logan gave a semi-involuntary chortle as she popped a placating smile into place. *Wrong crowd, kid.*

"Nope, I don't remember that at all. So, you feel that Violet took something from you?"

Missy faltered, her brows furrowing as she considered the question.

"I mean, Violet was just *like that*. She was one of those girls." She drew out the "o," then gave Logan a look like she was sure Logan would understand exactly what she meant.

"*What* girls?"

"The kind of girl who tries to *steal* another girl's boyfriend. You know, because she can't get one on her own. The kind of girl who just *needs* that attention. You know. A *slut*."

Suddenly, Logan realized she was developing a new artificial expression: concern-guided confusion. She felt it take over her face as she considered the girl in front of her.

"I was under the impression that Violet did have a boyfriend."

"Well, yeah," Missy uttered, clearly exasperated. "*Now* she does. Or did. Whatever. She was dating Derek. But, like, she wasn't *always* dating Derek. You know?"

"I don't. Tell me." She clasped her hands together and let her head tilt to the side, like she was eager to find out.

Missy rolled her eyes. The whole exercise was obviously quite a burden on her, and yet she kept on talking. "Violet always wanted what I had, okay?" She flipped a piece of hair behind her shoulder and pursed her lips again. "It's not my fault. I mean, when I first got together with Jason, she, like, completely flipped out. It was just sad. Nobody is going to date you if you let yourself look *that* pathetic. And, I mean, It's not my fault that I'm more popular than her, but she just couldn't deal with it.

Every time I turned around, she was basically throwing herself at him. I mean, god. But that's just who she was, I guess. Just another jealous little slut." She ended with a pointed look back at Logan.

As Logan gazed at the child sitting across from her, she imagined it wasn't hard to guess Missy's entire life in this little town. *What must it be like to live your life dependent on the approval of the crowd, with all those shifting loyalties and mercurial whims?* It was no wonder she came off so petulant and insecure, even in front of a stranger. Missy had put it into words herself: *you can't trust some people.* Or, in Missy's case, *any* people.

"It must have been hard for you to be friends with her," said Logan, her tone careful and measured. "I heard there was an incident at the Homecoming dance. Would you like to talk about that?"

She watched as Missy's eyes flashed, her face almost crumpling before she recovered herself.

"There's no need. I'm completely over it." She shrugged one shoulder, a half-smile struggling to spread on her lips. "Besides, I got my crown. That's what counts."

Logan had never, at any point in her life, wanted to be a homecoming queen. But she tried to imagine being the kind of girl who wanted that. And what it must have felt like to finally get it, only to have your boyfriend break up with you within a few hours. For your best friend, no less. *Your best friend who didn't even want him anyway.*

"Were you angry with her? For trying to tarnish your night?"

Missy's gaze remained pinned to the floor. *That pesky eye contact.*

"No. I don't get mad. That's for idiots and freaks. I just get even."

Logan kept her gaze neutral, refusing to let any expression pass. Her voice followed suit, sounding almost robotic as it escaped her lips. "Did you get even with Violet?"

Missy shrugged. Her voice, when she spoke, sounded hollow. "I got Jason back, didn't I? I'm gonna graduate high school as the Homecoming Queen, with the hottest guy on the football team as my boyfriend. And Violet is—"

She broke off, her expression frozen. Logan chose to finish the thought for her.

"Violet is not going to graduate high school at all."

"Right," said Missy. "Because she's dead." Finally she met Logan's eyes again. Her own looked muted and far away. "I win."

Logan heard no triumph in her voice. Only defeat.

Lunch, by the time it rolled around, proved a much-needed break from the drama of high school students. After Missy, she'd seen two kids in a row who openly and smugly admitted to agreeing to a counseling session just to get out of a class. They were both equally shocked by how quickly she sent them packing. Since she didn't know the schedules of any of the students on her list, she had to call Mrs. Wendell after each one to get her to send the next kid along. The third kid after that had been another crier who barely knew Violet but wanted someone to talk to. Though that was draining in its own way, she decided she would take a million of those over another encounter with Missy.

Mrs. Wendell had told her the day before when she should

take her break, and she took it on the dot. Since she didn't feel particularly in the mood for cafeteria spaghetti, she chose to forgo the actual meal and take a walk outside instead. A walk, and possibly a brief smoke.

Locking her jacket and helmet inside her "office," she shouldered her bag and went outside. The sun blazed down on her, heating up the day and urging her to roll up her sleeves, or even lose the over-shirt entirely. She ignored the impulse. Tattoos didn't work so well as an explanation for her deformations when she was supposed to be setting an example for teenagers. She couldn't help feeling a little resentful; if she were back in her home city, the weather would undoubtedly be cooler, likely with a crisp breeze rolling through.

She strolled out one of the back doors of the building, heading toward the field instead of the parking lot. The grounds currently lay empty, all students and teachers still cloistered in their air conditioned halls. Logan had never been great with heat, though she fared unusually well in the cold. Unusually for a human being, that is.

Once she passed behind a line of trees, she opened her backpack and fished out her emergency pack of cigarettes. She didn't smoke regularly anymore, but she kept a pack with her when she traveled as a kind of nervous habit. She'd picked up smoking a little before her eighteenth birthday, when she'd settled, for a time, in Los Angeles. Most days, she tried not to remember the LA months. LA was hot and miserable, and she'd been hot and miserable while she was there. She'd picked up a few good skills though—like how to hotwire a car, and how to disable a home security system. A few good skills, and at least one decidedly bad habit.

Missy had reminded her too much of other people, other moments. Logan popped a cigarette in her mouth and lit it, imagining Knatt's disappointment as she did. When she'd gone to LA, she'd been fresh from a brief respite at Other Side, which had meant that, for once, she was relatively washed and clean. The main advantage to cleanliness, she'd learned, was that it helped you stay anonymous in a crowd. If you had a distinctive scent, people tended to remember you with more ease.

She'd never wanted people to remember her. Especially back when she made her living by shoplifting and stealing wallets off men in suits.

She got about halfway through the cigarette before shame, and an unpleasant cough, overtook her. Then she stubbed it out and headed back, hoping the smell wouldn't linger with her if she walked briskly enough.

On her way back, she saw that a few girls had come outside and were now kicking a soccer ball around in one of the fields. She paused for a moment to watch them, glad of the reminder that, at the end of the day, most of the kids she had to talk to were just that: kids. Even the piece-of-work kids like Missy.

As she started walking again, she realized that she recognized one of the girls on the field. It was the angry girl from the day before, who'd slammed her locker and kicked it before running off. Logan paused briefly to watch her as she sprinted with impressive speed down the field. Well, perhaps soccer was a more constructive outlet for her energies.

Finally Logan pushed back into the air conditioning and made her way up the stairs, trying to steel herself for an afternoon of taxing interactions with teenagers.

The next student who walked through the door was an underclassman, a bright-faced girl in the freshmen class who idolized Violet. Logan got through that hour easily enough, though she could hardly say she'd connected with her. *But that's not what I'm here for, right? At least I didn't scare her off, I guess.*

Her appointment after that came quite late. Despite her interview with Missy, Logan once again determined that she shouldn't hold tardiness against him and did her best to put it out of her mind. Still, she'd clocked his name right after she came back from lunch, and she wasn't at all sure what she should expect from him: it was Jason Reed. *No one is any more a suspect than anyone else*, she thought to herself with determination. *All I know is that either he doesn't respect the concept of consent, or he doesn't understand it. But that does not a murderer make. Not for sure, anyway.* As he took his sweet time to show up for his timeslot, she considered what kind of questions she might want to take him through.

I am starting to understand why Knatt hates it when I'm late. But she forced herself not to dwell on it.

Finally, he knocked at the doorframe. He was white, tall, and somewhat nondescript in the face with a semi-vacant look in his eye. She waved him to the seat while she walked over and shut the door, then came to stand near the desk.

"Jason Reed?" she asked, her right eyebrow arching as she took him in. He'd slumped immediately on the chair, letting his legs spread wide before him. Entitlement wrapped around him like a cozy blanket. *Stop that*, she told herself.

"That's me," he said, letting an indolent smile slowly creep over his face as he stared at her.

Oh kid. Don't test me.

"And your preferred pronouns?"

His expression was blank and uncomprehending.

"My what?"

Logan kept her face frozen, resisting the urge to roll her eyes.

"Do you go by *he?*"

"Uh...yeah."

She glanced over at the clock.

"Tell me, Jason. Do you normally show up to scheduled appointments seventeen minutes late?"

For a split second, he looked uncomfortable. Perhaps he hadn't expected to be questioned. Perhaps the better question would have been—*when was the last time someone called you on it?*

The discomfort was gone in an instant, however. He covered it neatly with a new, more sheepish grin.

"Am I really that late? I guess I got more distracted than I realized."

Logan shrugged but held off on the placating smile. "I suppose it's your hour. You may waste it if you wish." Her head cocked to the side as she continued studying him. Underneath the smarm and self-satisfaction, his face was handsome. She supposed the sports jersey earned him some popularity among his peers, but it meant nothing to her. "Nonetheless, it would be polite of you to apologize."

"Uh...yeah. I'm sorry." His discomfort came back, accompanied by a dose of confusion.

Better than nothing. She turned on the conciliatory client smile. "That's not so hard, is it? Now, why don't we talk about you for a bit?" She eased into the chair across from him.

"You want to talk about me? I thought we were gonna talk about Violet."

"Whatever you like. Do you want to talk about Violet?"

"Uh, I guess so." He shifted in his seat, like he wasn't sure of his conversational footing.

"I understand she was close with your girlfriend, Missy. Were you and Violet also close?"

In an instant, it was almost like he forgot he was still talking to an authority figure. He cracked what he clearly thought was a sly smile, full of blunt teenage-boy innuendo. "You could say we were close, yeah."

Her own smile dropped as she zeroed in on him. "You could *say* so? What does that mean? Were you close, or were you not?"

He bobbed his head back and forth, more like an imitation of a rooster than a nod. "In a manner of speaking, yeah."

"Mm. Another qualified answer. Are you implying that you had a sexual relationship with Violet?"

He shrugged, that sheepish noncommittal smile back on his face. "Hey, I'm not saying anything ever happened."

"But you are implying so. Maybe you simply wanted something to happen?"

"Well, yeah, who didn't? Violet was hot shit, and she knew it. She loved to taunt guys, you know, wearing those tight little outfits and all. She looked good. Everybody wanted a piece."

Logan took a slow breath, hoping the boil of her blood hadn't changed her outer demeanor. *Good job staying neutral*, she scolded herself. She blinked and took another breath, centering herself.

"May I ask you something that might be a little personal?"

His gaze changed abruptly, growing more focused as he looked her up and down. Disgust overtook her but she pushed it back; she wished she'd worn looser pants.

"You can ask me anything," he answered, the suggestion in his voice ringing clear.

"Were you there with Violet the night she was killed?"

She knew she could have phrased it more delicately, and she'd deliberately chosen not to. Her words had the desired effect, acting like a cold splash of water. All the smarm died in an instant. He nodded soberly. "Yeah. I was."

"Was anyone else there?"

He bobbed his head again, his gaze traveling up and around the room as he avoided her eyes. "Yeah. Uh, me and Missy were there. And Derek was, too. I think there were a few more guys earlier, but they'd left already when…uh, when Violet walked off."

She nodded thoughtfully, wondering if that told her anything. It all depended on how thorough the summoner's control over the beast was. It was unlikely that someone at the party could have pulled it off without anyone noticing, but not impossible.

"I really am sorry she's dead, you know," said Jason. For a moment, she wondered if she might have accidentally unearthed his deeper side, or at least something resembling a decent one. Her question didn't live long. "I mean, there are only so many perfect bodies in the world, you know? And she sure did know how to showcase hers."

Rhode scholar, this one. Can't imagine why Violet wasn't interested.

"Hmm. That's the second time you've mentioned Violet's appearance and implied that she dressed a certain way to please others. Did she ever express that sentiment to you?"

"She didn't have to, ba—uh, man." Logan's right eyebrow twitched. Had he almost called her *babe*? *Well, that's gross.* "I knew, and she knew it. And she sure knew what she was doing to me."

"Right. Actually, I'm pretty sure when Violet Buchanan got dressed in the morning, she had very little interest in impressing you, Jason. None, in fact. At least, that's where the evidence points."

"Nah, every girl tries to look hot, man."

She tapped an impatient finger against a crossed leg. "No, based on both your files, I'd say Violet very much did *not* want to 'look hot' for you."

That sweet dull confusion returned to his features.

"Huh? What's that supposed to mean?"

"Violet filed multiple sexual harassment complaints against you. So, I doubt she would go out of her way to earn your attention, when she clearly didn't want it."

Jason scoffed. "Oh, you mean that time she went and told on me. Whatever, man. She was just being a stuck-up bitch because she could. Any other girl would kill to hook up with me. But Violet just thought she was such hot shit."

"A moment ago, you seemed to think she was *hot shit*, too. As a matter of fact, according to the timeline in the files, you continued to hound her long after you knew that she didn't want you."

"Oh, come on, she loved it! She liked being a bitch

sometimes, and, sure, she was a huge tease, but that doesn't mean anything. I never did anything she didn't want me to do."

"I've been told there was an incident at Homecoming. Is that correct?"

"What, did Missy tell you that?" He forced a puff of air through his lips, as though he were exasperated. *Join the club*, she thought. "God, she just won't let it go. Who even cares what happened back then? I mean, yeah, look, I get why she's mad, but it's not like we didn't get back together or anything. She should get over it by now."

"I didn't talk to Missy about it," she said. It was a minor enough lie, and it served her purposes to keep him on track. "I'm going off the files. Are you confirming that you attempted to hit on Violet at Homecoming?"

"Yeah, I mean, we flirted a little bit. I thought we might hook up, but nothing happened. I guess she decided to be a bitch again."

"I see." For a moment, Logan let silence fall between them as she studied him, sizing him up. For all her father's faults, she couldn't help but feel a little grateful that his hectic lifestyle had consistently kept her out of school and away from reprobates like this. "So, let's recap. You began aggressively hitting on Violet sometime last year, and she told you no repeatedly and asked you to stop. You didn't stop, and according to other students' accounts, you spread rumors about a fictional sexual encounter with her, and encouraged your friends to harass her over it. So she reported you to the school, and one of your buddies gave up the game. You received an in-school suspension and had to take classes over the summer to catch up. Even so, you refused to abide by Violet's only request—that you leave her alone. You dumped her friend so you could try to force yourself on her, and, surprising nobody but you, she turned you down. But now, flying in the face of all known earth logic, you've chosen to interpret that as—she decided to be a bitch that night. Have I missed anything?"

Bemusement settled and froze on Jason's face. She gave him a moment, but it quickly became clear that he had nothing to say to any of that.

"No, I suppose not." With a sigh, she figured she had the measure of him by now. "I'll tell you what I think, Jason. I think Violet saw you for what you are: a skeevy creep who wouldn't stop bothering her, no matter how many times she told you no. I think you were a nuisance to her. A piece of muck you have to sidestep on the street, but unfortunately for her, the confines of school gave you voice enough to harass her daily. I think she hated you, and your poor pathetic ego couldn't accept that. But you'd really better get used to it, Jason. The world is full of women who want nothing to do with you. So you really have to learn to take that *no*." She glanced up at the clock. "But you'll have to learn that on your own time. We're done here, you can go."

She didn't bother to watch him leave. Instead she got up and crossed to the window, satisfied in her power to send the slime back out the door. Of course, even as she reached the window and began to gaze out it, she could feel the first hints of regret tunneling their way through the back of her mind. *That wasn't exactly the responsible thing to do. Guess if I'm lucky, he'll be too embarrassed to tell anyone what happened.*

Unfortunately, she also didn't feel like she was making much headway on the case. Maybe, if he was the summoner, he'd hate her enough now to come after her, and that would reveal him. But in truth, she doubted it was him. He was too oblivious and too unlikely to undertake the work required. Whoever had killed Violet had worked hard to do so, and they'd done it out of sheer rage. Jason Reed didn't rage against her; he'd convinced himself he still had a shot with her. Logan doubted the summoner would turn out to be someone with the kind of social power that Jason Reed or Missy Vreeland had—though Missy might have had rage enough to do it. But when Logan imagined the profile of a likely suspect, she couldn't help but incorporate social isolation. Her image was of someone a little further down the totem pole.

Someone who didn't come by power naturally, so they'd chosen to take it by force.

That was her theory, anyway. She had plenty of time left to be proven wrong.

Logan couldn't remember ever feeling so grateful to see the inside of a downtrodden motel room. She tossed her jacket and helmet near the door and slid out of her stiff, uncomfortable counselor outfit, opting instead for loose cotton boxers. The air conditioning in her unit was predictably unsatisfactory, but by now the sun had gone down and the night had cooled, so she pushed her little window open for the breeze. Then she plopped herself in front of the ancient television and opened up the takeout she'd grabbed from the diner on her way.

It was hard to say exactly when she nodded off. She ate a small piece of her meal before leaving the rest in the room's mini-fridge. When she crawled backward toward the pillows, the television still blared. She was sure she was still watching it, though she knew she was losing the threads.

Her last full conscious notion was a resigned dread at the thought of another day with the tiny monsters up at school.

And then she was somewhere else.

At first, everything was a muddled blur of color. Then pieces materialized out of the mess. She was at a masquerade ball. All around her people whirled and twirled, ball gowns and coattails flying out behind them, distorting them into abstract shapes. She knew she was dancing with someone, but she didn't know who. Some part of her, a part that felt disconnected from everything else around her, knew that she wasn't safe. Wherever she was, she wasn't safe. There was something she couldn't see.

She turned to see whose arms were around her waist, but there was no one there. She floated freely. As she came to a stop, she felt skirts swish around her legs, weighing her down. She looked down at the cool, pale blue fabric, feeling its smooth silk under the tips of her fingers. Something about the fabric was wrong; it drew her in. But then someone spoke her name and she looked up.

Knatt stood before her, nodding solemnly.

"You must follow." It was his voice, but his lips didn't move. "You must run."

As she watched, his mouth broke into a hideous inhuman smile, warping his face into something else, and his arm lifted slowly, as if someone pulled it up with a string, pointing it to the back of the large ballroom. She turned to look.

She could see something moving, far back. At first it looked like a spider. Then it looked like a doorway. She went toward it, but she couldn't remember deciding that she should.

As soon as she moved, she was in another place. Bright colors and strange shapes still surrounded her, but they were of a different kind. As their edges hardened and evened out, she recognized it—a carnival. The alien sense of danger she'd felt earlier intensified, and her movements sped up and tightened.

She was looking for something, wasn't she? Yes. But also— something was looking for her. She knew that.

A soft chorus of human laughter sounded from behind her, but when she turned around, all she saw were the horses on the carousel. They were empty at first, but then she looked again, and each one suddenly had a rider. When her gaze focused, she saw that the first rider was Missy—disgust distorting her features. After her, she saw Jason Reed, leaning back in his horse and leering at her.

Next—the girl she'd seen at the locker and on the field. She looked away before Logan could get her attention. And then—the next girl was Violet. Only she didn't look like the bright happy girl in the photos. She looked like the body Logan had seen in the cooler at the sheriff's department. Her eyes were blank and empty, staring motionlessly forward. Her chest was a bloody mess.

For a moment, Logan thought she saw another rider behind her, but when she looked again, it was gone.

But someone—someone was behind her. She knew it.

She began to run. The carnival was endless, like it was stuck on repeat. The more she ran, the more the shapes blurred again, until she might have been anywhere. She could feel rather than hear her pursuer—but when she did manage to glance back, she saw a figure in a dark cloak right on her heels.

Finally, the carnival faded out. The colors around her turned to blacks and greens, and she knew she ran through trees now. Her pursuer grew louder—not his tread but his breathing.

This time, when she glanced back, the shape looked different. It had grown misshapen and strange, the proportions all wrong.

It was a wolf. It didn't look like a wolf, but somehow she knew that's what it was.

She stumbled and fell, her heavy skirts catching on a million branches all at once, trapping her where she lay. The wolf was on her, and she saw a violent flash of light sear the sky before her. A voice sounded in her ear.

I worship the wolf.

The wolf bit down.

Logan jerked awake suddenly, almost like someone had hit her. Her heart was pounding, and it took her a few moments to work out where she was. Her motel room. Nowhere, Montana. More accurately, Wolf Creek, Montana. The television was still on, and the sky was still dark. She checked the red light of the clock by the bed—2:00am.

Well. It had been a few years since she'd woken up from a nightmare. She would almost call it a novel experience. Except it still beat in her ears, and her heart didn't seem to want to calm down.

I worship the wolf.

She kept hearing that phrase. Her left arm reached up and back to touch the top of her shoulder, like she was checking in with the Key. It burned low, stinging her softly. Nothing she couldn't sleep through, if she could just get her heart to slow down for a minute.

She got up and switched off the television, then planted her feet and stretched both arms above her head. She forced her breathing into a slow, even rhythm, and focused her mind on an image of tree roots, pushing into the dirt beneath her feet, spreading slowly downward. It was an old meditation technique she'd learned at Other Side. She'd resisted Other Side's rituals and systems as a teenager, but during one of her longest stays a few years later, her aunt had introduced her to a teacher who had dragged acquiescence out of her, and eventually she'd embraced it all. Now, she attributed the continued success of her client smile to the centering techniques she'd studied there, as well as a few of her flashier tricks.

After a few minutes of slow stretching and deliberate mindfulness, she felt her body coming to its ease again. With one last stretch upward, she crawled back into bed and shut her eyes.

The words were on her lips as she fell into sleep once more.

I worship the wolf.

Chapter 4
Practical Revenge

Wednesday. When Logan woke up, she tried to remember the last time she'd looked forward to a weekend with such urgent need. She wasn't sure how much longer she could deal with high school.

Still, there was one thing she was looking forward to that day, though it hung more like a question mark than a bright spot over her horizon: she would be speaking to Judith Li today.

Judith Li and Suzanne Grubb were, in a sense, Violet Buchanan's last victims. If anyone had a reason to hate Violet, it was either of them. But Logan wouldn't get a chance to interview Suzanne Grubb—the girl had changed schools shortly following her incident with Violet. They seemed to have moved to another town, and according to Miss Swinson, they might have moved out of Montana all together.

So, while Suzanne was still a possible suspect, she probably hadn't even seen Violet in over a year. In Logan's experience, teenagers weren't famous for serving their revenge so cold. It was likelier that Violet had been killed by someone who still saw her every day—someone like Judith Li. So Logan felt pretty reasonable in her hope that Judith might prove her most useful interview yet.

Logan rifled through Knatt's clothing rack, searching for something a little bit cooler than what she'd worn the day before. She landed on a pair of boot-cut dress pants in a light-weight blue material, and a loose black blouse in fabric so light it was almost see-through. The sleeves fell short of her wrists, but only short enough to show the first mark on each arm. That would have to be discreet enough. She couldn't see herself getting through another day without some outdoors time on her break again.

Then, like before, she packed some snack food for herself and grabbed her jacket and helmet. It had been a grand total of one day, and already she felt herself chafing at the structure that school imposed. As she threw her leg over the bike and started it up, she wished she could take it anywhere else. Preferably somewhere she could go sleeveless.

Her ride was uneventful. Like before, she parked at the far end of the lot, though as she did so, her mind flashed on that first evening, and how she'd felt a presence when she left the building. But she didn't have time to ponder it now, so she shook it off and made her way toward the break room inside.

She was about halfway through pouring her oversized coffee when Esmerelda Swinson, the small older woman under a wild pile of hair, accosted her again.

"Good morning, Miss Logan," she said like an announcement as she planted her body between Logan and the cream. "I just wanted to come over and say thank you for everything you've been doing so far."

"Ah—that's very sweet of you, but honestly, it's not necessary. I'm just doing my job." With a bright smile and a wave of warning, she reached around Swinson for the cream and added it to her brew.

"Oh, but you're doing so much more than that," Esmerelda answered with enthusiasm. Her gray eyes were wide in wonder. "I know that Ashley Carson came to see you yesterday. I don't know what you said to her, but whatever it was, it was good. Oh, she was so distraught before. She's in my classes, you see. She was just so torn up about it all, but I know that talking to you really helped her. I could tell that she was doing a little better yesterday afternoon, so I asked if she'd been in to see you yet, and she said she had and she felt just *worlds* better. She's a sensitive girl, poor thing."

Logan nodded, taking this in. In truth, the main thing she'd done was listen. It wasn't a terribly difficult task. Ashley was a normal kid, though understandably shaken up. She was glad it had helped, though perturbed that it had required any intervention on her part in the first place. She had to hope that, if she hadn't magically elbowed her way into this situation, someone would have thought to talk to the kid eventually—or, rather, to listen.

"Ashley seems like a bright young woman," Logan answered blandly. "It was my pleasure to meet her. She's welcome to come see me any time."

"Wonderful!" Esmerelda Swinson exclaimed, clapping her hands together. Apparently satisfied, she tottered off once more.

Logan escaped before anyone else could stop her.

Her first appointment of the day was another non-starter. She kept her patience throughout, which wasn't too hard after getting through Missy and Jason the day before. Still, Logan couldn't help feeling like she spent the whole time metaphorically bound to the edge of her seat, waiting for Judith Li's inevitable appearance. What would she be like? Logan knew it was an inappropriate thought, but the part of her that had already tired of interviewing teenagers hoped that Li would turn out to be such an obvious killer that her work would be done by lunchtime. *Maybe the first thing out of her mouth will be a confession. Wouldn't that be nice?* Of course, Logan knew more than to put much stock in idle hope.

Then at the top of her second hour, perfectly on time, Judith Li walked into her classroom.

As she took her in, she realized with a start that she recognized her. Judith Li, it turned out, was the girl from the soccer field—the girl who'd slammed her locker that first day. She still looked like someone who wanted to disappear, in huge cargo shorts and another oversized sweatshirt. *Fascinating.* Brushing away her momentary shock, Logan carefully pushed her face into a welcoming smile.

"Come on in," she announced warmly. "Take a seat."

Judith set herself down a little awkwardly on one of the small chairs in front of the desk while Logan closed the door behind her. Now that they were face-to-face, Logan could mark the rest of her physical descriptors. *Asian, possibly 5'10.* Logan suspected she might qualify as lanky, but it was difficult to say for sure beneath the clothes that swamped her.

"Are you Judith?" she asked as she took the seat across from her.

"Yeah," Judith said, nervously tucking a stray piece of hair behind her ear.

"Excellent. You can call me Logan. Do you prefer female pronouns?"

Judith's hand froze, still holding onto that long chunk of hair. Her eyes whipped around the room before settling back on Logan.

"Is that a joke?" she asked.

"No, it's not." Logan paused, unsure how to continue. She couldn't remember if the book had any advice for how to diffuse a defensive reaction. "I'm sorry. Have I said something offensive?"

"N-no. I just…I don't know, maybe you heard…whatever. Yeah, I'm female. I like female pronouns for me."

"Lovely." Logan crossed one leg over the other, studying Judith and trying to gauge how best to proceed. "I'd like to ask you a question, but if you'd prefer not to answer it, please know that you are under absolutely no obligation to do so. I'd like to know…do other students give you a hard time about your gender presentation?"

Slowly Judith's hand detached from her hair and came to rest in her lap. Her face appeared serene and calm as she considered the question.

"Gender presentation? Like, my clothes and stuff?"

"Gender presentation can mean a lot of things." The guidebook had covered this pretty thoroughly. "Clothes included, yes."

"Hm. Well, kind of," she said with a shrug. She pulled a baseball hat out of one of her many pockets and started bending the brim back and forth. Another nervous habit, perhaps. "Some people aren't very nice. I think they look for weakness, so I don't give it to them if I can avoid it."

Weakness. There's a choice word for you.

"Are you saying you try not to be weak?"

"Yeah, I guess." More twisting.

"What do you think weakness is?"

Judith's mouth pursed and pushed to the left. "I don't know. It's like…you can't let it get to you. If someone starts messing with you, you can't let 'em see you get upset. You gotta go stone cold and act like it's just rolling off your back. Show them they don't have power over you. That kind of thing."

Logan recalled the incident in Violet's file. Judith, upon discovering that her clothes were gone, had marched to the front of the school in nothing but a towel in order to find them. Logan wondered how many times Judith Li had tried to turn herself to stone. "You sound like you've given this some thought."

"I guess. It's just what you do. If they see they got to you, they'll just keep coming until they rip you up." Her eyes looked cold and absent, like a part of her was somewhere far away. Quite suddenly, her gaze locked back onto Logan. "They swarm. Kinda like what happens in a game. If you stay in the same place, they keep coming, and they pile up."

Logan wondered if she meant a video game or something else.

"That sounds rather violent."

"A little bit," Judith nodded. She tore her gaze from Logan again and made a small show of staring out the window before forcing a heavy sigh through her lips and resuming her uncomfortably cold eye contact. "I'm in here because I'm supposed to talk about Violet, right?"

"If you like," said Logan. "Whatever you want to talk about."

"I'm supposed to be sorry she's dead." Judith's syllables were slow, her voice blank and hollow. "We're supposed to be all sad and traumatized. Is that because we're young, and young people aren't supposed to die?"

Young people aren't supposed to die. That concept didn't really track with Logan's experience.

"That's one of the reasons." Logan gestured around vaguely with her hand, roughly indicating the rest of the building. "Some people were friends with her, and they're sad because of that. Perhaps you weren't."

"No, I wasn't," said Judith. Something was missing from her voice. "I guess it's weird. It's weird that she's dead. Like, I never really thought that could happen, you know?"

"That someone in your class could die?"

"That *Violet* could die. I mean, of all the bad shit I wanted to happen to her, I never thought about her dying. I guess it just didn't occur to me. Am I supposed to feel guilty, now?"

Logan wasn't sure what to make of that. Somehow, Judith had managed a statement that seemed equal parts admission and denial. *Bravo, kid.* Logan took a stab at a clarifying question.

"Why would you feel guilty, Judith? Did you do something?"

Judith's nose scrunched up as she considered this. "Not really. But I wanted bad things to happen to her." She shrugged. "I'm not happy she's dead, I just…I don't care. I'm not gonna pretend I liked her. She was not a nice person." Her gaze went cold again, her mouth a hard line. "Sometimes people do things that shouldn't be forgiven." When she met Logan's eyes, her gaze almost seemed to dare her. What it dared her to do, she couldn't say. "I can deal with it okay. But some people can't, you know? Girls like Violet, they smell weakness. They're like sharks. They get off on picking someone to go after and tear down, especially when they choose someone who can't deal with it. And they just *get away with it*. Nobody cares, not really. They let you file a report, but they don't stop it from happening again. Nobody even gets in trouble for it. Violet was a golden child, a winner, and the people she messed with were weird losers. Nobody listens to us. They think we brought it on ourselves. You know, by being weirdos."

For a moment, Logan was silent as she let Judith's pronouncement sink in. *That's an awfully young age to think that way*. But was she wrong? Violet had written in her own admission that everyone dismissed Li as *that Asian dyke*, made double the outsider by her race and her perceived sexual orientation. They hadn't been kind to her friend Suzanne, either. And, really, what punishment had Violet received? By the time of her murder, her life had gotten back on track, almost as if it had never happened— as if she had never cruelly tormented and harassed her fellow students. There was barely a record to show for it. Suzanne, meanwhile, had felt compelled to change schools entirely.

"Do you want to talk about what Violet did to you?"

"No. Who cares what she did to me? It's what she did to— uh, to other people, people who can't deal with it. That's what matters. That's what's messed up."

Interesting. It seemed Li was angrier on Suzanne's behalf than her own. Or maybe, short stumble aside, that was the impression she wanted to give.

"I see. Does it mean anything to you that she turned herself in?"

"Why should it? She finally grew a conscience, a million years too late? She finally did something so bad, even she thought it was too far? I don't know. Maybe she just got cold feet at the last minute, maybe she thought someone else would turn her in and she'd actually get in trouble for once. I have no idea why she did any of it, but I'm not gonna pretend she was doing me a favor or something. Suzanne and I might be weirdos, but it's not like everyone just hates us. There were at least fifty people who saw what was happening. You can't get that many people to lie for you. Someone was gonna tell the truth eventually. She was probably just scared she wouldn't get into law school or something." Judith leaned back and crossed her arms. "Violet Buchanan is a vicious bitch who only cares about herself. I will never care what happens to her."

"Nothing else will ever happen to her again," said Logan dispassionately. "She's dead."

For only a moment, Judith seemed to pause. Then she shrugged. "That's not my fault. I shouldn't have to pretend I liked her now."

"That's certainly true," Logan nodded. "You're free to feel however you feel. You don't have to grieve for Violet just because she's dead. That being said, it's also true that sometimes when someone dies unexpectedly, even if we didn't like them, it can be jarring." She gazed at Judith, acknowledging that she wasn't entirely sure what to make of the girl before her. Maybe she was a killer, but she didn't feel like one. Not that Logan ever let something as vague as that determine a case for her. "For some of us, it makes us think about death more generally, possibly about our own deaths or those of the ones we love. Do you ever think about anything like that?"

Judith fell quiet. She went back to twisting the hat in her hands, but her expression was inscrutable. She might have been about to cry, or about to fly into a rage, or neither. Finally she spoke. "I don't know who I love. I don't know who I have that loves me."

A pang of recognition shot through Logan like a sharp spike. A petty voice in the back of her mind urged her to dismiss the sentiment as indulgent teenage angst, but she knew she couldn't. The pain was too familiar to her. She knew what it was like to wonder if you were loved at all. She could remember Knatt speaking to her in soft tones, trying to reassure her that despite everything, her father really did love her. *He just doesn't know how to show it.* The words rang as hollow now as they ever had.

But then Judith shrugged. "I guess I think about death sometimes. I don't know. It's sort of hard to…imagine it, I think. I don't know." Her gaze drifted away. "Sometimes you think about things. It's weird, that Violet died. I didn't think it could happen. It's…yeah."

Logan followed her gaze out the window, toward the far trees on the other side of the field. Beyond the trees lay plains and mountains, an endless expanse of empty terrain—so many miles to go before you'd encounter any kind of city, any kind of different life from this. Logan couldn't help her sense of desperation at the thought of it.

She imagined that Judith couldn't, either.

Logan had a number of other counseling sessions after that, but she couldn't stop herself from coming back to Judith. She kept seeing an image of her face as she talked about sharks tearing her apart. Or making herself cold. Or not feeling sorry.

I'm supposed to be sorry she's dead.

She hadn't spent a lot of time in high schools. The one she remembered most was the last one, but it had been private and stodgy, like an Ivy League university in miniature. She remembered the look and feel of the grounds better than any individual class she took—although at this point, it was difficult to be sure if even that memory was true, or if it was merely a conglomeration of media images pasted on top of remnants of the original.

Perhaps the reason she couldn't shake her interview with Judith was because she liked her; she reminded her of herself. Yes, she sounded angry, but understandably so. Even Logan couldn't argue for sure that Violet had learned any particular lesson from what she did to her. It was perfectly possible that she'd only been afraid of worse punishment if she didn't turn herself in. There was no way Logan could ever know with absolute certainty.

Don't expect me to feel sorry.

Unbidden, a long ignored memory swam to the surface. She remembered sitting in the dining hall at the private school, at a table by herself. Since she rarely stayed in school long enough to make friends, she usually ended up sitting by herself. It had never bothered her before, and she didn't stay in school long enough for it to bother her after this.

But that day, as she sat, a group of her peers walked close behind her on their way to another table. One of them whispered right as he passed.

"Fucking freak's got no friends." She could hear the laugh in his voice.

She'd kept perfectly still until they were a few paces away, but then she zeroed her gaze in on them, picking out exactly who had spoken. Perhaps in a way they were all culpable, but he was the one who had done it.

So he was the one who had to pay.

Don't expect me to feel sorry. Her words, played back to her over the broad expanse of time. How much had she really changed since then?

She liked Judith, but that didn't matter. It didn't matter what she thought of Violet, either. Whoever killed her was wrong, and they needed to be prevented from doing it again. Letha summoning could be rough and unpredictable. There was no guarantee the killer would keep control of their beast forever, nor any guarantee that Violet had been their only target.

Everything else aside, Logan had to find the beast and put it down. And she had to make sure that whoever brought it here would never be able to do it again.

Still, she couldn't help but wonder—what had that locker slam been about? Maybe nothing. Maybe something.

Logan started to roll her head in frustration, but then she remembered that she was supposed to be counseling the pretty white blonde girl in the chair in front of her. The girl was speaking. What was her name? Kelly maybe?

With an internal sigh, Logan forced her own thoughts out of her head and tried her best to focus on the task at hand.

The last kid on her schedule was someone she couldn't place from the files. His name was Kurt Redmond. By the time she got to him, she was already eager for the day to end, so she hoped he'd turn out as low maintenance as possible.

He knocked at the door frame right on time. With her wearied smile pasted back onto her face, she waved him in as she went to close the door tight behind him. *White, average height, oily hair.*

"Kurt?" she asked as she seated herself across from him. "Preferred pronouns?"

"Yes. Uh, what?" His dark eyes stared up at her in confusion. She was a little surprised to see that she was taller than him sitting down.

"Do you prefer male or female pronouns?"

"Oh. Uh. Male."

She nodded politely, smiling inwardly. Every time she'd done it, the act of asking teenagers what pronouns they preferred had been instructive in unexpected ways. She doubted the guidebook writers were fully aware of what their advice had done for her.

"How are you feeling today, Kurt?" she asked, leaning back in her seat, settling in.

Something passed over his face, like a split-second frown, but it was gone too fast for her to say for sure what it was.

"I feel pretty good today, all things considered," his voice was cool and crisp. It sounded practiced, much like her own this week.

"Did you know Violet very well?"

"Oh, I don't know," he said, smiling at her a little strangely— like they were already familiar somehow. Like he was letting her in on an inside joke. "I don't know if I would say that."

"Then what would you say?"

"Well, I would say that I admired her," he answered, his smile broadening. He reminded her of a politician who wouldn't quite acknowledge the attempt to pander to his audience. The comparison unsettled her. "She certainly was admirable."

"Why do you think so?"

His pander smile froze as he processed the question.

"Well, you know, she was so *involved*. You could really tell how much she cared about everything. She was an inspiration to the other students, I think. A role model, you could say. Everyone looked up to her." He nodded solemnly. "It's a shame, really, what happened to her. I think it's a loss for all of us."

Is this what kids sound like when they're trying to sound like adults?

Logan let her head tilt to the side. "Do you think it affects all of you? Equally?"

"Not equally, no. It's a loss, but certainly more for some than others. Like I said, I didn't really know her very well, though I will certainly miss her *presence* here."

As a point of fact, he hadn't said outright that he didn't know her very well. He'd avoided confirmation one way or another. She had a sudden thought.

"Hm. I'm curious, Kurt—were you involved in any extracurricular activities with Violet?"

"As a matter a fact, I was, though only recently. I joined the debate team last quarter, you see."

"Indeed. Do you do anything else outside of that?"

"I'm on Student Council as well."

Logan nodded, unsurprised. He had such an odd way about him—just a little bit more particular and a little less off-the-cuff than any other student she'd seen. Somehow it made perfect sense to her that he'd been involved in the closest thing to politics this small school had to offer. She guessed he'd made it into whatever position he now held despite technically losing out to the ever-popular write-in candidate *Giant Joint*.

"So did you primarily know Violet because you were both on the debate team?"

"We've been in a number of classes together as well," he answered with a nod, straightening his jacket with a twist of his wrists. It was at that moment that she clocked his entire outfit— he wore an ever-so-slightly ill-fitting sports coat over a collared shirt with no tie. The shirt must have fit him pretty badly, too— she noticed a lump along the buttons down the front, almost like he had some sort of protrusion in the middle of his chest. And the high-waisted khakis, of course. She felt an overpowering urge to tell him to buy some darker pants, but she resisted it. And she chastised herself for failing to observe this more quickly. Clearly time with teenagers had eroded her investigative abilities.

"So you had a fair amount of contact with her," Logan said.

He nodded again. "You could say that. In a way, I've known her for years now, since we've been in school together so long. She always was special, you know. I don't think you could know her without noticing that."

Tell that to Judith Li, Logan thought to herself. She weighed her thoughts a moment before answering.

"Actually, I'm not sure all your classmates would agree with you," she answered tactfully. "What was it that made you feel she was special?"

"She just was," he answered with a shrug, perplexed. In that moment, he looked far more similar to his classmates than he had this whole time. "She was smarter and nicer than anybody else in this school. You could just tell. We didn't really have the same friends, of course. Different social circles, you know. But I knew what she was like. She was…well, she was perfect. I mean, I know there were some rumors about her—something about that nasty girl on the soccer team. But those were just rumors. If you'd met her, you would understand. She was the kind of girl who made other girls jealous. And sometimes jealous people tell lies. But that's all they were. Just lies."

So many of Violet's fellow students, and even her teachers, seemed quite determined to pin down exactly what "kind" of girl Violet had been. So far Logan had yet to see any evidence that any one of them had gotten it right.

"I see," said Logan. There didn't seem to be much purpose to arguing the point with this one.

"That Li girl," he continued, his face turning a little darker. As his features twisted slightly with what looked like resentment, she thought he looked a little familiar somehow. But then it was gone. "She's—I've heard about her. Something Li. I've heard she's got a bad temper. I wouldn't believe anything that came from her, myself. Like I said, I'm sure she was just jealous."

"Right," Logan nodded. *Not sure jealous is the right word. Enraged, maybe.*

Suddenly, he wiped his face clear of expression and pasted on a placid smile. "You know, I hate to cut this short, but I was actually hoping to get out a little early so I could get a head start on this US History project I'm doing. Do you mind if I get going?"

"Not at all," answered Logan honestly. "I'm just here for whatever you need. Feel free to come back if you think of something you'd like to talk about."

"That's quite gracious of you," he said as they both stood. He reached out his hand to shake hers, and she couldn't think of a good way to refuse so she complied. "It was wonderful meeting you. Hope I'll see you around again."

"Sure," she said, matching his placid smile.

Then he went, and she watched him go. Were his feet a little splayed when standing? He shrugged in his jacket as he walked out the door, and the movement made him look briefly hunch-backed.

For a moment, she wondered if she should have pinned him down, tried to get something more solid out of him. But her days in this school seemed to drag on forever, and at the moment, she wasn't sure she could get her brain to grind out another question for anybody. Besides, he was her last appointment. She was free.

She pondered what kind of takeout options she might find on her way back to the hotel.

The answer had been the diner, but this time she'd chosen their self-proclaimed *New York deli style* vegetarian sandwich, boasting an intriguing nut-based veggie patty and pickled cabbage. She'd picked out seasoned fries for her side and added on a diet root beer.

Once she was back in the motel room, she immediately changed into her new after-hours outfit of a loose tank top and boxers before throwing the small window open wide. She felt restless and uncertain; she wanted to get out of this pointless small town and far away from the stench of adolescence. But her job was far from complete, and she wasn't yet sure what her next step should be.

She started to turn the television on, but then she changed her mind. Instead, she went over to the clothes rack and fished her ancient laptop out of the case that hung off one of the hangers. She planned to connect to her father and Knatt's database, which she'd migrated to the cloud herself, quite painstakingly, about a year ago. In lieu of any real action she could take, she hoped that research might make her feel a little less useless.

While the clunky piece of technology roared slowly to life, she opened up her still-hot bag of French fries and started munching. She didn't know what counted as *New York style* when it came to fries, but they were crispy and salty, so she figured they were good enough either way.

She had nearly finished the bag by the time the computer was up and running. Wiping her hands thoroughly on the provided napkins, she grabbed the slip with internet connection instructions and got started.

Someone had summoned a beast to kill Violet. She had a growing list of who might be the summoner. She figured she might as well start a list on what kind of beast might have been summoned. After all, odds were high that the beast was still around. And who could say if the summoner would be able to maintain control of it?

So that was what she wanted to do—start a list. But as she made her fourth go at getting the motel's internet to work, she started to suspect that the world was not prepared to cooperate with her plans.

Glancing over at the small bedside table where her sandwich still sat, she found the landline phone. She picked up the handset and dialed *zero*.

"Front desk," a young female voice said almost immediately.

"Hi," said Logan. "I'm in room 14B, and uh—well, I've followed the instructions on the card a couple of times now, but I can't seem to access the internet. Is there anything you guys can do about that?"

"Sorry," the front desk girl answered. "Internet's down for the whole building. No word on when it'll be up again."

"No word? Have you guys, I don't know, called the company, or—"

"Yeah, we've called," Logan could almost see her shrug through the phone. "But they just don't know. Happens sometimes. The internet goes out and it doesn't come back, sometimes for days. I wouldn't lay bets on getting it back anytime tonight."

Logan bridled her frustration. "Well. Thanks for your help." She hung up before she heard if the girl gave her any answer.

Of course the internet was out. She was stuck in the middle of Nowhere, USA, so why shouldn't her only connection to the rest of the known universe vanish? The feeling that she was trapped in this pointless little town intensified.

She pulled her cell phone out of her pocket and gave it one more shot. She tapped the necessary options to switch her phone into a hot spot and did her best to get her laptop running on it. But every time her laptop connected, the hot spot blinked out of existence. She let out a long sigh. At this point, it was impossible to say if this continuous technological failure was due to the uselessness of small towns or the lingering impression of the letha summoning. Either way, the result was the same.

Still, she reasoned with herself, it wasn't her only connection. She could attempt to call Knatt and ask him to connect to the database and go through it with her. She'd successfully used the phone as an actual phone already, so she had reason to believe that at least *that* function might work. Hell, he'd probably love that—he might even say something stupid like *happy to see you finally showing initiative.* He loved to act surprised when she did her job the right way. They were going on two years of official partnership now and she'd never once messed up anything that couldn't be fixed, but he still carried on like she might blow them all up at any minute.

She stared down at the phone in her hand and hovered over the idea. Did she want to talk to Knatt right now? She wanted access to the database, yes. But did she actually want it badly enough to subject herself to whatever piece of disapproval he might have waiting for her? After a moment of guilty hesitation, she put her phone down again. Maybe on a better day. She was about to give up on the whole idea and go back to her sandwich when it occurred to her that Knatt was not the only person she could call.

Running contrary to her entire life philosophy, Logan actually had accumulated a handful of friends over the years. Not many, but a few.

She couldn't say why exactly, but the first person she thought of was Alexei Marin. She'd met Alexei under slightly unusual circumstances; long before she'd returned to the estate to take over her father's side of the business with Knatt, she'd taken on a client who had called her south. If Knatt had ever had an unimagined reason to nag her, it would have been during that particular window of her life. She'd had no regular source of income then, and no regular place to sleep either. Instead of settling down into a job and a life somewhere, she made sporadic money contracting with disreputable clientele, usually for some kind of illegal activity. For the most part, she stole things. Since disappearing from her father's estate, she'd learned more than enough magic to do so easily.

Most of the clients who hired her had no idea that magic was real, and they hired her to steal from places or people who also had no idea magic was real. So, usually, once she was given a location to look for the desired item, all she had to do was summon a little shadow and she could sneak on and off premises with no problem. If she ever needed to get through a lock or into a safe, it helped that she had super-strength.

The equation altered somewhat if the client did know a thing or two about magic. Such was the case the week she met Alexei. She'd come to San Francisco to steal ("steal back," her client insisted) some precious gem from an impressive-looking townhouse at the top of one of the city's absurdly hilly streets. Only unlike most other townhouses in the city, this one was owned by a powerful letha practitioner who had bound his safe with demon power, making it almost impossible to break open.

Before this particular contract, she'd only taken on a handful of clients who knew about magic. What she didn't realize at the time was that she'd already unwittingly entered into a pre-established and uncommonly discreet subculture of the criminal underworld—one with more than a few connections to the paranormal underworld to which her father belonged.

Of course, none of that mattered on this particular job, as she'd lost the work before she'd gotten anywhere with it. On her way back from her initial meeting with the client, as she stomped down an unsavory back street towards her questionable hotel room, dizziness struck her, and her spine exploded in pain.

When she woke up some time later sprawled on the ground, she had an image in her mind and a direction she needed to follow. She called her client immediately to ask for an extension on the job, but her client refused. Already following the trail the Key had left for her, she politely declined the contract offer and expressed the hope that they wouldn't hold it against her, but the timing simply wouldn't work out.

She saw Alexei for the first time the day after that. She had chased a nasty creature down a dark alley before losing track of it, somewhere between a fire escape and a dumpster. Keeping her body as still and quiet as possible, she crept along the edge of the dumpster, hoping to get a jump on it. Unfortunately, when she spun around the last corner, it was nowhere to be seen. Confused, she partially straightened herself and turned back toward the open end of the alley.

And suddenly she found herself face-to-face with a dark, surprisingly handsome stranger. She almost felt like she was looking at a cartoon; his features were perfectly delicate and symmetrical, his full lips smiling sweetly, and she could have sworn his dark eyes actually sparkled. And, of course, she couldn't help but notice the stunningly obvious—those brilliant, impeccable three-piece suits he always wore, even when he had to make his way down alleys as dank and dismal as this one. This particular suit was midnight blue. She hadn't known it yet, but he was partial to blue.

"Are you lost?" he asked pleasantly, waving a hand to indicate her semi-crouching stance and the scene behind her.

She looked him up and down, somewhat bewildered.

"Are *you*?" She waved her own hand, indicating his outfit.

He looked admiringly down at himself.

"Well, I'll admit I didn't plan on interacting with the peasants very much today."

And that was the end of their conversation—for the moment anyway. The beast she was chasing moved again behind her, and she scrambled after it—following it all the way up a connecting wall, leaving the mysterious, gorgeous stranger behind. She came back later on the off-chance he'd stuck around, but of course he hadn't.

And she figured she would never see him again. Hell, a part of her figured she had hallucinated him altogether.

But she did see him again.

And now she had his number in her phone. How long had it been since she'd last talked to him? Had she called him since that job in Sacramento? She couldn't remember.

Well, maybe he can. She pulled up his name and pressed down to dial it.

He picked up after one ring. *Of course he did.* She imagined he spent a majority of his down time practicing how to be charming and unnerving.

"Why hello, darling," his velvety voice drawled on the other end. "It's not often I get to hear from the daring adventurer. How exciting. Is there danger afoot?"

For whatever reason, her mind conjured up an image of him tipping a glass of Scotch in her direction, possibly while standing in front of a large fireplace. Apparently she viewed him as an amalgamation of clichés.

"I guess you could say that. Isn't there always?" She gave her bag of fries a shake, hoping to find a few more down at the bottom.

"Of course." She heard him sigh. "Well, I have to admit I'm a little disappointed."

"Really?" Success—she grabbed the last half-burned fry. "Why?"

"For half a second, I thought maybe you just wanted to talk to me."

She felt a smile creep surreptitiously across her face.

"Does this mean I'm not interrupting anything? You don't have a date or something else on the calendar? I'm shocked."

"Yet. You're not interrupting anything *yet*. But if this takes longer than an hour, we'll be crossing into interruption territory."

Logan glanced over at the clock. "You have a date at 9:30 at night?"

"A bit early for me, I know." His voice fell somewhere between mock pomposity and mock resignation. "But *apparently* some people have to get to work in the morning."

"So I've heard." She fell back on the pillows, hoping to get a little closer to the breeze coming in from the window.

"So how are you, H.C.?"

"Well, I've been working with children all day. So not great."

"Good god. Why would you subject yourself to *that*?"

"I have to, for a while anyway." If she angled her head just right, she could see the stars through her window. "A girl died. She went to the local school. I'm investigating."

"Someone's paying you to investigate a school?"

Except for the "payment" part, yeah—but she couldn't say that. "Something along those lines, yeah. So for now, I'm stuck in Montana, interviewing high school students. You know, this might actually be my own personal hell."

"Ah, but think of it this way," said Alexei, and she could hear the twinkle in his voice, "once you get done there, maybe poor old Mr. Beirnbaum won't seem so bad."

She let out a quiet, unexpected snort of laughter. Mr. Beirnbaum had hired them jointly on a case about a year back. He was a little old man with four cats and an impressive and wide-ranging vintage pornography collection—which he had insisted on showing her about eight different times. And, as Alexei had been determined to mention daily, he smelled like old cheese and dust. On the other hand, he paid well.

"She laughs," said Alexei, his voice light and smooth. She conjured up an image of him again, all charming smile and thick, slightly overgrown hair. "It was all your fault, you know. You tempted him. You and your lady charms." He had the slightest accent; she could only hear it in his "*a*" and his soft "*r*."

"My lady charms? What are those exactly?"

"Why Miss Henrietta…how explicit do you want me to get?"

Logan rolled her eyes and let her head fall to the other side. "Please don't. My memory of poor old Beirnbaum couldn't take it."

"Speaking of explicit, did he ever show you any of his *engravings?*"

"Yes. Wait, did he show *you* his engravings?"

Alexei chuckled, and she imagined a light in his eyes. "Try not to be too jealous. He certainly preferred you, but he was perfectly happy to harass me instead, if you weren't around."

"Is it still harassment if you enjoy it?" She heard him laugh again. "You know, all things considered, that contract wasn't half-bad. Working with you wasn't half-bad, anyway."

"Yeah. We should do it again sometime."

She felt herself fall quiet. She liked talking to Alexei, but every time she did, she noticed a certain undercurrent to it, and it unsettled her.

"Hey," Alexei said into the quiet, "were you calling me to talk about something specific?"

"Oh yeah," said Logan, remembering. "I was gonna ask you about monsters that rip out people's hearts."

"Mm. You do know how to turn me on."

"Apparently I'm in the part of Montana that the internet hasn't reached yet, which means I have no access to the cloud."

Alexei made a clucking noise. "And no access to that huge private database of yours."

She shot an eyebrow up, even though he couldn't see her. She liked to think he could hear it in her voice. "Did I tell you about that?"

"Maybe," he answered. "Well, don't worry, darling. It may not be as comprehensive as your illustrious partner's, but I do have some research we can use."

"You're a blessing," said Logan. She gave him a description of the wound, and postulated a *theory* that the beast could sense heartbeats. Alexei didn't know anything about the Key, so it was better not to mention the vision. She also had him narrow down the field to beasts that could be summoned, and to some extent controlled. She hesitated for a moment, then added, "Also…can you look for any that…kind of look like a wolf? I—I'm not sure, but I think I remember reading about…well, wolf-demons that rip out hearts or something. My memory's a little vague on specifics."

I worship the wolf wasn't exactly a clear directive, but it was something.

He ran a search through whatever it was he was using, and came up with a list of options and basic descriptions, while she took down notes.

"It's not coming up here, but it could also be a draugr," he said after he'd read a few off from his search list. "The spell to summon a draugr requires an offering to the Viking god of death, usually in the form of a small statue of her. Draugrs can take on any number of forms, though it doesn't mention wolf specifically. Ah, and it looks like the last one on the list is a rekal, a pretty common revenge beast. There's not much of a physical description; it just says 'beast.' Oh, downside to rekals is it's impossible to get control back if you ever lose it." He paused for a moment, like he was considering something. "I think you need to figure out *how* it's being controlled. That might help us narrow this down a bit."

"Yeah," she agreed. She knew a few things about rekals, and she wasn't particularly eager to face one. She couldn't remember if she'd ever seen a picture of one or not. "Well, thanks for your help. I wonder if I should take a lap through the woods or something. I'm sure this thing likes to hunt."

"Probably so."

She pushed herself to sitting. "I should let you go, I guess. You need to get ready for your date."

"Oh, I was ready hours ago."

She imagined him sitting in his pristine apartment in a perfectly pressed suit for hours, ready to jump at the drop of a hat. The idea made him seem unusually vulnerable.

"You feeling the pressure to impress? Must be someone kinda special." She'd wondered more than once what sort of people Alexei voluntarily associated himself with. Most of her experiences with him had involved work one way or another.

"I don't know about special, but he is certainly well-coiffed."

Now she couldn't help but imagine two of him, both in beautiful, richly colored suits.

"That sounds special enough. Hope you have a good time."

"I don't have to go on the date, you know." Mischief laced his tone.

"And why wouldn't you go on your date?" As she spoke, she got the peculiar sense that she was playing with fire.

"Oh, you know. So I could stay here. And talk to you."

"You'd skip a date just to talk to me on the phone?"

"Maybe. If you promised to spice things up a little."

"And how exactly would I do that?"

He didn't miss a beat.

"You could talk me off."

She scoffed out loud; the urge to roll her eyes overwhelmed her. "And what do *I* get out of that situation?"

"I could talk you off, too."

"Alexei." She dropped the slightest hint of warning, and he backed away immediately.

"Apologies, darling. You know I'm only having some fun. Mostly. Well, feel free to call me if you need anything." Mischief still danced through his voice. "Now picture me winking at you roguishly."

When he said it, she could see it as clear as if he actually stood before her.

"Goodnight, Alexei."

"Goodnight, H. C."

As soon as she hung up the phone, she could no longer entirely evade a creeping sense of defeat. Fun as Alexei was, and good as it was to have the list, she didn't feel any closer to a real answer.

The truth was, Judith Li looked like her best suspect. Logan didn't like thinking about it; Judith had seemed far more reasonable than a number of her other interviewees, and Logan understood perfectly why she might have more than a little resentment towards Violet and her other classmates. But in lieu of any better suspects, Judith Li stood at the top of the list.

Logan got up and flipped the television on, then turned her attention back to her sandwich, which remained untouched in the bag.

As she made her way through the rest of her food and let herself start to drift in front of the television, she felt a new unease settle over her—similar to what she'd felt leaving the school that first day. It wasn't quite the same as the feeling that someone was watching her; it was more like there was something she hadn't figured out yet, something close at hand. Maybe she could touch it if she only knew how to reach. It stood like an ominous shadow along the periphery, promising danger.

Fortunately for her, Logan was accustomed to falling asleep through any sense of unease. Before she finally dropped off, she set her alarm early.

She planned to go hunting in the morning.

Chapter 5
Callous and Bored

On Thursday, she woke before the sun, and a pleasant early-morning chill greeted her. She stretched her way to wakefulness, then willed herself through a few sets of jumping jacks and mountain climbers. When her blood had warmed sufficiently, she marched over to her supplies and grabbed a pair of sandalwood candles. She sat herself cross-legged on the floor and lit both candles, placing them before her.

Though life on the road made daily practice difficult, Logan did make something of an effort to meditate regularly, even if she didn't need it just to fall asleep. It had been years since she'd seen her old instructor from Other Side, but when her practice was good, it felt like he was right there with her.

Regular meditation, for her, served two primary purposes: it kept her in tune with eira, and it kept a check on her power.

Power always struck her like a euphemism, like it was hiding the real truth. She knew where the power came from—or, at least, she had a pretty good idea. When finally pressed to explain her origin, her father had told her, in essence, that she was the result of an experiment. He'd been shallow on specifics, but the outline of it was that he had somehow summoned the "essence" of a demon and used it to create her. He'd made sure to inform her that she was "part human as well," but somehow that phrasing only served to underline for her the fact that, on some level, she was a demon.

Still, her father's explanation had never quite sat well with her. She had never heard of anyone summoning the "essence" of a demon like that; the closest magic she knew about was letha binding, but if that were the case, then she would have started out as a regular human child who had then been bound with demonic power. Yet Charles Logan had made it perfectly clear that his daughter had no human mother.

Eventually Knatt had offered her his own account, which had differed significantly from her father's. It had also rung far truer, despite the fairy tale strangeness of it. But even in Knatt's telling of it, there was no denying that, one way or another, she had sprung from demon stock.

Thinking about her father's myriad deceptions never failed to make her queasy. After all, when he'd finally deigned to tell her his unlikely version of events, he'd only been trying to use the information to coerce her into coming back home. He'd thought he could convince her that the demon inside her couldn't be controlled without his help—that she *needed* him.

Needed him. Logan had spent her life learning to get by without him. He'd demanded independence and self-sufficiency from her, practically from the moment she could walk on her own. He'd only decided he wanted her to need him when it was far too late—when she already hated the very thought of him.

When she lit the sandalwood candles, she had a specific

purpose in mind. Most of the time, she suppressed her heightened sense of smell and hearing. But if she was going to hunt, it would help to have both of those intact. With a deep breath, she began to perform a ritual of release.

She breathed in and out, focusing on nothing but the movement of her lungs. Thoughts of her father fell away, replaced instead by the image of an empty field, long green grasses stretching in every direction around her. The earthy smell of the candle filled her, and she let herself relax into it.

As she did, she felt the ridges on her arms push out through her skin, slower and more gently than they normally did. She felt something unhook in her brain, and a sense of ease washed through her. With her next intake of breath, she took in so many scents, one over another over another—like layers of transparent paper. All of it almost entirely invisible to her, only a moment before. She had smelled the bleach when she first walked in, but now she smelled the blood underneath it, coming from somewhere in the bathroom. A number of other human smells rose up before her, though she was pleased to note the cleaner on every surface and the detergent in the sheets, proof that someone had at least tried to clean the room before she came to it.

All of this was beside the point, of course. Her eyes popped open as her body grew taut, alert and ready. With a quick huff to blow out the candles, she jumped to her feet.

She needed to get to the woods, start searching for a good hunting ground. She threw on flexible cutoff shorts and a sports bra so tight it felt like armor, and then a loose tank top over that. Shoving her key to the room in a back pocket, she walked outside.

For half a second, the world was far too bright—even though the sun had barely peeked behind the mountains, and the sky remained a dark and slowly lightening blue. It was the sudden change that threw her now more-sensitive sight for a loop. Then her eyes came back to normal and she glanced around, determining the best direction to go. If the beast had been allowed to hunt, it wouldn't have gone more than a few miles out of town—provided its summoner still retained his or her control. A majority of the neighborhoods were on the south side of town, while her motel was towards the north. So she struck out along the road, heading south.

Once she'd walked past the last room of the motel and reasonably far enough beyond that she couldn't easily be seen, she slipped a few feet from the road and broke into a run. Within moments, she was moving fast enough to appear more than a little unusual to human eyes.

Her muscles felt strange at first; it had been a few weeks since she'd run like this. She couldn't help but bend and stretch as she ran, feeling blood rush into sinew and flesh. Her legs burned with unaccustomed pain, yet still seemed to ache for a harder push. She complied, forcing herself to the limit for a few exhilarating seconds. But almost immediately after that, she had to slow down completely, almost to a halt. She'd traveled far enough south to hit residential territory, which meant it was time to redirect her attention to the scents and sounds surrounding her.

Any wooded area was prone to host the smell of blood here and there, but she knew she'd need to be looking for something big. The beast that was hunting, if it was hunting, was large enough to feed on human beings, so it wasn't likely to settle for rabbits and vermin as prey. It might take down a large dog, or even an elk, if it could wrangle one.

There. She picked up a newer, fresher scent. She couldn't say for sure what it was yet, but it was something. It pulled her west, further from town. Once she had it locked in, she picked up speed again.

When she broke into a clearing, the scent hit her with full force. It was definitely blood, and it was near. She followed where it pulled, until she found herself on the other side.

There, in plain view, was the beast's latest victim: a grey and ragged coyote. Its chest had been ripped apart, the empty cavity gaping open. As Logan gazed down, she felt an alien excitement grip her, and she all but rolled her eyes. She hated that feeling—that arousal she couldn't control. When she let the wards down and relaxed like this, she put herself in a suggestible state. The sight of blood was enough to get the demon going, amp it up. At least, that was what she guessed was happening.

With a quick huff of breath to expel her own disgust with herself, she knelt down to get a better look at the gaping wound. Just like Violet Buchanan, the coyote's heart had been torn out.

She stood up again and dusted herself off. There was little point in remaining here long; she'd found what she needed, and the monster itself was clearly long gone. She adopted a brisk jog again, heading back in the direction of her hotel.

So, the beast was still in town. That much was certain.

Once she was safely back in her room, she lit her candles once more and cleared her mind. This time, she felt her spikes slowly retract, disappearing beneath her skin. She felt the world close itself off from her by degrees, until the layers of human smells in the room seemed to fade away. With one last deep breath, she blew out the candles and headed for the shower.

She found herself dressed and ready with ample time to get to school before the first bell, so she decided to stop by her new favorite diner and pick up the breakfast burrito the cashier had mentioned the night before.

As she stood by the counter waiting for her order with one eye on her bike, her mind flashed to the coyote's corpse, the wound, the short trail of blood leading back into the trees. The beast was still in town. Did its master have another victim in mind, or did they want to keep it around simply for the idea of its power? And the unwelcome thought came to her—what if they lost control, and the beast was set loose?

With a thump, the waitress slapped her bagged breakfast down on the counter. Logan slipped a few bills into the tip jar as she grabbed it and took off again, forcing her mind back to the road and the day ahead of her, and away from wild speculation.

Despite her reluctance to face another potential inquiry from Miss Esmerelda Swinson, Logan found herself back in the teacher's lounge again. Unfortunately for her, it was the only place she knew on school grounds that had coffee. Once in, she made a beeline for the coffeemaker, glancing around the room for a hint of danger. She spotted Miss Swinson a few feet away, mercifully already preoccupied in conversation with another teacher. Today it seemed Esmerelda had something other than her students' recent trauma on her mind.

Once Logan reached her target, she was close enough to make

out Esmerelda Swinson's not-quite-whispered conversation.

"Well, that's the superintendent for you," she said, distrust and contempt heavy in her voice. "You know what other bit of strange news I heard?"

"What?"

"Judith Li's parents called in this morning, to announce that she would be absent all day today."

"Is that strange?"

"Only if you happen to know that Judith Li has never once been absent, for the entire time she's been enrolled here."

"Is that so?"

"It is so."

"But she's absent today?"

"Yes, she is. And her parents gave no explanation except to say that she was sick." She gave a short, disbelieving laugh. "Must be the plague to keep that one home."

"That is strange!"

Logan might have scoffed at them if she'd been willing to call any attention to herself. The delight they appeared to take in this tiny whiff of a scandal, no matter how meager the evidence, struck her as absurd. Of course, unbeknownst to them, Judith Li happened to be a prime suspect in Violet's murder. So, in a world beyond Miss Swinson's narrow ken, Li's absence was indeed suspicious. Logan topped her coffee off with a bit of cream before slipping out of the lounge as quickly as she could.

Off the top of her head, Logan could list a number of reasons why Judith Li might be absent. She could genuinely be sick, though she'd looked fine when Logan had seen her. She could have gotten in trouble with her parents for something completely unrelated, and they could have intentionally kept her home because of that. Any number of family emergencies could have required her absence.

Or, of course, it could be something related to Violet Buchanan's death.

Reluctantly, Logan realized she would probably need to go to Judith Li's home to find out for sure.

As Logan climbed the stairs and zeroed in on her assigned office, her mind centered back on the day ahead. She had only one interview today that she was sure would be pertinent: the interview with Derek James—by all accounts, Violet's boyfriend.

Her first two interviews seemed to slip right by; one part of her mind kept itself occupied with potential questions for Derek through each one. When it was finally time for his appointment, he caught her almost unawares—she'd been gazing out the window, wondering if she'd be able to take a break from travel after this and whether she was missing a late spring festival back home right at this very moment. When he knocked politely at the door frame, she gave herself a little shake to refocus.

"Come in, sit down," she told him, hoping she sounded welcoming as she walked over to shut the door behind him. "You're Derek, right?"

"Yeah," he said, seating himself in the chair closer to the window.

I wonder what this one will be like. A part of her braced for a repeat of Jason Reed, all bravado and smarm, but for what felt like the millionth time, she reminded herself: *make no assumptions.* She took a moment to take in his appearance. His brown hair looked brushed and his tanned face looked clean, and he wore pants that fit properly and a plaid button-down free of obvious stains.

"And do you prefer male pronouns?" She took the other chair.

"Yeah, sure," he shrugged.

"Lovely. So how are you doing today, Derek?"

He shrugged again, this time adding a quick huff—almost like a laugh, but not quite. "Uh, not great, actually. My girlfriend is still dead, so, you know. Everything is pretty fucked-up and stupid right now."

He gave her a look of mild defiance, like he wasn't quite sure he was allowed to curse in front of her, but he was willing to defend it if she took issue. Instead, she nodded. Cursing seemed perfectly appropriate to her.

"I think we can agree on that. It's not fair, what happened to Violet. Or what's happening to you. Tell me, have you thought about taking some time off school?"

He looked at her sideways, out of the corner of his eye, like he suspected she was laying a trap for him. "Are teachers supposed to say it's okay to skip school?"

No idea. But seems like a fine idea for a fake grief counselor. I think.

"Well, I'm not a teacher," said Logan out loud. "And it's not really skipping if you need to take some time. I would say something like this is a more than a good enough reason to take a few days off."

Derek's face relaxed, the suspicion melting out of it. "Oh. Okay. Yeah, I don't know. It might be nice to not have to…see everybody else for a little bit."

As his defensive demeanor relaxed, she saw an unexpected vulnerability rising to the surface instead. His eyes looked tired, his shoulders hunched. He seemed burdened, beleaguered. Perhaps that shouldn't have surprised her.

"I think that would be a good idea for you. I can write you a note to bring to your parents, or speak to them directly if you like." She leaned back, studying him. "Would you like to talk about Violet at all? You don't have to, but you certainly may if you want to."

"Uh, yeah," he said. His eyes locked with hers briefly, and he nodded, looking all the world like he was perfectly ready to speak. But then he didn't say anything else. He held her eyes a moment before letting his gaze fall to the floor, where he proceeded to stare at the dull grey carpet. His face looked blank, like it couldn't quite hold on to any particular thought. After a moment, he scrunched up his nose and brought his hand up to swipe roughly at his eyes. Was he crying?

"Take your time," she encouraged him, settling back into the hard, unyielding plastic. "We can take as long as you need. There's no pressure here."

He took a deep breath, then another. Then he spoke.

"I just…I keep forgetting it, you know?" The words came out of him slowly, as if he had to pick each one individually from a turbulent sea. "Like, I'm in math class, and everything is normal, and I forget, so I turn right to ask her a question—only her seat is empty. And when I see it's empty, I kinda remember but I kinda don't. I think she went to the bathroom or something. And then I think I'll ask her later, but that's when I remember that I won't see her later. And then class keeps going, but all I can think about is the last time I saw her, and everything we were still supposed to do. I don't know."

Logan nodded slowly, giving him time to add more before she interjected. "It sounds like she was very important to you."

His gaze drifted up, floating along the posters taped up near the front of the classroom. "I had most of my classes with her. We tried to pick everything together this semester. I don't know. Some of the classes I don't care about that much, but she wanted them and she said they were good for schools to see in our college applications. She wanted to learn more about business, but that class is boring as fuck. Oh shit—uh, I mean—I'm sorry. I didn't mean to do that."

Logan let a real, unpracticed smile unfurl across her face. "I don't care if you curse, Derek. Say whatever you want."

Derek smiled back at her, a little sheepishly, a little shyly. "Cool," he declared. "I never get to say real shit at school."

Logan kept her smile in place and gave a small shrug. "I know we're on school grounds, but you don't have to think of this as school. I'm here as resource for you, not as a disciplinarian. And after what you've been through, I'd say a little cursing is not only allowable but perfectly appropriate. Your situation sucks. It *fucking* sucks. It's okay to say it."

"Thanks. That's cool." He wore a surprised half-smile himself, but after a moment, his expression turned softer and more contemplative. "I do miss her, you know," he said. "She was great sometimes. I feel like nobody really got it, but she was the smartest person I knew. And she was funny, but I don't think she wanted anyone to know that." His expression turned darker. "I guess it isn't always a good thing to be funny like that, though.

Funny and smart, maybe. I don't know, sometimes I think she was too smart. Too smart to be here, anyway."

Logan already agreed with him, but she wanted him to unpack his thoughts a little more. "What do you mean she was too smart to be here? You think nobody appreciated how smart she was?"

"That's part of it," he said, nodding. "But also…I don't know, I think she'd get bored. And when she got bored, she got mean." He made a kind of clucking noise as he shoved his hands in his pockets. It looked to her like he wanted to shrug out of responsibility for what he was saying. "I never got why she liked doing some of that stuff, but now I think it must have been because she was so bored. It's like if she couldn't get a real challenge, then she was gonna do whatever else she wanted."

"What do you mean? What else did she want to do?"

He paused, a look of concern frozen on his face. Perhaps he felt he shouldn't incriminate her in any way, even if she couldn't get in trouble for it.

"It's okay," Logan assured him. "I know she had some conflicts with a few of the other students. You don't have to tell me anything you don't want to."

"No, I do want to tell you. I don't know, I guess I feel bad remembering some of the bad stuff. It feels like I'm only supposed to remember what was good about her, like that's all that matters now. I mean, it's not like she can defend herself anymore. You know?"

"Hm," Logan answered, no real hint of agreement in her voice. She studied her boot for a moment, noting the piece of dried grass stuck to the side. "You can't help what you remember about her. She wasn't perfect, just like you and I aren't perfect. Most people have little defects and shortcomings; it's part of what defines us. If you intentionally try to block those things out of your memory, then you aren't really remembering the right person at all. And I don't think Violet would want you to remember her wrong, do you?"

Derek took a moment to absorb her words before he slowly nodded. "I guess that's true. I don't think she ever tried to hide what she did, anyway." He looked out the window for a moment, like he was gathering himself back up. Still gazing at the clear blue sky, he spoke. "She could be kind of dark and awful sometimes. I never…sometimes the things she said, I didn't know where it was coming from. I'd ask her if she wanted to see some movie, and she'd say no, but she would go see it if I wanted her to. But it felt like…it felt like she wanted to go just so she could make me feel guilty for making her do it. So then I'd try to find a movie she wanted to see—literally *any* movie, I would go through and name anything that was out, anything that was playing here. But she didn't like a single one. Ever. No chick flicks, no action, no comedy, no anything. She said they were all too dumb. So one time I asked her if there was anything playing at the theater in the next town—you know, maybe if there was something that wasn't coming here. Still nothing. And I asked her why, I mean *really* why, and she said she couldn't stand to spend two hours being reminded how stupid people were, how so many people could be tricked into believing it was worth it to waste their money on the same stupid thing, over and over. And…I don't know, I think I pushed her too far. She got really quiet, and she said there was no point to anything. Everyone had always been stupid, from the beginning of time until now, and everyone always would be, until we do something so stupid that we all die. And…god. I just shouldn't have…her voice got kinda weird. She said the only interesting thing she could think of to do was kill herself. I don't know. It seemed like a joke to her. But some people really…really try to do that, you know? So it's not funny. I mean, she wasn't trying to be funny. But, like, you can't even…you can't say that shit, even if you don't mean it. Because some people do mean it, man. They really do."

"I take it you don't believe that Violet did mean it?"

"Not really, no. I think she was bored by everything, and I think she hated most of our friends, and her parents, and this town. But she never tried to hurt herself. She just liked to say some shit. She told me once that she'd never do it, because she needed to know what the rest of the world was like. See, I finally did get her to go to a movie one time. I found this theater over in Billings that plays more, like, those indie films and foreign films. When I told her about it, she was so excited. We spent the whole day in the city, and then we went to go see this Argentinean movie. I think that was probably the happiest I ever saw her. Finally something new, you know? After that, she said that no matter what, she had to travel the world someday. She wanted to see every other kind of place there is, you know? See everything. I mean, she'd still say all that other shit, too. As soon as she was upset about anything, all of a sudden the whole world sucked again and she might as well kill herself. But I knew she wouldn't ever do it." His gaze drifted again, like he couldn't look Logan in the eye when he remembered the worst of it. "But some people really do it, you know? They do."

Logan felt her right eyebrow rise with intrigue, but she pushed it back to neutral. "What do you mean, Derek?"

Derek shifted uncomfortably, his eyes gaining focus once more. "I mean, I only know what I heard. I didn't really know her that well. I mean, we had, like, one class together, so I spoke to her a couple of times. Mainly for class. But I don't think she'd say I was her friend or anything. I probably should have talked to her more, but I didn't even know, you know? Her name's Suzanne, and I guess a lot of people think she's weird. I always thought she was pretty normal. She helped me out one time when I missed a class, so I thought was cool. But I think a lot of the girls thought she was ugly, and they liked making fun of her sometimes. I never got why Violet was into that. She used to make up these shitty names for her and get the other girls to say it. I think she just liked that they would do it because she said so. She liked it when people did what she said. But I never thought it was funny. Anyway, when we started going out, she hadn't done it in a while I think. Finally got bored of it maybe. Or maybe she felt bad. I don't know. She wouldn't talk about it. I didn't even know about what happened with Suzanne until, like, a month ago. Missy told me. I think she hoped it would make me break up with Violet or something. I don't know."

"What did Missy tell you about Suzanne?"

"Oh, well, I knew about the flagpole prank that someone played on Suzanne, back in sophomore year. But I didn't know that Violet was behind it. So Missy told me that. And she told me that before she switched schools, Suzanne tried to kill herself. She tried to hang herself in her room, I guess." Pure disgust washed over his young, still-forming features. "Missy made sure to mention that Suzanne was too fat for her noose, so she just fell down on the floor instead. She's so full of shit. Why the fuck would you ever say that to me, you know? You really think I'm gonna laugh at some girl who tried to kill herself, just so you can pretend you're funny? Damn."

Logan nodded silently, letting the full cruelty of Missy's statements wash over her. Perhaps, after everything, it was a kindness that she'd never gotten to stay in any one school for too long of a stretch. "It must have been difficult to discover that Violet was responsible for that."

"I guess I wasn't that surprised." She could hear a bitter, brittle note in his voice. "I never really knew what Violet got out of pushing people around like that, but I knew she did it. Anyone…I don't know, anyone a little *off*, anyone *weird*…she made fun of them at some point. I mean, she wasn't as bad as she used to be. She didn't rile anyone else up anymore. But if we were alone, she'd just talk shit. About everyone. I guess she talked about her friends a lot, too." His mouth pursed into an empty almost-grin. "Sometimes I think I was the only person she actually liked. Maybe she didn't even like me that much."

Logan paused. She was starting to feel an uncomfortable affinity for Violet Buchanan, though the girl remained something of a mystery. Not as dissimilar from Judith Li as either girl likely believed, Violet seemed like another kid who didn't quite fit, who couldn't quite find contentment. But what did that matter now? Besides, maybe Logan was wrong. For all she knew, Violet's cruelty had nothing to do with feeling out of place herself. But there was little point saying any of that to a grieving teenage boy. So instead, she stepped back from her own head and tried to think of something more comforting.

"It sounds like Violet might have had a hard time expressing her affection for other people. But that doesn't mean she didn't care about you."

"I guess." His eyes made a rotation around the room again, and she could see his brain working in his face, his thoughts searching. "I know she had a hard time sometimes. It could be hard…looking the way she did. Honestly, most of the time, I wished she didn't look so good. It kinda sucks sometimes when every other fucking guy wants to hit on your girlfriend, you know?"

A smile of recognition washed over Logan's face before she could stop it. "Was it hard to feel like you had her to yourself?"

"Yeah, it was. That was it. You know, these guys, they just come after her. Jason was the worst, but he wasn't the only one. Some of these dudes, they'll just keep coming. It was like I couldn't even leave her alone at a party without them all swarming around her like she was a fucking buffet or something. I don't know. Violet used to say it felt like they all thought she owed them something, just because she was there. No matter what she said, they'd keep coming. And, man, I don't know for sure what it was, but these last few weeks…I just wonder, I guess…."

He trailed off and his eyes glazed over a bit. Logan fought the urge to lean forward, and instead kept her posture neutral, allowing only a slight tilt to her head.

"What do you wonder about, Derek? What happened in the last few weeks?"

His eyes focused again, and his back straightened out as he

met her gaze. "Violet got kind of weird. Not like…I mean, she was just really stressed out. She thought someone was stalking her. I don't know. She got these notes, and she thought someone was in her yard. I don't know if it was real or not. It's like, I totally believe it could be—some of these guys go too fucking far, you know? I mean, Jason's a fucking idiot, but it doesn't take brains to follow someone home, I guess. But then I think—maybe she was imagining it. Violet wasn't crazy, but—maybe it's, I don't know, kinda normal to think someone's stalking you after you've been dealing with all these assholes, you know?" He shrugged, and she got the sense from the motion that he was giving up all hope that he'd ever know the truth. "Or maybe someone thought they were being funny. Or maybe it was Missy being a bitch. Maybe it was fucking anything, you know?"

Logan nodded, studying him carefully. When she spoke, she let her words form slowly, hoping he wouldn't take her more seriously than necessary. "What if we assumed, just for a second, that someone was following her. What would be your first guess about who it was?"

"I don't know. Someone who hated her, I guess. Maybe someone she fucked with. Maybe someone who hated her for some other reason. Who knows, you know?"

Logan felt a forlorn half-smile push across her lips. "Someone who thought she owed them something, perhaps."

He nodded. "Yeah. Something like that."

Something like that.

Logan took a cursory lunch from the cafeteria, despite the fact that a single glance at it told her that she might have found a primary source of the country's health problems. She brought it back to her makeshift office and shut and locked the door, determined to procure a few minutes of freedom. With Violet's file spread across the desk before her, she picked up her plastic fork and took a stab at the puddle of green beans on her plate.

Naturally, at that moment, her phone buzzed in her pocket. Without looking, she knew it was Knatt. Only rarely did she get calls from anyone but him. She answered the call and set it to speaker phone, then placed it on the desk near her plate.

"Why Knatt," she said with feigned surprise, "how sweet of you to want to keep me company on my lunch hour. It's the little things like this that show you care, you know."

"That is not why I have contacted you, Miss Logan." He sounded as stiff and British as ever.

"No, really? But you're usually so sentimental."

"I require an update on your progress in the case you are currently pursuing." She would have said he sounded even more like a stick in the mud than he normally did, but she wasn't sure such a thing was possible.

"You *require* an update. That's interesting." The sinking feeling in her stomach told her that she already knew what was coming, but she felt an urge to pull it out of him as painfully as possible.

He allowed a split second hesitation before he spoke again. "Require, request. Whichever you like."

"Require, request. You've never been much for inexact phrasing, Knatt. And the word you chose was require." She paused to take a bite of her green bean mush, chewing as slowly as she could. "It's an interesting choice."

She could almost feel the impatience rolling off him. "Do you have an update, Miss Logan? Have there been any developments?"

"Sure there have." With another bite, she finished off her greens, which ultimately bore a texture closer to soup than vegetables. Then she moved on to the pitiful apple slices in the next section of the plate.

Knatt's voice sounded strained, like someone had wound him too tight. "Are you going to tell me what you've learned so far?"

With a loud crunching sound, she finished her chunk of apple. "Well, for starters, I've learned that teenagers are assholes. Well, I guess I would say I *relearned* that. I'm sure I used to know it when I was one."

On the other end, Knatt let out a frustrated cluck. "Is anything you've learned so far actually relevant to the case?"

"Sure it is."

"Would you care to tell me what?"

"I don't know, Knatt. The thing is, I don't feel terribly compelled to share information with someone when I'm pretty sure that they're withholding something from me." She crunched on another piece of apple to give him a moment.

Finally, he sighed. She imagined the exasperated lines of his face growing taut on the other end. "Very well. Your activities in Montana have not gone unnoticed by the community at large. I received a call this morning from a member of the Order of Shadows."

The sinking feeling she'd noticed at the beginning of their conversation intensified. "I see. So. Have they been monitoring me?"

"I asked. They said no."

Logan didn't bother to repress the sneer that pulled on her upper lip. She mistrusted the Order almost as much as her father. "So how did they find out?"

"Mr. Atherton informs me their psychics picked up on an unusual uptick in paranormal activity in the area." She could hear the contempt in his voice; it mirrored her own. Psychics were generally charlatans who knew how to manipulate suggestion magic and passed it off as soothsaying. In other words: Atherton's explanation was bullshit.

"Right. And somehow they picked up on me specifically?"

"Mr. Atherton did not expound on their detection methods. He merely called to let me know that the Order are standing ready, should we require their assistance."

"He called you personally?"

"Indeed."

Logan fought to keep the image of smarmy James Atherton out of her head. "Right. So, you require an update in order to know if we require their assistance. Is that right?"

"Roughly. Yes."

Logan was down to the soft, wilted square of cheese pizza. "I don't require any assistance. If anything, the *assistance* of the Order would only get in my way. I don't know if you're aware of this, but getting kids to tell the whole truth is something of a delicate business. It requires a subtle approach. In this case, subtle does *not* mean a bunch of old bluebloods running around in stupid black capes. You get me?"

"I surmised as much. Unfortunately for us, Miss Logan, while the Order have thus far only offered their assistance, they may soon insist upon it. Any quantifiable update you can give me would help to keep that inevitability at bay for a few days longer."

Logan almost loathed to help him out with this, but she did see his point. "Fine. I have a couple of suspects, and one of them didn't show up at school today, so I'm going on a field trip tonight. Is that enough of an update for you?"

"It will do for now." She disliked the sound of his satisfaction. "Thank you, Logan."

"Yeah. Later, Knatt."

She clicked off the phone without a second thought. Somehow, the limp pizza slice looked even less appealing than it had before.

But she did need to force a few more calories into her system. And she needed to put in a call to Mrs. Wendell to ask for Judith Li's home address.

If she was lucky, she might have a better update for Knatt by the morning.

Getting Judith Li's address was the easy part. Mrs. Wendell gave it to her without a question, and she threw in a paper map of the town as well. Logan had prepared a reason she needed the address—that she'd scheduled a second session with Li and was concerned about her absence, and she hoped to offer her a chance to reschedule. But she need not have bothered; Mrs. Wendell didn't ask a single follow-up question.

So she stood now in the front office, staring at the map and trying to figure out her route. She felt a vague sense of dread as she pondered the evening in front of her. Talking to children for the past week had been bad enough; she had no desire to experience any of their parents.

Nevertheless, she knew what she had to do. Once she had a clear picture in her mind, she swallowed her unease, folded up the map, and marched out to the parking lot.

She wasn't sure what she should expect when she got to Judith Li's house. Would Li even be there? Did she want her to be?

Maybe Li's absence would prove to be a coincidence after all. Maybe she had a cold.

Or maybe not. Logan zipped up her jacket as she swung onto the bike again.

The route she'd mapped out brought her back into the suburbs to the south. She ended up on a street of identical ranch houses, all a uniform rusty red color with uniformly manicured lawns and SUVs of various neutral colors parked in the driveways. When she saw the sign for Li's street, she went just past it, deciding it was best to weigh anchor out of sight. She didn't want to have to explain to anybody's parents why a high school counselor rode a motorcycle.

After she'd kicked the stand down and hopped off, she took a chance and slung her jacket over the seat, placing the helmet on top of it. She had a feeling theft wasn't an overwhelming problem in this town, and she wanted to maintain whatever shot she had at coming off as nonthreatening and harmless. With a quick tug to straighten her tucked-in collared shirt, and a glance to check for sweat stains, she took off down Judith Li's street, toward her home address.

Each lawn on the street had a mailbox at the end, and each mailbox had been helpfully printed with the address of the accompanying house. Judith Li's house was halfway down: *5914*

Acorn Street. Logan stopped right in front of the box and gave the house a quick once-over.

She wasn't sure exactly what she'd expected, but the house hardly looked like it held a murderous mastermind. It didn't even have a garage; it had a carport. As she glanced around behind into the yard beyond, she could tell that it backed up not to the plentiful forests all around them, but to another row of cookie-cutter suburb street—not exactly ideal for hiding a monster. A small window set into the side of the house, so low its ledge rested in direct contact with the earth, told her that the house at least boasted a basement, but she saw no indication that the basement held any exit to the outside world larger than that cat-sized opening. In short: if Judith Li had a monster for a pet, Logan doubted she was keeping it in this house.

With a deep breath, she put on her best client face and made her way up the sidewalk to the front door. The door was white with a white-based screen over it. A shining gold doorknocker rested under the peephole, but Logan pegged it as decorative only and opted for the deep gray doorbell to the right instead. The hollow ring echoed through the rooms beyond.

After a moment, the door cracked open an inch, then inched onward at a turtle's pace until it finally held wide. A well-dressed Asian woman in her fifties, wearing pale peach, stood behind it, hesitating briefly in shadow as she gave Logan a once-over. Finally, she stepped forward, meeting Logan behind the screen door with an expression of pure suspicion on her face. As far as Logan could tell, she looked to be in her late forties; her frame appeared light and fit, and her perfectly black hair hung straight to her shoulders before ending in an abrupt line, meaning that the only available indicator of her age lay in the fine lines crackling just around her eyes, displaying an as-yet-unearned air of character and critical thinking. She cocked her head sharply to the left as she spoke.

"Who are you?" Her voice was crisp and sharp.

"My name is Miss Logan," Logan answered immediately. Something about this woman's voice demanded promptness. "I work up at the high school, where Judith Li attends. Is this her residence?"

"Is Judith in trouble?" One of the woman's eyebrows shot up, clicking into a perfect upside-down checkmark above her eye. "Are you a teacher? Did Judith do something bad at the school?"

"No, that's not why I'm here," said Logan, in what she hoped was a reassuring tone. "I'm actually—I'm a counselor at the school. One of Judith's classmates died very recently, and I've been offering grief counseling sessions to the students. Judith was scheduled for a session with me today, so I wanted to come by and see if she'd like to reschedule. May I speak to her?"

"No," said the woman abruptly, shaking her head with stern force. "Judith does not need that. You may leave now."

Her voice was commanding, but she didn't shut the door right away. Logan let a broad smile spread across her face.

"Tell me, are you Judith's mother, by any chance?"

"Yes, I am Mrs. Li," the woman answered with a nod. Her hand rested on the edge of the door, but she still didn't close it.

"It's so nice to meet you, Mrs. Li. I must admit, I was a little worried to hear that Judith called in sick. I hope she managed to get some rest at home today?"

The woman stared at her silently with no answer, suspicion

blossoming anew across her features. Just then, a child's voice sounded somewhere in the room beyond her.

"Mom! I finished the worksheet."

Without a word, Mrs. Li turned around and walked a few paces into the house. Logan leaned furtively forward, glancing inside as her eyes adjusted. She could see a dining room table with two children seated behind it—they looked like they were no older than six and eight, respectively. Each child slumped over a pile of papers, with more piles of books beside them. Logan did the easy math—these kids, likely Judith's siblings, though close in age to each other, looked nearly a decade younger than Judith was. Logan couldn't help but wonder what that might imply about the potential for loneliness in Judith Li's life.

"If you're finished, you put it in the stack by the end of the table and start on the next one. I'll check the work in a few minutes to make sure. If it's good, we will take a snack break when your sister finishes hers. Now start the next one."

Then she turned around again and walked back to Logan. Her face bore the exact same expression as before, almost as though they had experienced no interruption.

"What do you want with Judith?" asked Mrs. Li.

"I was just wondering if I could talk to her for a moment. I'll be very quick, I promise. I certainly wouldn't want to interfere with her convalescence. I'm only concerned for her emotional well-being, Mrs. Li."

Like a pot collapsing in slow-motion, Mrs. Li's expression melted from suspicion into resignation. Then she sighed.

"Judith is not here." Her lips pursed into a hard line as she continued to survey Logan with something less than warmth.

"She's not here? Does that mean she's not sick?"

"That girl is not *sick*. Her *body* is not sick. She is wrong. Something is *wrong* with that girl."

"Wrong with her?" Logan allowed surprise to flood her voice but kept it neutral apart from that, devoid of judgment in any direction. "What do you mean?"

"She's not right. I don't know how it happened. Something is not right with that girl. I did what I can, but I have two children in this house. I can't spend all my time correcting that girl."

Two other *children*, Logan thought, but she didn't say it.

"Are you saying Judith is not here because she no longer lives here?" As she spoke, she found that her voice sounded just as crisp as Mrs. Li's.

"Yes, she is gone now." Mrs. Li gave a small shake of her head. "I don't know where she went. I have to take care of my children. It's not good to keep her in the house with them. They don't understand."

"Mrs. Li...in what *way* is Judith wrong?"

Mrs. Li stared at her, a new emotion that Logan couldn't immediately identify spreading across her face. Logan tried again. "Earlier, you asked me if Judith was in trouble. Has she been in trouble before?"

Mrs. Li's new expression solidified; she looked...*afraid*. That was it.

"That girl *is trouble*." Mrs. Li shook her head resolutely; she bore the expression of one who had been through fire, or at the very least, wanted their audience to believe so. "We fight all the time, in front of her siblings. I tell her not to bring this rottenness into my house, in front of young children. But she does it all the same. She does not stop." She fixed Logan with a stare like a lamplight. "She goes against God. If she wants the devil to take her, then let him have her." Her voice wavered slightly, and she cut off her stare. "I thought maybe—at the school—someone could have seen her—but, no. No, I don't want to talk about it anymore. Thank you for coming, but we don't need any help from you. You may go now. No, wait." She turned away and walked out of sight briefly. When she came back, she held a small piece of cardstock in her hands. For the first time, she opened the door and reached out, in order to pass the little postcard-sized piece through. "Take a coupon. Everybody needs to eat."

Logan glanced down at the paper in astonishment. In bright yellow letters, she read: *Little Italy Palace*. When she looked up again, Mrs. Li was staring her down with intention once more.

"It's a family business. You should eat, we make very good food. Best food in town, I guarantee. Everybody needs to eat. Okay?"

Logan blinked.

"Okay. Thank you, Mrs. Li. I appreciate it."

She turned away without another word. As she walked back down the path through Mrs. Li's front yard, she stared down at the cardstock in mild disbelief. *Weird business strategy*, she thought. As a matter of fact, the whole conversation had left her feeling strangely unsettled.

Judith Li had been kicked out of her home. Mrs. Li had tiptoed around spelling out a reason, but perhaps it wasn't unreasonable to think Judith may have done something violent.

As Logan made her way back to her bike, she realized that she didn't have the faintest idea where she could start looking for Judith. Despite conducting an entire counseling session with her, Logan hadn't gathered enough information to have any real idea where the girl would go if she needed to leave home. Maybe she had gone out to some secret hideout in the woods, where she was keeping her monster hidden. Or maybe she had an accomplice—a friend, perhaps another victim of Violet's childish cruelty—and they kept the monster housed on their property. But Logan had no idea who that accomplice was likely to be, or what section of woods Judith would have chosen for a lair, if she had done any such thing at all.

There had to be something she could track. Surely.

It was likely only a matter of time before someone else was attacked. The presence of the coyote carcass told her that much. She glanced at the time—well past 5:00pm, so Mrs. Wendell was probably home for the night. In the morning, she would have to ask her everything she knew about Suzanne Grubb and how to find her now, on the off-chance that Suzanne was Judith's accomplice.

In the meantime, she couldn't be sure that the beast in the woods would restrict itself to wild animals for long. As she pondered what options she might have to track it, or pick up on any sign of it, she felt an itch developing in the center of her back. The itch seemed to burn in a small circle, dead center between her shoulder blades. It was almost as though the Choronzon Key wanted to remind her of its presence.

Almost as though…Logan bent her arm behind her back to touch the lower edge of the Key where it now lay tattooed on her hidden skin. She should have expected as much—the Key felt hot to the touch.

She hated anthropomorphizing the body art she'd never chosen, but the truth was that sometimes the Key *wanted* things, and it let her know when it did. Like right now—she knew it wanted something from her, though she couldn't immediately say what. So with a small sigh of resignation, she closed her eyes and opened her mind to whatever suggestion it wanted to place.

She imagined nothing. Instead, she cleared away all her lingering thoughts and focused on empty space. Her breath came in and out. The hot almost-summer air pressed down on her, and her temple formed a thin line of sweat.

An urge to move came over her. She pulled on her helmet and swung onto the bike, then revved it forward at a much lower pace than normal. Turning her Ninja down streets that seemed to come to her like whims, she headed out of Judith's subdivision and rode a little further south.

After a few minutes, she found herself slipping down a lonelier, emptier road. A simple playground with a small gravel lot stood at the end; when she met it, she came to a stop.

If someone had asked her, she couldn't have explained why, but she felt like now was the time to leave the bike behind. She parked it in the gravel and left the helmet and the jacket sitting on top of it, knowing somehow that she'd need to move a little more freely than either would allow her.

As she gazed on at the woods before her, she got the sense that she'd been here before. Her feet propelled her forward, along the short stretch of grass and straight into the line of trees.

When she found a path no more than a few feet into the woods, she wasn't surprised. She'd known it would be there— or, rather, the Key had. She followed it deeper into the dark, ducking around branches and high-stepping over bramble. Though the sun had not yet faded from the sky, the woods here were dense enough to block out most of the remaining illumination, leaving her in an ersatz night.

She knew she had arrived before she saw any signs of what she might be looking for. With a burn so brief it barely hurt, the Chorozon Key released its hold on her, and with it the urgent physical need to move dropped away. As she hesitated with her foot in midair, suddenly uncertain, she met a low-hanging branch and stumbled. Righting herself again, she took a few surer steps forward and found herself facing a small circle of empty space within the trees.

Across from her stood a tall stone, possibly positioned purposely, covered in stains and deliberate marks, the melted stubs of burned-down candles littering the top edge. The floor of the hollow looked burned out, almost like someone had cleared away the debris with fire—or something else. She had seen the after-effects of letha summoning before. She took a step into the clearing, past the arbitrary boundary created by the line of trees, but despite all the clear evidence of magic, she felt no involuntary shiver down her spine. Instead, when she looked at this empty burned-out husk in the middle of the woods, she felt nothing. It didn't tell her much, but it suggested that since the beast had been summoned, its summoner had not used the site for any further casting. She doubted Judith or anyone else had come by here at all. It had that unused feeling to it.

Glancing around the site, she took note of all the various signs of spell work, from the minor singe marks along the ground to the last vestiges of blue powder in the visible crevices. Once she'd gotten a good look around, she walked over to the rock on the far side—tall and thin, almost like a naturally occurring gravestone.

For the most part, the stains and markings on the stone were too faded for her to make anything out from them. But in the very center of its face, there was one clear image she could still interpret.

It was some kind of rune—a rune displaying a wolf's head.

She remembered clearly the voice she'd heard in her vision, then again in her dream. *I worship the wolf.* And here she was, staring at a wolf's head.

It was starting to feel like someone was trying to tell her something.

Chapter 6
Full of Surprises

She dreamed of a carnival again. First she saw ball gowns, but when they started to twirl, they expanded. They grew all the way out until they were fifteen feet wide, and little rider-less horses started to take shapes out of the cloth.

She knew she was dreaming. When she rounded an unexpected corner, she got the sense that something was watching her. She tried to look out into the dark, hoping she could make out something new—maybe now, maybe now that she knew she was dreaming, she could find out what information the dream had to give her.

Was it the wolf? Was the wolf watching her?

But the edges of her dream faded and blurred, too uncertain for her to tell. She pushed forward, forcing her dream-legs to move even though they felt like lead dragging her down. Someone was near; she could feel it. Her gaze covered everything, everywhere it could. Who was watching her? Who was following her?

Something shifted. She heard a sudden crack and felt her real-world body jolt.

No—who was—she had to stay—

But she couldn't. Before she could even turn around, her

body woke up completely, dragging her from the dream.

As she sat up in bed, she looked toward her open window and the rain streaming down it. Another crack of lightning flashed through her room; the sounds of the storm must have been what had woken her. Perhaps if she'd managed to shutter the glass before drifting off, she'd still be exploring that carnival…but it had been so hot in the room….

She turned over and let herself slip away again. As her thoughts turned to mush, she knew she probably wouldn't fall back into the carnival. If it held any lessons for her, she'd have to find them out some other way. Maybe it was nothing; maybe she was imagining it all.

When Logan arrived at school the next morning, she had a very particular task in mind: locating Suzanne Grubb. Nothing guaranteed that Suzanne could lead her anywhere, but in lieu of any other ideas—even vague and unfounded ones—she figured Suzanne was as good a place as any to start searching for Judith Li. Besides, there existed the outside possibility that Suzanne might even be Li's accomplice—if Li was indeed the summoner after all.

So, before making her usual stop in the staff room for coffee, Logan headed toward the front office. Inside, a young woman in her early 20s glanced up at her from behind a monitor that looked like it hadn't been updated since the late 1990s. The girl's gaze was equal parts contempt and disinterest.

"I'm looking for Mrs. Wendell," said Logan. Just like she'd been doing with the students, she kept her tone carefully neutral.

The girl didn't say anything. Instead she slowly raised her left hand and pointed over to the office behind her.

"Thanks," said Logan as she pushed past her, searching out Wendell's blunt bangs and overlarge square glasses.

She found her easily, peering out the window of the inner office, watching all the students trundle in to start their day. Logan knocked on the door frame as she entered.

"Miss Logan!" Wendell exclaimed as she turned around to face her. "What a pleasant surprise! How might I help you this lovely morning?"

"I have a slightly unusual request," answered Logan as she took another step into the office. "It's perfectly all right if you can't tell me. I was just wondering what happened to that girl who changed schools—Suzanne Grubb. Do you remember her? Do you think you can find out?"

"Of course I remember her," said Mrs. Wendell with a dismissive wave of her hand. Logan would have been amused but unsurprised if the next words out her mouth were *I remember everyone*, but no such luck. "Let me see what we've got in her file."

She strode out past Logan into the hallway connecting all the inner offices, then pushed into the next room over. This room fell somewhere between an office and a broom closet in size, making it difficult for more than one person to navigate it at a time. So Logan hovered awkwardly just before the threshold while her counterpart entered. Wendell dug through a few file drawers with vigor, before pulling out an open folder and flipping through the first few pages.

"Oh dear," she sighed finally. She closed the folder as she met Logan's waiting stare. "This is unfortunate. It looks like we don't have any record of where Miss Grubb moved to. If memory serves, it was somewhere in Montgomery County, but I don't have an exact address to give you. Sorry I couldn't be more useful."

"Oh, don't worry about it," Logan answered with a shrug. "It's not important, anyway. Thanks for the effort."

She turned to go again, already anticipating the injection of caffeine that awaited her in the staff room, but Wendell called her back again.

"Miss Logan?" Logan turned to face her. "I wasn't sure if you were aware, but there's a home baseball game tonight, over in the field with the bleachers. It's a small post-season game, but a lot of the students usually go. Just thought I'd let you know, in case you wanted to go." She allowed herself a little smirk. "Or in case you wanted to avoid it, either way."

Logan let her eyebrow drag upward as she appraised the older woman.

"Will you be avoiding it, Mrs. Wendell?"

"I didn't say that, did I?" Wendell answered, but she had an unmistakable sparkle in her eye.

"Well, thank you for the heads up. I appreciate it."

She turned away again, making her way down the thin inner hallway and back out into the main thoroughfare that was the entryway.

Inwardly, she sighed. While Mrs. Wendell was free to avoid the baseball game, Logan knew where her own duty lay. She had to go.

The game would be a large social gathering, and at least part of it would happen at night. If that wasn't the perfect recipe for an attack from the beast, she didn't know what was. So she was going.

She headed in the direction of coffee. She was going to need a lot of it.

After her last appointment ended but before the game began, Logan managed to sneak back into town to pick up another sandwich from the diner. She brought it with her out to the field, where she chose to seat herself in a high, far corner of the bleachers, apart from where most of the crowd was sitting. She kept her motorcycle jacket on as she perched on the cold metal, scanning the area around her to check if she had any blind spots from this vantage point, and to assess where she might want to train her attention.

As she sat there surveying the field, the stands around her began to fill up. Almost unconsciously, she inched further to her left, away from the people. She didn't expect to find much in the way of entertainment that evening, so she tried to hold off on eating her sandwich for as long as she could. Though she had her book shoved into one of the jacket's inner pockets, she'd need to stay aware and alert once the sun started to go down. Of course, for now, the sun barely skimmed the rooftops, so she could bury her nose in it for a little while.

At some point, the noises ahead of her told her that the game had begun. She kept going with her book for a few more minutes, until she noticed the temperature start to drop. She glanced around and silently cursed herself; the sun had indeed started to fall, but her eyes had adjusted so well, she hadn't noticed. With a sigh, she put the book away.

Based on decorations she had seen around the school, she guessed that the school colors were red and white, which meant that the team currently up to bat surely belonged to the school. *Her* school, for the moment. She watched a student she didn't know walk up to the plate and bend his body into an awkward batting stance. The allure of baseball was lost on her. She honestly couldn't fathom why so many students had gathered to observe this pointless and uninteresting performance, except for the sheer lack of other possible activities available in town. As she adjusted her position to allow a small shoulder stretch, she observed the students nearest to her. They still sat just far enough away to allow her a bubble of semi-privacy, which she attributed to the uninviting nature of her straight-backed posture and unwavering scowl.

The kids near her were laughing and chatting away with abandon. She continued to observe them surreptitiously, and after a few minutes, she saw the quick flash of a metal flask as it passed between two of them. Her mouth threatened to quirk into a partial smile, but she repressed it. The flask told her exactly why so many students would come to this blasé attempt at a diversion: the game provided them cover.

Satisfied for the moment, Logan decided it might be time to make sure she had enough fuel to get through the night and, accordingly, opened her takeout bag from the diner. She felt her eyes close of their own accord as the taste of slow-roasted eggplant and three types of cheese hit her senses. Far too soon, she had devoured the thing in its entirety. She still couldn't wait to get out of this town, but she had a feeling that she would miss that damn diner for the rest of her days.

Her gaze returned to the field. During her brief meal, the teams had switched places. She gazed around at the members of the red-shirt team, wondering if she might recognize any of them. Sure enough, she noticed Jason Reed almost immediately. He had abandoned his left field post and walked in, up to another boy on the field. It looked like he had grabbed one of the spare bats and dragged it out onto the field with him. As she watched, he took hold of his bat and positioned it in front of his lower torso. He leaned his shoulders back and thrust his pelvis forward, positioning the bat above his genitals, allowing it to jut forward. She watched his head fall back in laughter, beset by the force of his own hilarity.

A moment later, she was startled to realize that the boy he had walked up to was Derek James, Violet's boyfriend—and probably the most likable of the boys she had interviewed so far. Jason, in all his unappealing swagger, had briefly overwhelmed her field of vision.

Jason waved the bat in his face, and Derek forcibly pushed it away. Jason laughed again, and again came aggressively toward his counterpart. Derek pushed it away a second time, and for a moment, it seemed Jason might finally leave off. But no. He waved the bat a third time, this time nearly letting it collide with Derek's face. Pushed obviously past the limit, Derek swooped his arms and shoulders in a tight backwards loop, a clear gesture of exasperation, before darting forward and snatching the bat out of Jason's hands. Without a moment's hesitation, he ran infield and flagged one of the coaches to hand it right over to them. They took it and put it out of sight while he ran back over to his post. From Jason's own arm circles, thrown violently wide, she guessed that he was yelling angrily at his teammate, but Derek's neutral posture betrayed no reaction to it of any kind. Eventually Jason walked away.

Logan let out a small sigh of relief when he finally relented. For the life of her, she still couldn't understand why anyone ever willingly brought themselves to a baseball game. This town was a mystery.

The game ended without incident. As the crowd started to stand and walk away, Logan didn't know whether to feel worried or relieved. She was sure the beast was still in town, and she was sure it would attack again. When it killed Violet, it chose to come for her during a social gathering, a party with her friends. Wouldn't it be likely to follow the same pattern? How long would she have to stay in this town before it made its move?

As two students passed closer to her on their way down the stairs, she got a hint at her answer.

"Hey, are you going to the after-party?"

"Hell yeah, I am! Beaker's Grove, right?"

"You got it!"

Damn. Logan had no idea where that was. As surreptitiously as she could, she stood up when the girls passed her and began to follow them. She'd need to follow one of them to wherever they were going. Of course, she could only hope no one else noticed what she was doing. After all, a grown woman choosing to follow teenagers without their knowledge probably wouldn't look too good to anyone.

She trailed the girls as they made their way around the school and out to the parking lot. When they split up, she followed the one who turned to walk toward the back of the parking lot, closer to where her Kawasaki was sitting. She kept one eye on her target as she peeled away from her and made her way to the bike. She swung onto it and turned it on, then waited as the girl disappeared inside an SUV and it roared to life. When it drove past her, she pulled forward to follow it out.

Her motorcycle wasn't exactly inconspicuous, but somehow she doubted this particular teenager had the wherewithal to take note. She followed about thirty feet back as the SUV drove off down a long, empty road headed out of town. When she finally saw the girl come to a stop in the gravel parking lot that denoted the start of a hiking trail, she drove past on the off-chance that the girl had noticed her. Finally she parked her bike a quarter mile away, partially hidden in the trees.

Once she'd swung successfully off the bike once more, she popped open the hidden storage compartment underneath her seat. She had a small knife already tied to her ankle, but if the beast really did attack, she'd need more than that to fight it off. She strapped a longer dagger, sheathed, to her upper thigh, and pulled out a battleax and holster that fastened to her back.

Off she went, back toward the parking lot where the girl had left her vehicle. She hoped the girl's path would be obvious, but if it wasn't, she figured the smells would key her in. As she approached the lot, she slowed, alert to any possible movement. Though a few other cars had come to rest by the first girl's SUV, it seemed their passengers had already moved along. Logan slipped across the gravel, quiet as a mouse, and entered the woods by the only visible trail.

She could already hear the telltale sounds of a party in full swing. Assured that she would find them with ease, she slipped off the path again and traveled parallel to it instead. She didn't want to let anyone know she was there if she could avoid it.

Sure enough, within moments she was in sight of them. They had chosen to gather in a wide clearing less than half a mile in. She guessed there must have been a second, larger path that led to it, as some of the kids had actually driven their vehicles right into the clearing and now appeared to be using them as mobile amplifiers for their terribly bland, aggressively catchy music. As she peered out from behind an old, thick trunk to scan the scene, a teenage boy in a baseball jersey passed right before her, so close she could have touched him. If he'd only looked to his right, he would have seen her. She pulled herself in, pushing her body completely behind the tree.

Fuck, she thought as she let out a metered breath. It was bad enough that she had to attend a high school party in secret just to make sure none of the students were brutally killed by some hell beast. But if she got caught sneaking around? She imagined she'd be lucky to make it out of town without fending off a lawsuit from an overbearing parent. Well, that wasn't entirely true—Knatt would probably find a way out of it for her, magically or otherwise. Of course, that would provide him with enough material to nag her for the next six months—which was almost worse than a lawsuit.

She didn't have any meditation candles with her, but she knew she needed to concentrate. Leaning back against the tree, she closed her eyes and imagined a calm ocean, full of gently rolling waves and invisible fish. She allowed herself to smell the salty air, to feel the breeze and the ocean spray on her face. Then she conjured up an image of a cave, full of shadows and dark depths, only a few feet down the beach from her. She moved toward it, knowing that it held within it her release. All she had to do was step inside…so she did.

As she imagined stepping forward into the cave and letting its recesses envelop her, she could feel the shadows gather around her, enshrouding her body. The restful ease of the eira summon clicked into place, and as it did, she allowed her other senses to open. A sudden rush of sounds and smells hit her, disorienting her momentarily. Once she adjusted, she took a deep breath, taking in all the sensory information she could from the clearing beyond. She had shadow cover now as well, so she peaked out again, hoping to get as full a picture as she could. There were over thirty students scattered throughout the clearing, and the smell of alcohol was strong. She made a mental note of the general layout of the scene, then she slipped further back into the trees once more.

It was too hard to say exactly where the beast might come from, if it came at all, so she decided to keep watch by marking a wide circle around the clearing and pacing along it, her senses all on alert for any signs of disturbance.

With a sigh of resignation, she started walking and began her watch.

An hour passed. She wanted to go home. Since her book would have been too distracting, she'd left it with the bike. This meant she had nothing to occupy herself with except the overheard conversations of teenagers. They'd grown infuriatingly boring within 10 minutes.

Another half hour passed. The woods had long since gone dark, the clearing lit by headlights and a pit fire. She made another lap around, feeling her spirit drag along the ground behind her, wondering when she might be able to go home.

At long last, some of the kids decided to pack it in. She watched a few of them pack themselves into cars before taking off down the wider path. She would be a little surprised if the beast never showed itself at all, but by now, all she could really think about was her waiting motel bed. Another 20 minutes passed.

The sound, when she heard it, came from out of nowhere. She was farther away from it than she would have liked.

As she climbed over a low bush, she heard a blood-curdling scream somewhere south of her. Immediately she whirled around and ran as fast as she could in that direction. Branches caught her legs and dragged across her skin, but she pushed on. First she followed the pre-beaten path she'd made on her rounds, but the source of the scream was further than that, so she jumped forward into unknown terrain.

Finally she burst into another clearing, much smaller than the one behind her. Ahead of her a prone figure lay on the ground— a white girl with a long blonde ponytail, still wearing her red-and-white cheerleader's outfit. Logan couldn't see her face well enough to tell if she knew her. But she could see the gash along the girl's arm.

And she could see the beast hovering over her, positioned directly between them.

Logan's considerable grace chose that moment to fail her; a root in her path escaped her notice and she tripped over it, instantly losing her meager surprise advantage over the beast. It roared and reared back, never once turning to face her, and came down and forward, toward the helpless girl before it. By the time Logan launched herself upward again with dagger in hand, she knew she would be too late.

Fortunately for the girl on the ground, Logan wasn't the only other person in the clearing with them. Someone else came into her view for the briefest moment—someone she hadn't even seen the moment before. The unknown person yelled incoherently into the night, and the air around them exploded with a white brilliance. For several seconds, Logan couldn't see anything at all. Somewhere ahead of her, the beast let out a grunt of pain.

Her brief glimpse of the unknown figure hadn't told her much, but she had managed to clock a baggy gray sweatshirt and what might have been a backwards baseball cap. One student sprang to mind, but she pushed the speculation away. She had other things to focus on for now.

Whoever the figure was, they had screamed out a spell word as they leapt forward, though she couldn't make it out. But that couldn't be right. Logan had never heard of a letha spell that successfully summoned light—as far as she knew, it was impossible. Still, here she was, trying to get her eyes to work again through the haze of some strange, glowing white light. So whatever that spell was, it had certainly done something. *Maybe it was eira?* she wondered. *Maybe the words were superfluous, or random noise…*

Even as her thoughts threatened to distract her, Logan rushed forward, straight through the fog of light, toward the spot where the beast had been moments before—but there was nothing there. She kept going, dagger held high before her as she came out of the strange enveloping cloud. On the other side, her head turned to the sound of crunching branches before her, and she saw the beast retreating.

She took after it at full speed, but within moments, she knew it was pointless. The beast could traverse these woods as easily as if it were open ground, while she found herself blocked by rocks and bramble, thickset bushes and trees. She couldn't explain why it had such an easier time with the terrain than she did; perhaps it was more familiar with it, having spent its last few nights marking its territory and hunting grounds. Or perhaps it simply saw better in the dark.

Soon enough, the beast had gotten so far ahead of her that she knew it was time to admit defeat. She slipped her long dagger back into its sheath and turned back toward the two students she had left behind.

Before she took her first step back toward them, she heard a strange noise—the sound of a flute, floating on the air from likely miles off. She didn't know what it was, but it struck some chord in her memory. Unearthly and cold, it struck her. She took mental note of the sound.

As she came out of the densest underbrush, she could see that the bright, blinding light from before had already dispersed. And she could make out the two figures now standing before her.

The first was the girl she'd seen on the ground in the cheerleader uniform. She stood upright and cradled her right arm, which was bleeding heavily just above the elbow. Now that Logan had a moment to study her face, she was sure she'd never spoken to her before.

But she recognized the other student immediately. As she watched, Judith Li pulled a blue bandana out of the pocket of her oversized sweatshirt and reached out to wrap it around the other girl's wound.

"What the fuck was that?" the blond girl whispered to Judith Li, her voice panicked and wild.

Judith began to mumble something in return, but then paused and glanced up as she heard Logan enter the clearing again.

"Hey! Uh, you wouldn't happen to have a real bandage on you, would you?" She looked Logan over, her eyes lingering on the leather sheath, clearly visible on Logan's upper thigh. "Alongside your…battle…knife? Uh, that's not a secret teacher thing, is it?"

Guess I could have tried to hide that. Logan sighed internally, but outwardly she shrugged. The cat was at least partly out of the bag; Logan was morally opposed to all kinds of memory spells, and she was well aware of how often they went wrong, so she hadn't left herself many options. Besides, Judith Li was her mystery figure. She had proven only moments ago that she knew a little something about casting, even if the spell she had used was one that Logan had never heard before. Logan almost laughed, wondering how many bizarre and unworkable spells she must have made up when she was younger, playing around in her father's study whenever he wasn't around.

"It's not a secret teacher thing, no. It's a…it's a secret that's specific to me, actually." She gave Judith a piercing look, deciding to study her closely as she got her answer. "Kind of like how you, an ordinary high school girl, somehow knew how to blind a hell beast. Along with anyone else caught in the crossfire."

Logan watched carefully as Judith scratched her head through the baseball cap, looking sheepish and contrite. Beside her, the blond girl watched her silently, her eyes wide with fear. "Yeah, sorry about that. I, uh, I didn't really think that would work. I just...I needed to do something." She looked over at the blond girl. As Logan watched, she tenderly touched the girl's arm, but only for a moment. "I couldn't just let it kill her."

For a moment, Logan kept her silence, still studying Judith Li intently. Every thought she'd had about Judith Li since the moment she'd first seen her raced through her head, begging her to make sense of it all. *What are you doing here, Judith Li?* Surely if she were the demon's summoner, she wouldn't have chased it off from the kill. And even if she'd wanted to, why would she need extraneous magic to do it?

"Of course not," said Logan finally, turning her attention on the cheerleader. "Are you all right?" She closed some of the distance still between them, hoping to get a better sense of the amount of blood loss.

"I don't know," the girl answered vaguely. She met Logan's eyes, and her own looked lost and confused. "What the hell was that thing?"

"I'm not exactly sure," said Logan. From a technical perspective, this was an honest answer. She knew it was a demon, yes, but she couldn't confirm what kind yet. "The important thing is that you're both okay. Do you feel faint at all?"

The blond girl gave a shake of her head. "No, I don't think so." She looked back to Judith Li, and her expression warmed. "You really—you did *magic*, and it *worked*. You saved me."

Judith smiled back at her, before self-consciously glancing down at the ground. The other girl reached out and touched her arm, taking a step closer. With a small start of surprise, Logan realized she was witnessing something of an intimate moment. Then the girls seemed to remember her presence, and they stepped apart again, both trying to look everywhere but at each other, as though they could pretend nothing had happened. Logan coughed. She felt more intrusive and out-of-place by the moment.

"Uh…sorry, what was your name?" she asked, hoping to break the awkward silence.

"Amy," said Amy. "Amy Williams."

"Amy," Logan smiled. "Do you mind if I take a look at your arm, Amy? I'd like to figure out if you need medical attention. May I?"

Amy's face crumpled into an expression of worry and concern, but she nodded and held out her arm, offering it to Logan. Logan strode forward and gently took hold of the girl's elbow, loosening the bandana so she could get a good look. While the cut did cross the width of her arm, it was surprisingly shallow. The bleeding had already stopped.

"It's not too bad," Logan reassured her, tying the bandana back up. "We should get you straight home so you can wash it out, but it looks like it will heal on its own. Be careful how much you move the arm, and try not to bump it into things if you can. Can your parents take you to urgent care in the morning to get it checked out?"

Amy looked stricken. "What am I supposed to tell them? I can't just say a monster tried to eat me."

Logan nodded, thinking. Internally, she couldn't help but correct the girl: the monster wouldn't have eaten her, he would have torn her heart out...probably to eat it. But she understood the folly of relating this sentiment, so instead she said, "Can you just tell them you fell?"

Amy considered this. "I don't know. They might assume I was at a party...which, I was, so, like...I think they might get mad."

Logan looked back and forth between the two girls, pondering exactly how severe the consequences might be for either of them if Amy's parents did get mad. After all, if Judith no longer lived with her parents, Logan had very few guesses about whom she might be staying with instead. "Will you promise me you'll wash it out very carefully? Use alcohol."

Amy nodded solemnly. "Yes, I will."

"Will you also promise me that you'll go see the school nurse on Monday? You can tell her you fell on your way into school or something."

"I will."

Finally, Logan nodded too. "Okay. Let's get you home."

Relief washed over Amy's face like a wave, and she took a few steps forward, back toward the clearing and out of the woods. Judith, on the other hand, stood still and stared at Logan in confusion and disbelief.

"I don't get it—why are you being so nice to us? Don't you want to...I don't know, make sure we get in trouble or something? I mean, we're at a party, and there's drinking and stuff. And we were...well, you had to save us from some fucked-up thing." Her gaze slid off to the side. Logan had a feeling that she had sidestepped mentioning something about why she and cheerleader were away from the rest of the crowd in the first place.

She remained silent for a moment, mulling her answer. Earlier that day, she had considered Judith Li her number one suspect—and yet it was almost impossible for Judith to know that, and therefor improbable that she should have any reason to try to prove her own innocence. Even if she had summoned the beast, surely she would have had a better way of running it off than throwing up a wall of light? And if she was the summoner, why had Logan heard that unearthly flute playing as the beast fled? Logan acknowledged the outside possibility that Judith Li did know she was a suspect and had arranged all of this to throw her off the scent, but she deemed it unlikely.

A far simpler explanation for it all lay at her feet.

"You two are dating, yes?" She motioned between the two of them. Amy had turned around by now, and her pretty face grew worried once more as she looked to Judith. Judith nodded slowly, cautiously. "And when I went to check on you at your house yesterday, your mother behaved the way she did because she discovered you and doesn't approve, and she kicked you out. Yes?" Judith nodded again. "And if I force Amy to admit to her parents that you were at this party, they might kick you out, too. Yes?" A nod. "Well, there we are then. How are we getting you two home?"

Amy raised her hand, as if she were in class. Then she looked at it, startled, and put it down again. "We came in my car," she said.

"Good. I'll walk you back to it. Lead the way."

Amy turned and started up the path again, and this time, Logan and Judith followed suit. Logan kept abreast of Judith for a moment, hoping to probe her backstory a little more.

"Tell me," she said, so quietly that Amy, a few feet ahead of them now, wouldn't be able to make it out. "Where did you learn that spell?"

"Oh, uh, I—well, I found this book on the internet that claimed it could teach you magic," Judith answered. She still sounded sheepish and embarrassed, possibly still unaware how impressive her earlier act had been. "I didn't think it was real, you know? But I bought it as a joke, and I've been messing around with it. I, uh, I haven't been able to do much—before today, I mean. I'm sorry if it fucked you up. I didn't mean to hurt anyone, I've just never tried it around anyone else before. Anyway, sorry."

I'm supposed to be sorry she'd dead. Out of everything Judith had said in her interview, that was the line that had stuck with her.

"Do you always apologize when you save someone's life?"

Judith froze in place, so Logan followed suit. Amy got a few more feet ahead of them before Judith shook herself, and they started walking again.

"I didn't save anybody," Judith insisted, shaking her head. "You were already there when I said it. You probably could have killed that thing if I hadn't been so stupid. I just got in your way."

"Not at all," said Logan, now shaking her own head. "I wasn't going to get there on time. If you hadn't done what you did, Amy would probably be dead. You saved her life today. Don't apologize for that."

Judith didn't say anything in response. After a moment, Logan risked a glance over at her and found a faint bemused smile settled on her face.

"So, you just bought a spell book on the internet one day? You never had any reason to believe that magic might be real before that?"

Judith paused again, this time taking care to catch Logan's eye and examining her face for a moment before she answered. Logan guessed she was looking for signs that Logan might turn on her if she told the truth. "Well, not exactly," she said. "I've never told anyone before. Most people wouldn't believe me, so why bother, you know?"

Logan nodded. "You don't have to tell me if you don't want to. All I can do is promise you that I won't tell anyone. And I will believe you."

Judith nodded and kept walking. Logan could see her thoughts working her way over her face while she debated whether or not to divulge herself. As she considered it, they stumbled to a halt—they had reached Amy's vehicle. Logan sighed.

"Well, I suppose I'll let you two get going," she said, trying not to shoot Judith a hinting sidelong look.

"Wait," said Judith immediately. She turned to Amy. "Can you give me a second? You can get in and turn the car on, I won't be long."

Amy looked like she was about to open her mouth and question her, but instead she nodded silently and climbed into the SUV, shutting herself in as she turned the ignition.

Judith turned back to Logan and looked her straight in the eye as she spoke.

"I can't prove it, but when I was five years old, I set a girl on fire in my class just by wishing it." She paused, blatant terror on her face, like she expected Logan to punish her on the spot.

"Keep going," said Logan.

"I didn't mean to do it. I mean, I did want her to catch on fire, but I didn't know that wanting it would make it happen. She pushed me down at recess and then made fun of me, and the teacher wouldn't believe me. So when she got up to answer a question, I just wished that she would catch on fire…and she did. The teacher grabbed her sweater and beat the fire out immediately, and she wasn't badly hurt. I don't think she even has a scar." She shook her head. "Obviously, I've never wished something like that again. I mean, sometimes I still hate people, but I make sure that I never think anything *specific* about them. I've tried setting other stuff on fire, just to see if I could. Like pieces of paper and stuff, nothing big. But it's never worked. I don't think I can do it if I'm not mad." She looked back at the car for a second, probably checking to see if Amy was trying to listen to them. Her face remained in profile, perfectly blank as far as they could see, and music emanated faintly from inside. Judith continued. "I have made other stuff happen. One time, I tripped over something in the woods, but somehow my body magically slowed down before I hit the ground. And…and…not always, but sometimes…I think I can hear what other people are thinking. Just a little bit. I can't control when it happens, so it's mostly just annoying. Like, I know that Amy gets embarrassed by how I dress sometimes, even though she's never said anything or even looked at me weird. And I always know when we're having a pop quiz." Her eyes narrowed as she fixed Logan with a penetrating stare. "And I know that when you first saw me, you thought I looked like I wanted to be invisible. You recognized it because you remembered what it felt like to know that nobody sees you."

Logan didn't have to think back to that moment to know that Judith was absolutely right. She thought the same thing every time she looked at her. Judith's discomfort with herself was painfully obvious, and Logan's recognition of those feelings was painfully strong.

"But you can't hear every thought?" Logan kept her mind as blank as possible as she watched Judith for an answer.

"Nope," Judith shrugged in return. "I usually just get a flash when I first meet someone, or if they feel a really strong emotion or something."

The possibility remained that Judith may have known she was a suspect before. But if she did, why give Logan the one piece of information that could hint at her foreknowledge?

"So, at some point, you decided to find out more?" asked Logan.

"I read a few library books that were mostly theoretical," Judith answered. "Then I did a lot of internet research. The book I bought—it seemed the more legitimate than most of the things I'd seen." She shrugged. "It talks about summoning the elements, and it says you have to be in tune with nature and, like, in a meditative state and stuff. I've tried summoning light a bunch of times, mainly just in my room with the lights off. But for the most part, I haven't been able to do much. I've thought a couple of times that it was working, but it was so faint I couldn't really say if it was actually magic or not. What you saw in there was the biggest thing I've ever done."

Eira, then. Definitely.

"That's more impressive than you seem to think it is," said Logan. A part of her wanted to stay right where they were and keeping talking until she felt sure she'd gotten all the information she could out of Judith, but she knew that wasn't safe. Her only other option was to drag her back to her dingy motel room, which posed its own problems. So instead, she had to cut it short. "Well, I think you should probably get going now. But feel free to seek me out at school if you'd like to talk about it a little more. Oh, and make sure that when you two get home, you get inside immediately and don't go out again until dawn. Understand?"

"Yeah, completely," said Judith, nodding vigorously. "Straight inside. Got it."

"One more thing." She paused for a moment, glancing briefly at Amy Williams, sitting inside her car. "Amy seems like a nice kid. But I'd be careful how much you tell her about any of this, and I'd caution you against telling anyone else." She let out a measured breath and shrugged. "It's not always a matter of how much you trust someone. Sometimes you just can't know how they'll react."

"Yeah, totally. There's no one else I'd ever tell anyway."

With that, Judith gave Logan a brief, bright smile and a wave, then ran around to the other side of the car and got inside. Logan stayed put until they had driven out of sight.

Then she sighed and decided to head back to the hotel. In so many ways, she was back to square one.

Still, the flute gave her another jumping off point. She'd think about where to go with that after she got a little rest. The day had turned out quite long.

Logan woke well after the sun the next morning. It was now Saturday, so she didn't need to worry about going back to the school. Swamped by a reluctance to climb out of bed at all, she lay face up on the mattress for several minutes, watching the fiery hot sun beat down on the world outside. Eventually she decided to vent her frustration with this intractable mission by going on a short five-mile run over the rough terrain that had tripped her up the night before. She dressed quickly, slipped the room key in her pocket, and took off into the heat, already oppressive at 8:45 in the morning. As she sweat it out along the uphill path she'd set for herself, the events of the evening replayed themselves before her eyes.

Who was Judith Li, anyway? Logan had met all kinds of spell-casters before, both affiliated and self-taught, but almost none who had claimed to possess the kinds of gifts Judith had mentioned—or, rather, none who claimed to possess them without any formal training whatsoever. A true eira Master, or even an eira student with years of training under her belt, might be able to summon light like Judith had, and even an inexperienced eira student might manage to summon a fire for a brief moment. But the ability to read thoughts was rare, even among eira Masters. Logan had met a lot of casters in her life, both eira and letha trained, and she only knew two people in the world who could do it. Of course, it was possible Judith was exaggerating, or outright lying. Hell, it was still technically possible that she was the summoner, and everything she'd said had been misdirection.

But Logan seriously doubted that. She didn't know exactly why, but for some reason, she couldn't help but believe Judith

Li. In fact, a small part of her still harbored the urge to chase her down at her girlfriend's house and request her entire life's story. Of course, she knew that wasn't the best use of her time. Not yet, at least.

Her girlfriend's house. Logan felt a stab of pity for the girl. She remembered the leering face of Jason Reed and knew without a doubt that this was not a town where it would be easy to be strange. She could hardly imagine what growing up here must be like for any girl, let alone one as deeply and irrevocably different as Judith Li was.

Before she knew it, Logan had reached the end of her predefined trail. By now, her body had begun to protest her decision to forgo any kind of fuel, so she reluctantly turned back to town. This time, instead of thinking about Judith Li, she focused her efforts on finding rocks and underbrush to climb over, hoping to improve her agility in the wooded terrain. She found her failure to gain any ground on the beast the previous night faintly embarrassing, and she refused to allow a repeat should she encounter it again.

Eventually she had reached her hotel once more, so she slipped inside to take a shower before inflicting her presence on the general public.

As she stripped off her workout gear, she inspected her body for any signs of damage. She'd gone to sleep with a few cuts on her legs and some bruising on one knee, but her skin looked perfectly unblemished now—apart from the old scar still evident on her right side. Though she found some satisfaction in her body's quick recovery time, she often wondered what might happen if the wrong person ever noticed. She passed the small bathroom mirror on her way to the shower and caught a look at her naked upper body. If the light was dim enough, her bizarre markings could almost go unnoticed—almost. They stretched now from her collarbone to the edges of her shoulders, and she wondered when they might start to stretch down her arms. *If. If they might.* She reached her left hand to touch her right shoulder, and though it still felt similar to skin, there was no denying that it was a little bit rougher than most human skin, and when she pressed down, it had significantly less give. She tried to press down until it hurt, but she couldn't seem to press hard enough. *Maybe scales have no nerve endings,* she thought.

She was dawdling. She pushed away her pondering and jumped in the shower, washing herself quickly but thoroughly. Though she still believed that the beast would only come out at night, she hoped to find something productive to do with her day anyway.

Once she was clean, she dressed in shorts and a sleeveless shirt that covered up her shoulders. Nobody had ever given her trouble about the markings, but she didn't particularly want to take the chance that someone would someday. Shoving her wallet into a back pocket on her way out the door, she decided to forgo her jacket for the sake of the heat and hoped she didn't get struck by a surprise vision as she pulled on her helmet and climbed on the Ninja.

It only took a few minutes to get to the diner, and parking was mercifully easy for a motorcycle in this small town. She went inside and sat at the counter, and the same waitress she'd seen every day came over and placed a menu and a hot cup of coffee in front of her immediately. She scanned for the woman's nametag. *Sherene*. Sherene was damn good at her job.

A part of her wanted to order the biggest, greasiest thing on the menu, but she had started to feel concerned about the effect diner food was having on her performance. Maybe she was only being paranoid—it was hard to know for sure sometimes what affected her part-demon physiology and what didn't. There were no reference books to consult about it. But she figured the human half had to enter into the equation somewhere, too. So she scanned the menu for something a little healthier.

Oatmeal with fresh fruit. That should do it. And an egg on the side for protein. Maybe two.

When Sherene came back, she gave her the order. Her cup was already half-empty, so Sherene filled her up, too. Logan took a mental note to make sure she gave her a more-than-decent tip.

As she sat waiting for the rest of her breakfast to arrive, the bell on the door chimed behind her, indicating a new customer arrival. In her boredom, Logan decided she might as well test herself. She trained her eyes on her coffee, but her ears focused in on the rhythm of the footsteps, counting to see how many people entered. By her tally, two. And there was something else—ever so faintly, soft as a heartbeat, a thud against the flesh. Non-paranormal hearing would never have picked up on it. At least one of them was wearing something heavy at waist level—a gun? *Two cops?* She kept herself from turning around. After a moment, they rounded the counter and seated themselves at a booth in the far corner.

She was right. There were two of them. And they were cops—or, rather, a sheriff and his deputy. Law enforcement. An opportunity seemed to present itself. Slightly unethical, perhaps, but they had entered a public place. Surely they knew it was possible they could be overheard. *This could be interesting*, she thought. She took a breath to relax a bit, then focused through the ambient noises of the diner until she had them.

"—spoke to Johnston to make sure."

"And the funeral is today?"

"Yeah, so there's no chance we're getting that body back now. Not that I expected we'd find anything new if we could get it back."

"The doc seemed pretty sure it was just an animal attack."

"What kind of animal you know pulls out the whole heart and leaves the rest untouched? The doc also said he couldn't explain how clean the wound was. It was like whatever it was knew *exactly* where a person's heart should be, and exactly how to tear it out the most efficient way poss—oh, g'morning Sherene. Uh, how's things these days?"

Logan stifled a surge of annoyance at her saintly and overly competent waitress, who had made a beeline to the new table to get them started as soon as possible.

"These days? You mean since the last time you were in here, which was yesterday?"

He chuckled. "Would you believe it if I told you I didn't get too much sleep this week?"

Logan listened to the clucking noise that sounded between Sherene's teeth. "Oh, I would, honey. You can bet I haven't slept much myself this week, not since what happened to that poor girl. I've had a prayer for that girl's mother every day this week. Have you boys had to deal with it much?"

"Not too much, actually," replied the one Logan identified as the Sheriff. "It was an open-and-shut kind of thing. It's tragic, but when you live out here, you have to expect these things will happen from time to time."

"I suppose so," said Sherene with a sigh, though to Logan's ears she sounded somewhat skeptical. "Well, that's enough talk about it for now, I think. Do you boys know what you want, or should I come back?"

"Same as always," said the Sheriff.

"Me too," said the deputy.

"Got it. Two Meat Lover's Specials, coming up." The clicking of her flats followed her away from their table.

"Sir," the deputy said timidly, "if you don't mind my asking—why'd you tell her that?"

"Tell her what?"

"Tell her it was open-and-shut? Weren't you just saying—?"

"Ah, you know," the Sheriff cut him off, then paused. "Well, some talk just isn't fit to repeat to civilians, you know? Besides, like you said, the doc said animal attack. No reason to let anybody doubt that, especially just for the sake of telling them that maybe we don't know *what* it was. Ah—you shouldn't be repeating that either, deputy. Understand?"

"Yes, sir," said the deputy immediately.

The topic seemed closed. When the Sheriff opened his mouth again, it was only to say something about some local sports team. With a slight sigh of disappointment, Logan slowly let her concentration waver. It seemed that was all the information she'd be getting out of them today. Besides, once the topic changed, it only took seconds for it to bore her to tears.

Mercifully, Sherene put a plate in front of her. Perfect—
something far better for her to concentrate on for a while.

After she'd finished her meal, Logan hopped on the bike and
made her way to the nearest grocery store, where she picked up
some fruit and vegetables and cheese, hoping to cut down on her
diner trips for the rest of her stay in town. Backpack full of
produce, she rode on back to her hotel headquarters.

Almost as soon as she'd walked in the door, her phone rang.
As always, she knew who it was before she ever looked.

"Hi Knatt," she answered with some resignation.

"You didn't call yesterday."

"No, I didn't."

"Do you have any updates to the case?"

Logan sighed. Her answer was obvious, but somehow he
couldn't make the leap. "Knatt, if I'd had real updates, I would
have called."

"So in three days' time, you haven't made any progress
whatsoever?"

Making sure to lock the bolt and close the chain behind her,
Logan stifled a second sigh. "You make it sound like I'm not
doing anything at all. I promise you, I am working this case every
second. True, it's not moving nearly as quickly as I had hoped,
but I can't help that. Some cases resist solving a little better than
others."

"You told me three days ago that you were going to follow a
lead, and that you would get back to me."

"And I did follow that lead." She walked over to the mini-
fridge in the corner of the room and started unloading the

contents of her backpack into it. "But, as sometimes happens with leads, it didn't go anywhere. The girl that I thought was my main suspect had nothing to do with it."

"How can you be so sure?"

She could have rolled her eyes, but there would have been no point. Knatt loved to micromanage, to force her to trot out every decision she made so he could judge it himself.

"I can be sure because the beast attacked again last night, and when it did, I discovered my suspect protecting its intended victim."

For a merciful moment, Knatt was quiet—possibly stunned into silence. "I see. And in what manner was she protecting this victim, exactly?"

"She threw some kind of cast at it," Logan answered with a silent shrug. The room's tiny fridge was now filled to capacity, so she shut the door and made her way over to the bed so she could collapse onto it. "It was—well, honestly, I'm not sure what it was, and I don't think she knew, either. Anyway, the beast ran off in the middle of the fight. As far as I could tell, someone summoned it back with some kind of flute. I couldn't tell where it was coming from, but it seemed pretty far off. I tried to follow, of course, but it lost me. So, my suspect is no longer a suspect. I'll get back to interviewing on Monday, and in the meantime, I'll be patrolling the town at night. And the flute thing should narrow down my list of possible monsters."

Again, Knatt was silent. She knew he must be working furiously to find something to criticize about her investigative strategy. When she heard him sigh, she knew he'd given up.

"Very well," he said with a soft cluck. "And what do you

propose I tell the Order when they inevitably ask for my update?"

"I don't know. Stall them, I suppose. You know they'd only get in the way here."

Now it was his turn to sigh.

"I do know that. Well. Call me the moment you have any more news."

And with that, he was gone. Her phone clicked and his side went dead.

Love you too, she thought to herself. Even in her own mind, it came across more bitterly than she intended.

Though the rising heat throughout the day made it hard on her, Logan pushed herself through her usual workout routine, then, for good measure, forced a second round through the woods near her hotel. Every second that passed in this town saw her frustration levels rise. While the low burn at her back reminded her that the Key wasn't done with her yet, she couldn't help but feel like she was spinning her wheels. She was trapped, and all the better missions she could be pursuing lay far beyond this stunted wasteland.

But she couldn't get to any of that until she was done here. Until she killed that damn elusive beast and moved on.

After she'd pushed her body to the point of weariness, she finally returned to her room. She had precious little she could do to entertain herself, and the longer she was awake, the more the heat seemed to get to her. With the air of someone accepting defeat, she stripped off her clothes and lay down on the bed, making sure to set an alarm just in case. After all, she needed enough energy to keep her going all night if necessary. However long it took to find the beast again, she would do it. She had to.

She woke again at dusk. Her watch was about to begin.

The night air had grown mercifully cooler than the day. Logan perused the freestanding clothes rack until she found a pair of comparatively lightweight, stretchy jeans and slid them on, glad to discover that they neither added bulk to her frame nor prohibited her range of movement. In the base of the rack sat a plastic tub full of underwear; popping off the top, she scanned the contents for her favored sports bras. The one she landed on had two layers, hooking separately in the front, and held her as sturdily as leather. Over that, she slipped a loose white T-shirt and strapped the battleax sheath over her shoulders. She rotated her shoulders around a few times, moving her arms in wide circles to make sure that didn't restrict her movement, either. Knatt preferred her to enter the fray armed to the teeth, but she'd gone astray following his advice at least once before. He'd instructed her to strap herself with four separate knives, an axe, and a crossbow before one particularly memorable case they'd gone on, early in their partnership. Not only had she only needed one knife for the job, but the crossbow had gotten caught on a low-hanging tree branch, eventually causing her to trip and fall flat on her face. In full view of the client. She'd chosen to lean on her own judgment to decide her armament from then on.

She went ahead and strapped one knife to her calf, but left it at that. The axe could strike a good killing blow, but she figured it was best to rely on her natural talents for most of the fight itself. She had a hard enough time navigating the terrain here without adding weight.

And then she was out the door. Forsaking the bike altogether, she made a beeline for the trees behind the hotel, and took off running as soon as she hit the edge. She couldn't do the bulk of her patrol from the bike, since the sounds and fumes would inhibit the senses she most needed to find her target. And since she now enjoyed both the cover of darkness and the dense foliage, she didn't have to worry too much about a civilian spotting her supernatural speed.

She took off so fast it almost felt like flying. It always felt like that, if she really let loose. She stumbled more than a few times as she went, but before long, she started to develop a rhythm with it. Run, stumble, slide and lean, straighten up, run, stumble. It was a good thing she already knew how fast all her scrapes and bruises would heal. Otherwise she might hesitate.

Over the past few days, she'd gotten a feel for the lay of the land. It only took a few minutes of flat-out running southward for her to come parallel with the center of town. She slowed her pace, sure she must be closer to the beast's preferred hunting grounds by now.

Her disadvantage on this terrain was still uncomfortably obvious to her. Though either jobs or Key missions could take her anywhere in the country (technically, anywhere in the world, though that was rare,) she still usually spent the bulk of her time in urban areas. Or at least areas more urban than this. She could chase a monster across a hundred rooftops, down a hundred alleys, through a hundred train tunnels. But the sliding rock face of a mountain, or the craggy underbrush of a forest? It just wasn't her home turf anymore, and she could tell it in every step.

Even so, she pushed herself forward—kept running,

jumping, sliding, running. Slowing when she needed to rest. Eventually, she reached her first destination and stopped, checking the details to be sure she was in the right place. *The ritual site.* She was near the site where the summoner had made their sacrifice. Good. She went a little further south, a little further downwind, until she found herself a nice, thick tree to climb. This was where she would wait.

Getting up the tree was easy enough. The lowest branch stood just out of her reach, so she backed up a few feet and took it at a running jump, wrapping her arms around the wood as soon as she had enough lift. After that, one solid kick propelled her body over the top, and a quick twist pulled her upright. Glancing back to the forest floor, she figured she was now about eight feet up. She turned toward the trunk and grabbed onto the next branch, and climbed her way up as far as she could go before the branches would no longer support her weight. When she was sure she'd reached the highest possible safe height, she settled herself in, back against the trunk, and looked around.

The wood at the top had thinned a little, but it was still far denser than she'd like. Visually, she clocked, at most, a 30- or 40-foot radius all around her. So, seeing the beast was unlikely.

That meant she'd have to go a different route for surveillance. As she relaxed her back into the rough surface of bark against it, she imagined a wide, empty field. It felt as though her senses were all around her, spread far and wide—but with one deep breath, she willed them closer. She imagined a million rays of light heading toward a single spot, just ahead of her. One more deep breath, and they converged.

Her third deep breath came involuntarily. Each time she

released, she suffered a tiny shock to the system. In a moment, it was gone, and she swam her way to concentration. Hearing came first, so she followed that. Wind-rustled leaves wove in and out of the tittering and crawling of creatures. Most of it was white noise. She pulled air sharply through her nose, familiarizing herself with a base palette of mud and fauna.

Unwilling to risk a glance at a brilliant phone screen, she guessed the time. Sometime after 11:00pm, but unlikely past midnight yet. She had hours left to burn.

At around 3:00am, she finally heard exactly what she was waiting for. Far, far in the distance—the sound of a flute.

A strange, unearthly flute. Or maybe that was the echo. She focused in on it, trying to determine its position in relation to her.

Suddenly, over the flute, she heard a roar. It, too, seemed unearthly. And it was…north. North and east.

Unfortunately for Logan, sitting high up in a tree for hours didn't do much to keep your muscles warm. She'd made sure to stretch and move regularly, but she wasn't exactly primed for fighting. As she swung down through the branches, she could feel how cold and stiff her shoulders and hips had gotten. She braced before she hit the ground, landing softly on her feet. Instead of taking off after the beast immediately, she dropped into a deep crouch, pushing into her tight muscles, and listened.

She could hear the beast traveling south. From its careless snuffing and growling and crunching of underbrush, she determined that it didn't seem to have much mind for concealing its own presence. Perhaps it, too, was yet only stretching its legs.

As she slowly came to standing again, making sure to

straighten out her hamstrings, she brought her fists to chest height and swung her elbows back and forth in quick succession. At the end of the day, it didn't matter to her much if a little cold muscle caused her injury, but she had to make sure she had enough mobility to throw power into her strikes.

Then she started running. She went north first, hoping she could sidle up parallel to it and stalk it awhile. She was pleasantly surprised to find herself navigating the forest floor now with far greater skill than she had two nights prior. Of course, she wasn't quite up to her city-based level of deftness, but she was certainly making far less noise than her target.

Unbeknownst to the beast, it drove toward her as surely as she to it. She could tell it still had no idea it was being surveilled; it behaved like a monstrously overgrown puppy let loose from a cage. She found its exact location with ease, and began to follow at a discreet distance.

But she didn't attack yet. The beast was likely at its full strength, and she'd been growing cold and tired for hours. Though the run had woken her up, she knew an imbalance remained, and she hoped to diminish it before she engaged in combat.

It would hunt soon. She intended to observe.

The possibility remained that if it chose to hunt, it might hunt human prey, but she doubted it. She couldn't be sure, but she had a feeling that its master knew someone had caught onto them. At a minimum, the summoner must have wondered why the demon came home clean of blood the night before—and why there had been no news of another death. Any reasonable master of a beast so powerful would have to wonder if someone other than cheerleader Amy Williams had interfered, if someone else had fought or scared it off before the task was complete. A cautious summoner would wait before sending its beast after a human target again. But Logan knew the time could only stretch so long before control began to wane.

So she watched. Gradually, the beast slowed, grew more cautious. More quiet and subtle. Either the pent-up energy had faded quickly, or hunger had overcome it. She had no way of knowing if the summoner had been feeding the demon, or even if it could eat anything other than a fresh heart.

Though she'd been following it a few minutes now, Logan still hadn't gotten a good look at the thing. She recognized its smell, and its overall size and shape was consistent with the silhouette of what she'd seen before. But apart from general hulk and dark coloring, she couldn't say much about what it looked like. On the other hand, she could have written a chapter on what it smelled like. She'd never thought someone could be reminded of something they'd never experienced, but the stench of the creature reminded her, undeniably, of hell.

Ahead of her, she heard the beast stop moving, so she stopped, too. Had it caught a scent? She'd kept herself downwind as a precaution, but the wind could always shift. As she listened, the beast sniffed the air and growled. It *had* caught a scent. It shifted its weight, likely dropping itself lower, and began to move again.

Now the beast became harder to follow. Once it started the hunt, she understood that it was, in fact, perfectly capable of near-silent movement. Her extra-perceptive hearing was already stretched almost to the max; if she pushed it any further, she'd make herself vulnerable to any sudden cacophony that might occur.

It sped up, but it kept quiet. She tried to smell what it had smelled, but there were too many organic scents, all too undifferentiated. She'd never trained to use her sense of smell for hunting small game. Her only choice was to follow the beast.

It sped up for a moment, then it slowed again. From the shift, she'd say it had dropped into a full crouch. She was still too far back to get a visual, but she guessed that it had come upon an opening in the trees, and now it circled the edge.

She closed in on it, certain that the distraction of an impending dinner would muddle its focus. She crept forward until she could see its outline and the beginnings of details, distorted as they were by dappled darkness. In thin moonlight, she could make out long, shaggy fur rippling over the hump in its back. Then it ducked down again.

With almost no sound, it sprang up and pounced. Something screeched—a funny, tinny sound—maybe a deer. When the beast sprang and stretched, she got a good view of its hulk. The thing was four, maybe five times larger than she was. She knew she wouldn't have an angry soccer player throwing spells to help her this time. She had to make her first blow count.

A little height might do it. On the very edge of the opening stood a thick trunk, its lowest branch not even seven feet off the ground—and it stretched south, away from the scene. Even if it looked, the beast wouldn't see her when she jumped.

The beast was consumed by its kill; it had abandoned silence and stealth in the face of its victory. It didn't matter if she crouched, so long as she was swift and quiet. As it tore into its meal, Logan closed the distance between herself and the tree with a silent run, ending in a running jump onto her intended branch. Then she was twelve feet up, so she picked a northern branch and climbed away from the base.

Once she was in position, she shifted her leg upward until she could reach the knife strapped to it. The beast roared beneath her, as vulnerable as it would ever be. Its face was buried in the kill. Gripping the knife, she pinpointed exactly where she wanted her hit to land. Then she jumped.

The beast didn't hear her as she dropped. It had no idea she was there until her body crashed down on it, her poised knife sliding cleanly into flesh. Then it roared, rearing back. It would have thrown her if she hadn't already locked her legs in place, clinging on. She grabbed the hilt of her knife, which had found home to the left of its shoulder blade, and she yanked. The beast jerked wildly beneath her; she tried to bring her knife down again, but she was rapidly losing her grip. As she pulled up to swing down, the beast gave a mighty shake and dislodged her.

She fell hard on the forest floor, landing on her side with her arms outstretched, the knife flying free from her hand. The fall knocked her wind out, the shock reverberating through her bones. The monster jerked before her, trying to reach a massive claw over its back to where she'd wounded it. The claw fell short, so the beast let it drop. It stood there for a moment. Then it slowly started to turn back toward her.

Her muscles didn't seem to want to obey her. She wrenched her arm back to her side, tried to locate her next weapon. But it was strapped down—there was no way she'd get to it in time—

The sound of a flute floated down to her ears. She couldn't

say why exactly, but it filled her with dread.

The beast froze before it finished its rotation. Its massive head cocked to the side, turned, as ever, away from her. For a moment, it remained perfectly still. Then it crouched down and ran, heading in the direction of the sound.

Logan's muscle control came back to her all at once. She sprang into action and bounded after the monster, swooping down to grab up her knife along the way.

Within a moment, she was in full pursuit. The creature wasn't quiet anymore, crashing along the forest with abandon as it followed the call of the music. Logan didn't bother to disguise herself, either; if it wanted to turn back on her now, all the better.

They both swept through the forest floor at top speed. Though she still stumbled, the small amount of practice and her massive surge of adrenaline from the drop combined to give her an edge now. The beast was slower than it had been before—likely both from the meal and the injury. As she flew through branches and leaves scratching at her legs, she spied the trails of blood that the demon left in its wake. In the light, it looked black.

She was almost upon it now. She could hear its ragged, labored breathing as she passed an especially large pool of blood. It slowed in front of her, and her excitement soared as she anticipated its defeat.

But then it made an unexpected move. It dodged suddenly to the right, changing course entirely. She corrected and followed it, wondering where it would lead her now.

Within a few moments, she was forced to come to a halt. Her stomach dropped as the beast tore forth from the trees—right into someone's backyard.

In seconds, her momentum vanished. She watched helplessly while the monster easily outstripped her, even as its pace slowed ever further. For half a second, she geared herself up to follow it into suburbia, maybe with the help of summoned shadows—until the house right in front of her lit up like a little bomb. Lamps with the power of small suns flooded the yard with light, and her still super-powered hearing picked up the small click of a lock beginning to open.

So Logan retained her hiding spot, letting herself melt into the darkness behind and around her. She stayed long enough to watch a man walk out into his yard, the beast slipping ever farther into the darkness beyond. Finally, it was so far she knew she'd never catch up in time. With one last bitterly wistful glance, she turned away.

It was time to head back home. She'd lost for the night. There was no use denying it.

She ran most of the way back, wondering vaguely if there might be anything she could do to feel like she'd actually accomplished something with her time, but nothing came to her. By the time she reached her hotel room, her mind, for all its weariness, remained a perfect blank.

It didn't matter much anyway. Within a minute of hitting the mattress, she was lost in sleep.

Chapter 7
Power Balance

Her failure the night before washed over her afresh as soon as she woke up, somewhere around noon. As she reluctantly pushed herself into sitting, her only consolation was that it was a Sunday, which meant she had a little more reprieve before her next round of student interviews. Even so, disappointment covered her like a shroud. She wanted nothing more than to get out of this stupid small town. But she couldn't do that until the job was done.

With a final self-steadying sigh of resignation, she stood up and stretched, taking in the full stilted glory of her stuffy hotel room. She needed a quick fix for her restlessness, so she pulled off yesterday's clothes in favor of running shorts and a racerback tank top. Then she jumped out the door and into the blazing sunshine.

Even after all this time, it still amazed her how quickly her body could bounce back. When she'd first fallen into bed, she'd felt like one big bruise. Her right thigh and the right half of her torso carried the impact of her fall to the forest floor, while her legs had started to ache from the prolonged running and crouching in trees. But as her muscles warmed during the first few minutes of her up-mountain run, she felt nothing. No pain, no stiffness. When she'd hit the ground the day before, it had been the kind of impact that breaks human bones. She wouldn't have been surprised if one of her ribs had cracked, the pain temporarily masked by her surging adrenaline. But now? She felt fine.

Apart from her irritation and disappointment in herself, of course. Perhaps her disappointment was unnecessary. As she ran through the events of the night before one last time, she conceded that there was little else she could have done. She'd gotten off an excellent hit with her first volley, but the beast had rebounded anyway. Maybe she could have run after it into the yards, throwing caution to the wind in pursuit of her target. But Knatt wouldn't have approved, and if the Order really was watching her now, she might have faced censure from them. Besides, it had already proven more adept at fighting her than she would have liked. It's possible it would have beaten her if she'd caught up to it.

Of course, if another student died because she'd failed to catch it when she'd had the chance, then what did it matter? She might face censure still, and she'd have to live with the knowledge that such a petty threat had allowed her to fail her real duty.

She ran for over an hour, but when she got back to her room, she felt no better than she had when she started. At least she'd gotten her blood running, she told herself. Demon physiology or no, it was best to keep her body at optimal working conditions.

Once she stepped into the blissful shade of her room, she went straight for the refrigerator and grabbed an apple and a piece of string cheese. Then she pulled out her laptop and plopped down on the bed with it. A slight breeze swept in through the ever-open window and stirred her sweaty hair.

Almost without conscious thought, she went to a web browser and tried to pull up her database. Something was gnawing at her. She couldn't connect, of course. She should have remembered. For a moment, she turned toward the phone on the side of the bed, almost tempted to give the front desk another call. But what would be the point?

Instead, she munched down her food and located her cell phone, which she'd thrown somewhere in the vicinity of the free-standing clothes rack. She checked, but once again, the hotspot refused to flash into life. She checked the time—a little after 2:00pm. Seeing as it was a Sunday, odds were fair that he'd be home. Hungover, perhaps, but likely home.

She scrolled to the last number dialed and clicked on it. Images from her vision mixed with things she'd seen that week and swirled through her mind, leaving a tapestry of half-formed thoughts behind. Had she ever gotten a good look at the beast? She'd been blinded during her first real-life encounter, and when she stalked it the second time, she came up from behind. What did it look like from the front?

The phone rang three times.

"Well, if it isn't my favorite daredevil," said Alexei as soon as he answered. His voice was smooth and warm, like silk pooling in the sun. "You know, you call a boy twice in one week, he might start to think he's special."

"Wouldn't want that," said Logan. Her initial impulse was to ask him if he was wearing a suit, but she resisted. "How are you doing, Alexei?"

"Not bad at all," he purred. "Better now that I'm hearing from you. Are you still up at that—it was a school, right?"

"Yes, it was," she said with a short sigh. Her failure still seemed to cling to her like a cobweb; frustration bubbled in her chest. "And yes, I am. To be honest, I had hoped to be done by now. I've run into the demon twice, and twice it's gotten away from me. I'd really love it if I could just kill the damn thing already."

"So impatient," he said, almost wistfully. "Tell me, are you always this keen for a fight?"

"I'm just keen to get the hell out of here," said Logan without missing a beat. "It's not like I *like* violence."

"Of course not," he said, but his tone implied something else. "You don't like violence. You like…action?"

"You're not saying that like it actually means something different."

"It does if you want it to."

Logan sighed and reached her arms up into a stretch. It hadn't taken even a minute for them to get completely off-topic, and the topic they were veering toward made her uncomfortable. As if it meant to remind her of her task, the Choronzon Key sent a spike of heat up her spine.

"This isn't really why I called," she said.

"Right," said Alexei. "I'm guessing it's about the case?"

"You are correct," said Logan. She had finally crystalized the question she wanted to ask, but she couldn't bring herself to blurt it out. "I did find the summoning site, and I found no direct evidence of an offering to the Viking god of death. Of course it had been a few days since our culprit had been there, so that's a little inconclusive. I do, however, have a good idea about how it's being controlled."

"And that is?"

"Every time it runs away from me, somewhere in the distance, I can hear this—this cold, off-putting flute music."

"Flute music," said Alexei, recognition in his voice. On the other end, she could hear the faint sound of keys clacking on a keyboard. "Yep. I've got at least one account of someone using a flute to control a rekal. It's not all that difficult, actually, provided you have a very special flute. Any idiot with a basic grasp of summoning magic and a taste for the grotesque could do it. Getting your hands on the flute, however, might pose a challenge. I'd be curious to know how your culprit managed to get one."

A rekal. Logan had suspected as much, but she'd wanted to make sure everything fit.

"If I ever find out how they did it, I'll let you know," she answered.

"The good news is that you don't need anything special to kill it."

"I was just about to ask."

"Yep. Just chop of its head, stab it in the heart. Any old axe or sword will do it. I recommend you choose something sharp."

"Good, I love sharp things." Picturing the silhouette of the beast, she asked, "Where is its heart?"

"Good question," he said. More clicking sounds. "Hmm. Dead center, close to the spine. Hmm. Some of them have a kind of exoskeleton piece there, like a bit of bone armor. You might have an easier time beheading it."

"Beheading it. Sure." She paused. "Was there bad news, too?"

"Ah, just what I told you before—if the summoner loses control, that's it. A rekal off leash can't be caged again. They'll wreak havoc on everything around them—and I do mean havoc. There's an account of one being set loose on a small town in Romania back in the 1700s. By the time a demon hunter showed up, the town had already been decimated. No survivors. The hunter barely made it out alive himself."

She remembered something then—her father, telling a client that a rekal was out of the question. His words floated through an unmoored memory: *No one in their right mind would summon such a beast, unless he was fully prepared to deal with the consequences.*

"So how does the summoner lose control?"

"If you lose the instrument, or whatever else you're using to control it. Whoever summons a rekal has to maintain contact with the instrument they used in their initial ritual at all times. Your summoner must have that flute strapped to their body every single minute of the day, even when they're asleep."

"That sounds fairly precarious."

"Yes, it is. According to this, there was a rash of rekal summonings during the early days of the Order, and it wasn't pretty. Most of the rekals ended up devouring their masters, as well as anyone else in the vicinity. They were one of the first beasts the Order ever outlawed." He gave a short cough. "There are a few quotes in here from Order members tasked with taking them out. Apparently they were commonly referred to as '*the pests of the night watch.*' So, there you go. Just think of it as pest control."

"Right, pest control." Logan noticed a small lump of tightness developing in her abdomen. It accompanied the persistent press of her final thought. "One last thing. Have you got an inscription of the words used in the summoning ritual?"

"I've got a version of it, though it might not be the only one."

"Does it include the words *I worship the wolf*?"

For a moment, he was quiet, presumably reading through the files he had. "No, I don't see that here."

"Does it come up anywhere else, in any of the stories or anything?"

The faint clacking of keys floated up to her again. "Nope, sorry. Nothing."

She considered that a moment. "What about the image of a wolf? Like in a symbol or something?"

"Mm. Not that either. Why are you asking about this? You mentioned a wolf last time, too, didn't you?"

Logan sighed. "Oh, it's just a hunch I have. Apparently it's nothing. Thought I remembered something from a book, but I guess I'm just…I don't know, hallucinating, I guess. Thanks for humoring me, Alexei. I'll let you get back to your life now."

"Happy to be of service, H. C. If you need anything else, I'm always within cell phone reach."

"Thanks. I'll let you know."

She heard the click on the other line and dropped her phone. As she let out a long breath, she could feel herself deflate. She felt empty, bereft. The rest of her answers remained just out of her reach. At least she knew for sure that she didn't need some impossible exotic artifact to slay her demon. *That's something.*

As she rolled over onto her side, she accepted that she did, in fact, have to return to school tomorrow. All things considered, her best bet was to start over from the top until she found a new suspect. Unless she caught the beast on her rounds tonight, of course.

It was still perfectly possible that the summoner was someone she hadn't even encountered yet, in person or in file perusal. But she didn't want to think about that too much—she had enough potential suspects lined up for herself already.

She pushed herself to standing and made her way over to the shower, hoping to wash a little grime and disillusionment off herself. As she pulled off her sweaty workout clothes, she found her thoughts wandering to sullen, uncertain Judith Li. She couldn't quite banish the girl from her mind.

Under the hot water streaming down from the showerhead, she almost didn't notice the ever present radiating heat of the Choronzon Key.

Monday morning came far too quickly. She got up an hour earlier than she had been, in order to have some time to herself before her sessions started. She showered quickly and dressed simply, making sure her crisp collared shirt covered up all her markings. To be safe, she strapped a knife to each ankle, hidden safely under pant legs. She also grabbed a few bulkier weapons to store in her hideaway spot on the bike.

When she stepped outside, the air was blissfully cooler than it had been for the past few days. She was sure it would heat up by the afternoon, but she decided to enjoy it in the meantime. With her weapons safely stored, she pulled on her jacket and got underway.

She ended up stopping in at the diner that never closed for another breakfast burrito, then took the rest of her ride at a leisurely pace, enjoying the cool air as much as she could. When she arrived, the door was still locked, but she found that one of the keys Mrs. Wendell had given her solved that problem.

She needed coffee before she got started, so she made a beeline for the empty staff room. As the coffee started percolating, she found herself drifting over to the row of windows set in the far wall. They provided her with a view of a small courtyard, and just a glimpse of the field beyond. She could see movement out there—maybe soccer practice. Maybe Judith Li's soccer practice. She wondered if Amy Williams had come up with a convincing reason why Judith had to stay with them all weekend, or if they'd decided it was easier for Judith to hide out unannounced instead. Or maybe they'd been honest from the beginning, and her parents had understood.

The coffeepot clicked behind her. She filled up her giant thermos and went on her way, back out into the hall and upstairs to her designated classroom office. Once inside, she decided to lock the door—better not to chance any interruptions at an inopportune moment.

She pulled out a few pertinent files from the drawer and arranged them on the side of the desk. Drinking deeply from her thermos as she went, she took out a piece of paper and wrote down a list of names—every single student she'd interviewed so far. Then she went through and crossed them off, one by one.

The first several she crossed off were kids who didn't raise any kind of warning bells for her and didn't seem to have a clear connection to Violet. She was left, primarily, with a list of Violet's friends…though in truth, she wasn't convinced "friends" was an accurate description.

First on the list was Derek James, Violet's boyfriend. Out of Violet's social circle, he was the only one that Logan genuinely believed had more affection than resentment toward her. He seemed well aware of her imperfections, but he'd loved her anyway—as much as a teenage boy could. Logan hoped the summoner was anyone but him, but she knew she couldn't rule him out just because she wanted to.

Next on the list was Missy Vreeland. Logan couldn't pinpoint any particular reason why Missy might have wanted Violet dead, apart from general jealousy and spite. But there was certainly enough of that to keep her on the list.

Then there was Jason Reed. She almost scratched him off based on stupidity alone; she found it unlikely that he could have the wherewithal to pull of any kind of summoning magic. But she had to admit to some small possibility that he was smarter, and angrier, than he outwardly seemed. So he stayed.

Fourth was Suzanne Grubb—she had replaced Judith's name on the list. Logan had seen no evidence that Suzanne was even in the vicinity of town anymore, but it seemed foolish to ignore her as a possibility entirely.

A few other names remained at the bottom of the list, but none of them had such a clear connection to Violet. She trailed her finger down each one, and while she didn't cross them off, she didn't have much to think about any of them, either. Slowly she folded up the paper and put it in her back pocket, making a note to herself to ask Wendell to schedule follow-up interviews with each of them. If anyone pressed her for a reason why, she'd make up some bullshit therapy reason.

Once she'd finished contemplating her list, she still had just enough time to enjoy her breakfast before she had to open her door and let in the teenagers.

She decided to take her time.

At lunch, Logan spent some time poring over Violet's file again, though she didn't expect to encounter anything new in there. If anything, she hoped that maybe she could tempt the Key into transmitting another psychic spike of information…but it never did. So she ate her soggy square of pizza under a shroud of vague disappointment.

The rest of the day passed in a haze of boredom. None of her appointments that day gave her any new information worth considering.

After her last scheduled student walked out the door, she gathered up her jacket and readied herself to go find Wendell to set up her follow-ups. Then she turned toward the door.

To her surprise, she found her way blocked by a now-familiar face. Judith Li stood in her doorway, fist frozen over the frame like she'd been about to knock.

"Uh…hi," she said, smiling sheepishly. "Can I come in?"

"Of course," said Logan, dropping her jacket back down on the desk. "Come and sit down."

As Judith took the seat in front of the desk, Logan shut the door behind her. She'd already put her own chair back behind the desk, so she opted to sit there instead of pulling it out again. When she looked across the plywood at Judith, she felt something slightly off in the configuration. This seating arrangement seemed to place her in a position of power; what was she supposed to do with that?

"I know I don't have an appointment," Li said sheepishly, gazing at the floor. "If you want to go home soon, I understand."

"Home for me right now is a dingy motel room with cockroaches for roommates," Logan answered easily. "I'm in no rush to get back. What's on your mind?"

Judith's brow wrinkled, like she was screwing up her courage to talk.

"It's just…I wasn't sure who else I could go to. I don't…I don't really have anyone I can…well, anyone I can talk to. I couldn't even talk to my parents before they kicked me out, and now…I'm not sure what they would do if I showed up at their house again. Call the sheriff, maybe? My mom thinks I'm a bad influence on my siblings. You know, because I'm an abomination."

Logan clicked her tongue involuntarily and let out a slow breath. "Your mother is…entitled to her beliefs. I don't share them. Honestly, I find them repugnant."

Li chuckled, finally raising her eyes enough to meet Logan's. "I bet she'd love that. The American devil criticizing her parenting."

Logan felt her eyebrows shoot up of their own accord. "American devil?"

"My mother likes colorful language."

"I see." Logan shifted back in her seat, settling in. "I'm sorry you have to go through this."

"It's okay," she shrugged. "Well, no, I guess it's not. I thought about…I don't know, like, talking to Amy's parents, but…they probably wouldn't be any better. They're only letting me stay there because they think we're just friends." Inwardly, Logan checked an invisible box where that question had lingered. "I told them my parents are having the house fumigated. So...I think I've bought myself maybe, like, a week there. But after that, I don't really know where I'll go. I don't have any teachers I'm close to. I don't even have any family members that I'm close to." She glanced over her shoulder toward the window, her face clouding over with fear and uncertainty. Then she looked back at Logan. "There isn't anyone that I really trust. But I thought...I mean, I know I don't know you very well, so you could be an axe murderer or something, but I just thought...if there's anyone I can trust at all, maybe it's someone who already saved my life. Plus you didn't even tell on us when you totally could have."

Logan let a smile creep across her face. Looking at Judith now, she still saw herself at sixteen—so certain she couldn't trust a single soul, so certain that life would never get any better than it was at that moment.

"Axe murderer, huh? Well, I promise I've never killed a human being with an axe," she said. "I can't give you much more of an assurance than that."

"Good enough for me," said Judith, cracking a small smile. Almost immediately, her smile faltered, and fear settled in once more. "I just don't know what I'm supposed to do now, you know? Two weeks ago, I had my whole future planned out. I got into all these schools, and my parents picked out their favorite. I had a partial scholarship for soccer, and my parents were going to pay the rest. I was going to do pre-med like they wanted, and marry a nice Chinese guy." She gave a humorless laugh. "I think they would have taken a white guy, too. Just not a black guy. And obviously not a girl." She glanced out the window again, as if she could see any answers out there. "But then I fucked it all up. They caught me with Amy, and…everything just imploded. I couldn't lie to them anymore."

She fell silent then, and Logan considered her a moment. Despite the uncertainty, she noticed a determined set to Judith's jaw.

"Do you wish you could?"

Judith sighed and came back to the room, meeting Logan's gaze once more.

"No, I don't. I never wanted any of the things they wanted. But…but I don't know what I do want, either. I mean, the whole world is—everything is different now. I always suspected, but…magic is real." Her eyes, locked on Logan's face, went wide. "How can magic be real?"

Logan shrugged. "I can't answer that."

"But you do know about it, right? I mean…you showed up that night with some kind of battle knife. You're supposed to be a grief counselor. Why do you have a battle knife?"

"Well. I'm not really a grief counselor," said Logan.

"And why were you even there that night? How did you know where to be? You saved us."

You saved yourself. Logan took in Judith's eager expression, her expectant body language. *Where is this leading?*

"You're still selling yourself short," said Logan. "Your spell scared the beast off before I could get to it." She paused, tapping her forefinger on the desk as she considered how much she ought to divulge to this kid. Her intuition told her to trust her, but the thought of what Knatt might say made her hesitate.

As if she could read her mind, Judith chose that moment to speak up.

"I would never tell anyone about you, if you're worried. As far as I'm concerned, I owe you for helping us, and not telling Amy's parents. I wouldn't repay you by blowing your cover."

Logan nodded, but remained silent a moment longer. Where should she begin?

"Magic is real," she said finally. "You're right about that. But there wasn't anything magical about how I found you on Friday night. I heard one of you scream, and I came running."

"Were you at the party?" Judith asked, surprise writ large on her features.

"I wasn't *attending* the party," she clarified. "I thought the beast might attack that night, so I went where it was most likely to go. When I heard a few girls talking about a party in the woods, I figured that would be a prime target. So I went, and I spent the night patrolling the woods, waiting for it to show."

"What beast is it? Why is it here? *How did you know?*"

Logan laughed quietly. "Are you wondering if the beast has lived here the whole time and you only just noticed?"

"Yes! Is that true?"

"Of course not," Logan assured her. "Someone summoned it. They summoned it to kill Violet Buchanan."

Understanding broke like the dawn over Judith Li's face.

"Oh. I see." She nodded, her face contemplative, like she was mulling it over. "So...so you came here because Violet died."

"Yes," Logan answered, pleased at how easy it would be to

sidestep any mention of the Key. "Violet was killed by the beast, and I came to find out who summoned it. And to stop the beast from killing anyone else."

"Like Amy," said Judith, nodding. "And you've been... you've been interviewing everyone so you could find out who it was."

"Yes."

Judith's brow furrowed momentarily, then released. She grinned.

"You thought it was me, didn't you?"

"I did. Sorry about that."

"No, I get it. I hated Violet. I'm a good suspect. Hell, I'm the best suspect. I would have thought it was me, too." Suddenly her expression darkened, and she locked eyes with Logan again. "But if you thought it was me, then...then who's your main suspect now?"

Logan clicked her tongue again. "I no longer have one."

"Oh. Shit."

So they had reached the crux of the situation. Logan glanced up at the clock and realized she had probably missed her chance to grab Mrs. Wendell and schedule her desired follow-up sessions. What should she do now? She glanced at Judith again, pondering her options. *Well, I've told her so much already...*

"Judith," she started, "apart from yourself, who do you think wanted to kill Violet? Or, better yet—do you know anyone who might have wanted to kill Amy?"

"God," Judith sighed, collapsing her shoulders inward. "I honestly can't think of a single person who would want to kill Amy. I mean, I'm probably biased, but—Amy isn't like Violet at all. Violet was cruel, and she pissed off a lot of people. But Amy? Amy doesn't even get mad at people when she should. She's probably the nicest girl in our whole school."

There are other reasons to want someone dead. "Did she date anyone before you?"

"No, she didn't. Or, at least, not that I know about. Do you have, like, a list of people? I don't know, maybe I could look at it or something."

"Sure," Logan answered, reaching into her back pocket to pull out the paper, folded into fourths. She slid it across the table, and Judith picked it up.

"Derek James?" Judith asked, a little nonplussed. "He always seemed cool to me. We had Chem together, and he actually talked to me. I mean, he talked to me like I was a person and not a troll or something."

"He's the boyfriend," Logan shrugged. "I don't think it's him, but it would be stupid not to consider it."

"Missy makes sense. And Jason. They're both so stupid though, I don't know if they're capable of it." She scanned the rest of the list, shrugging slightly. "Oh. Huh. Kurt Redmond? That weird kid who dresses like a forty-year-old?"

"Yes. I don't have too much reason to suspect him, though he did seem…a little off. For a teenager, anyway."

"Yeah, he's kind of a weirdo."

An image of him swam into her mind—his duck-footed walk, his ill-fitting clothes.

"He had only positive things to say about Violet. He, uh, seemed to regard her as a kind of role model for other students." She decided not to mention his incredibly poor opinion of Judith

Li, since that would be neither relevant nor helpful.

"Really? Huh. Honestly, that doesn't really sound like him. I mean, not that I think he had a problem with Violet or anything."

"If he didn't have a problem with Violet, then why do you think it doesn't sound like him?"

"Well, it's not Violet so much as, like, *all* girls, you know? I mean, he's kinda bitter, I guess. I think that's why, anyway." Her expression was puzzled.

"Why do you think he's bitter?" asked Logan.

"Oh, I had English with him last year, and for one of the essays we did, part of the assignment was to read it out loud to the rest of the class. The one he read was…well, it was kind of unsettling."

"What was it about?"

"Well, it was about…girls. He started by talking about how girls have power over men because of how they look, and then he said that most of them don't appreciate their power, so they devalue it by being huge sluts. Oh, but they're only huge sluts for all the wrong kinds of guys, which is why the wrong men are always in power. And then he ended by describing the perfect woman who could save the world, and it was basically a description of a '50s housewife, only mute. It was so creepy. I could kind of tell that most of the girls in the class felt really uncomfortable. Oh, you know, I think Violet was in that class with us, actually. And I remember thinking that she looked pretty wigged out after Kurt read his little manifesto. I think the teacher had him stay afterward to talk to him about it, not that it matters. I kinda doubt he would listen to a female teacher's opinion about it."

An uncomfortable recognition settled over Logan as she took this in. She'd thought the kid was weird and possibly manipulative, though she hadn't detected an angry misogynist vibe. But perhaps the manipulation itself was a clue: even during a counseling session, he had attempted a power grab. And from the sound of Judith's story, power appeared to be a core issue for Kurt Redmond.

"But you know," said Judith, "I could see him having a better opinion of Violet, I guess."

The comment pulled Logan from her contemplation. "You could?"

"Yeah," Judith nodded slowly. "I mean, you know, guys always liked Violet because of how she looked. And, I mean, Kurt can write an essay about how shallow girls are, but that doesn't mean he isn't shallow, too. I mean, a dude writing an essay about shallow girls is practically the best proof there is that he's actually really shallow himself. And he might have liked Violet for more than that, too. She was really nice to him once."

She couldn't say why, but Logan felt a spike of cold dread at the thought of Violet's sudden kindness to this particular boy.

"Do you remember what she did?"

"Oh, yeah. She stood up for him to another boy." Judith glanced down at the list, then pointed at one of the first few names. "I'm pretty sure it was Jason Reed, actually. He was, uh, picking on Kurt one time in the front hall, and Violet came over and yelled at him and told him that Kurt was way better than him, or something like that."

Based on her conversation with Jason Reed, as well as Violet's complaint against him, it seemed to Logan that Violet's outburst had

had far more to do with her hatred of Reed than any affection she might have had for Kurt. Although perhaps that was selling her short—perhaps she had intervened in the moment because she thought it was the right thing to do, or because she felt plagued by the guilt of what she herself had done to Judith and Suzanne.

Logan was still considering this line of thought when Judith spoke again, quietly and ponderously, and primarily to herself.

"I wonder if that's why he left that note in her locker that one time."

That spike of dread shot through Logan's system once more. Her neck straightened as her gaze narrowed on Judith once more.

"He did what?"

"Yeah, weird, right? Man, that was so weird. Uh, this one time, I came back into the girls' locker room in the middle of soccer practice, and he was in there. He was just standing there, staring at some dumb shorts that Violet had left on the bench. I mean, I think she left them there, because that's where her locker was, but I guess they could have been anyone's. Anyway, when he saw me, he put this note on the door of her locker and ran away. Weird, right?"

Kurt left the note. Kurt was Violet's stalker. Kurt was an ineffective, bullied boy with a thirst for power and a nasty, vindictive view of women. What were the odds that he had only put the note on her door, and not also called her only to breathe into the phone and hang up, or lurk in the shadows outside her house?

Kurt was her new best suspect. Without conscious thought, Logan rose to her feet and swung her jacket around herself, sliding it back on over her arms.

"Judith," said Logan calmly, "I need to ask you a question, but first, I need you to promise me that you are going to remain cool and calm and do exactly as I say for at least the next thirty minutes. Can you promise me that?"

Judith, apparently lost to the gravity of the situation, chuckled.

"Well, like, I definitely can't promise you I'm gonna be cool, because I've literally never been cool." She smiled sheepishly up at Logan, and as she met her eyes, her grin crumpled. "Oh, shit, you're being serious, aren't you? Uh—yeah! Yeah, I promise I'll do whatever you say for the next thirty minutes."

"Good." Logan kept her gaze level. "Now, tell me—did Kurt have any reason to like Amy?"

At first, Judith looked surprised and confused by the question, but after a moment, her features darkened with comprehension.

"Yeah, a little—she did a project with him one time. I think he asked her out—but she told him that her parents wouldn't let her date anyone." Judith shrugged in begrudging acceptance. "It's not like she could tell him she had a girlfriend. Anyway, she—she told me he took it really well, like he didn't seem mad at all."

Logan allowed a humorless smile to spread over her mouth. "I don't think Kurt has a very direct style of conflict resolution. But on the plus side, I have a feeling Amy is safe, at least for a little while. Kurt has to know by now that his attack on her didn't work, and there must be a reason why. I'm not sure how much he can communicate with the rekal, but if he can, then he might know that someone used magic to protect Amy, which should give him some pause before going after her again. Of course, the only reason to keep a rekal alive is if you aren't done with it, so he must have at least one more target in mind." She chuckled darkly, briefly imagining the vile inner workings of a young misogynist's brain. "One more girl he wants to punish for her lack of interest in him."

Judith stared at her blankly, as if she were overwhelmed.

"Uh…what's a rekal?"

"Kind of demon," Logan answered automatically. "We need to get going. Are you ready?"

Judith stood up and gave a half-salute. "I'm ready to do exactly what you tell me. And, uh, I'm calm and stuff."

"Good. Let's get started."

"Yes, sir!"

Logan walked over to the door to open it, Judith right at her heels.

"Hey," said Judith hesitatingly, "what—what exactly are we gonna do?"

Logan shrugged as she tugged the door open. "I'm not sure yet. Either find Kurt or miraculously find his target. Whatever happens, I have to stop him."

"Or he'll hurt another girl."

"Yeah."

Logan nodded and didn't elaborate any further. Yes, if he hurt another girl, it would be tragic. But by now her worries were larger than that—by now she worried about his inevitable loss of control over the beast. And once that happened, she worried how many might die. And how quickly.

Chapter 8
Invisible Forces

The damn thing escaped and scampered down the hallway and out of sight. As I tore after it at top speed, a half-formed thought ran through my mind: the best laid plans...

At least it was only a shadow ghost. The harm it could do was innately limited. I rounded the corner into the next wall so fast I almost crashed into the far wall, but I managed to look up just in time to see its translucent silver form slip out through an open window. If I'd had the time, I might have had a word with Henrik about that—I'd been very clear when I told him that all windows and doors to the house needed to be shut before we began. But I didn't have time—I had to launch myself out of that window before the creature got too far for me to track it effectively.

We were two floors up, so when I sprang from my crouch on the windowsill, I braced hard for the impact. Even so, as I landed, I felt an ominous pop in the vicinity of my right ankle. But there was no time to stop and check for injuries. I could see a streak of silver disappearing into the trees ahead of me, so I broke into a flat run once more.

When Henrik had called, he'd told me off the bat that he was only contacting me because he was too afraid to contact the Order. Afraid they'd sanction him, he said. He wasn't supposed to be doing this kind of magic, and for precisely this reason—he wasn't experienced enough to ward off the potential havoc that experimental magic could wreak. Like the accidental summoning of a shadow ghost. A shadow ghost he'd trapped in his study—a ghost he couldn't take care of on his own.

If I hadn't been so desperate for work, I might have said no. I was barely 18, and I still worked irregularly enough that going one more night without a job would leave me no choice but to shoplift snacks from the nearest convenience store. When I could get work, my primary income was crime-for-hire, but by now I'd taken on one or two paranormal jobs as well. Henrik was one of those. He told me he'd gotten my name from a fence he knew who specialized in ancient artifacts, and he'd made the leap that I could handle a casting-gone-wrong based on my name alone. It took a little pushing to coax out my memory of him, but eventually I recalled that I'd met him as a child, tagging along on one of my father's jobs. I'd hesitated at the connection to my father, but his desire to avoid the Order endeared him to me, and he'd implied that he wished to avoid my father as well, though he kept his reason to himself. Henrik was a sweet old man, and if memory served, he had a penchant for tipping big. So I'd said yes.

And now here I was, bounding my way through the underbrush.

Fortunately for me, shadow ghosts had little ability to fight back, and they weren't very clever. Their only advantage was speed, which was precisely why I'd wanted to keep it trapped in the house. But it was a bit late for that now.

The trees thinned out quickly, and suddenly I was chasing the *ghost through a wide open field. Deciding to press the change to my advantage, I unleashed my full powers and burst into top speed. I was on top of the thing in seconds.*

This particular shadow ghost was about the size of a small dog. I might have almost felt bad about what I was about to do, were it not for the fact that I knew full well that the shadow ghost wasn't truly alive in the fullest sense. It had movement, yes. It could certainly inflict some damage on the world if it was left to its own devices. But at its core, it was little more than magical residue.

So I didn't hesitate when I caught up to it. I tightened my grip around my knife and hurled myself down at it, driving the knife right through its center—where its heart would be if it had one.

The ghost gave out a shrill shriek as my steel made contact. Then it glowed brightly and swelled almost imperceptibly in size—and popped right out of existence. My body thudded to the ground in its absence.

Relieved and excited by such an easy kill, I returned to the house. An overjoyed Henrik paid me in cash, and his tipping did not disappoint. He insisted I stick around for dinner as well, so that evening, we sat in his enormous, ornate dining room and dined on expertly broiled black cod, roasted asparagus, and garlicky mashed potatoes. He brought out chocolate cake adorned with strawberries for desert. It was the heartiest, most filling meal I'd even seen in months. By the time I left for the evening and began my hike back into town to get to the bus terminal, I felt giddy and light-headed, and more than a little pleased with myself. That cake sure was something, *I thought, indulging in a mini twirl as I took a bend in the road.*

A part of me recognized how fleeting this victory was, but I did my best to ignore that part. Sure, this kill only provided me security until that short stack of cash ran out, but it was still the fattest one I'd received on a job yet. And, hey, I'd gotten a full stomach out of the deal, to boot. I gripped the small to-go Tupperware that Henrik had pressed into my hands as I'd walked out the door, and I decided that once the bus deposited me back in Portland, I was getting myself a hotel. Maybe I'd even spring for something mid-level. Might be a two-hour trip, but at least I know there's a real mattress waiting for me on the other side.

The journey back to town was long, but I ran it when the road was empty. In half an hour, I was back in town, and 10 minutes after that, I purchased my ticket at the terminal before loading myself into the bus and settling in toward the back. Only a week ago, I'd been camping in a field, staring up at the stars and wondering if every single decision I'd ever made had been a mistake. Would I ever get myself together? Do something important? Would I ever be stable? Of course I hadn't actually gotten an answer to any of those questions. But with such a full belly, it was a little harder to care.

By the time the bus pulled in to a stop on a well-lit street in Portland, it was nearly midnight. I'd been sitting in the same position so long, I'd gotten a cramp, but that wasn't enough to dampen my spirits. I walked a little closer to the center of town, until I saw a hotel chain I figured would fit my price range. The man at the front desk didn't disappoint, and soon I found myself ensconced in one of the nicest, cleanest rooms I'd ever seen. Sure, I'd want to find something cheaper after tonight. But I didn't mind. I'd sleep until check-out time, and I'd love every minute of it.

But after I put my leftovers in the tiny fridge, unpacked a few things from my bag, and changed into sweatpants and a T-shirt, I found I couldn't quite drift off to sleep just yet. I lay on the nice, plush bed, staring through the open curtains of my fourth-story window, out at the stars and the blinking city lights, and my mind would not quiet. Maybe it was adrenaline that caused my blood to rush. Or maybe it was the thought of that stack of cash and the feeling that, for the first time in a long while, I had options.

I stood up again. I needed to move my body and still my mind. I grabbed the room key, a lighter, and a pack of cigarettes and slipped them into the pocket of my sweatpants, then pulled on my boots and walked out the door.

The hotel was fifteen minutes east of the river, so I started walking west. The night air was cool on my face and arms; if I'd been anyone else, I might have found it cold. I took in the sights as I walked, enjoying the shifting store-front lights playing out on the sidewalk ahead of me. A small tug at my heart reminded me that home was only a few hours further north, and if I wanted to, I could go. Except I couldn't. Not if I wanted to keep myself.

Eventually I reached the river, and the very sight of it calmed me. Portland wasn't home, but it was familiar enough to be comfortable.

With a quick glance around to be sure I was alone, I pulled out the pack and tapped it against my thigh. I'd taken up smoking in a blind rage against my father, though I still couldn't say what exactly I'd hoped to accomplish. Maybe it was really myself I'd been raging against. Every time I did it, I wondered what I was doing to myself. Could demons even get cancer, or was that a terrestrials-only thing?

As I took my first drag, I noticed something funny on the surface of the water. Was it glowing? I was still high on the slope that led down to the bank, so I took a few steps further down it. A small spot about two feet wide was, indeed, glowing near the surface of the river. I couldn't quite make it out through the ripples of current, but it looked like a big, golden circle. I kept walking until I stood nearly at the edge.

As I approached, I began to feel pleasantly warm, though I knew the night air was still cold. The sensation was familiar, and as I looked into the water, I realized the shape there was, too.

There, maybe a foot under the surface of the water, was the Choronzon Key. It looked gold, not bronze, under the water, but it still glowed inexplicably, like it had before. It had been a year since I'd seen it, but I recalled that meeting in perfect detail. As I gazed at it, my only conscious thought was a question—would it stay this time?

I felt a funny shift in the air. The warmth around me seemed to concentrate itself at my back, like someone had lit a fire right behind me. Then I felt a phantom pressure there, as if something was pushing against the thin fabric of my t-shirt. I reached my hand back automatically, feeling around to check if something had blown into me, but nothing was there. I brought my hand back down and took another drag off the cigarette, still gazing down at the Key in curiosity.

That was when it vanished. While I still staring right at it, it disappeared into thin air. I twirled around, as if I thought it had somehow jumped behind me.

Then something crashed into me. I fell to my knees, and the cigarette went flying.

Before I could even catch my breath, my back exploded in pain. Certain that I had somehow caught on fire, I dropped the rest of the way to the earth and rolled on my back, hoping to put out the flames. But the pain didn't stop. After a moment, I realized that there was no warmth, no sound of flames licking at my flesh. There was no fire.

Still, the pain didn't stop. I rolled back onto my stomach and reached back—this time, I could feel something. It felt like metal, but I couldn't make out the shape. Warm to the touch, but not hot. As I touched it, it seemed to reduce in size. I reached around a little more and felt my t-shirt come clear away from my skin. Feeling along the edges, I realized…it had been burned. Something had burned through it, leaving a hole whose shape I couldn't yet determine.

I touched the metal again. By now, it was much smaller than before—in fact, as I touched it, it seemed to…disappear.

What was happening? A moment after I felt it disappear, the pain receded. I let out a breath I hadn't realized I'd been holding. When I reached back again, my skin was sore to the touch and there seemed to be a ridge of scar tissue running through it, but it was skin. I breathed in and out, feeling my pulsing heartbeat begin to slow. I could feel the ground beneath me, and I pushed against it until I was sitting up on my knees. A light breeze pressed against the bare skin of my back where my shirt had burned away.

I looked around again to make sure I was still alone, then I delicately removed my shirt and placed it on the ground in front of me, back facing up. Small pieces of fabric fluttered away like flower petals—little shapes burned out in outline.

As I stared down at the pattern, I understood exactly what I was looking at—the shape of the Choronzon Key, a bit smaller than I'd seen it before. Though it was impossible, somehow I knew exactly what had happened: the Key had adhered itself to me—it had marked me. I knew something else, too: this was not the kind of mark you could simply remove. It stays with you. As long as it wants.

But why? And why me?

Starting to doubt that I would ever get any more answers, I shook the spare pieces from the shirt and pulled it back on over my head. Sure, it was only half the shirt it had been. But I didn't have a lot of shirts, and it still covered my front well enough, so on it went.

I had barely made it to standing when I fell to my knees again.

This time, the Key gave me something other than pain.

It gave me images.

During the first sixty seconds of her forced servitude, Judith Li proved an adept follower. She kept pace with Logan down the hall, remaining completely silent, until Logan stopped her at the head of the stairs leading into the main hall.

"Li, please tell me honestly—is there any chance Amy will be out at another party in the woods somewhere tonight?"

Judith's face remained serious and stricken as she shook her head.

"Are you kidding?" she eked out. "We were barely brave enough to sneak out to that party on Friday. Even if someone is throwing a weird-ass Monday-night rager somewhere, she wouldn't go near it. She'll be home with her parents all night."

"Good thing it's Monday, I guess," Logan shrugged, before turning back to the stairs and practically jogging down them. Judith Li kept pace at her heels. As they reached the bottom, Logan came to a decision. "Still, it might be best if I take you back there. You can warn her and keep her safe, and, frankly, locking you up in her house might keep you safe, too."

"You don't need to keep me safe!" Judith cried. "I can help you! I can help you figure out who his next target is. Come on, you know I know this school better than you do."

Logan allowed her head to nod, but something else had caught her attention and pulled her out of the moment. They were walking down the stairs, and she had automatically turned to the right…

And suddenly she remembered why Kurt had looked familiar—unplaceable but still familiar—when he'd come in for his session. She'd seen him before.

As her gaze roamed before her, taking in the entire entryway and the hallway full of lockers beyond, her mind filled in the scene with her memory from her first day there, now exactly one week past.

There he'd been—to her left, standing at his locker. She'd thought he looked out of his depth, uncomfortable in his own skin. Resentment poured out of him, flooding his direct surrounding area. His eyes when he saw that she could see him— so angry. Then he'd huffed and stumbled his way down the hall with his awkward splayfooted limp.

He'd walked up to a girl. He'd pushed a note into her hand. When she'd looked down at it, she'd looked startled and confused. Logan didn't imagine that the note's contents had resonated particularly well for her.

"Shit. I think I know who his next target might be," said Logan. "Except I have no idea what her name is." She did, however, hold a perfectly pristine image of the girl in her head. With her eyes trained squarely on the spot where she'd seen the girl, she allowed her memory to fill in the rest, clear as a picture. There she was, just as she had been. "Her locker is over there, number 730. I saw her around this time, maybe a little earlier.

After classes. Black hair, a little longer than her shoulders, curled. Kind of golden skin—Latina, I think. She was wearing bright colors—a coral skirt and a green sweater. Uh, I believe the kids call the color *mint green* these days."

"Yeah, I don't really pay attention to what colors girls wear most of the time," Judith shrugged, her expression curious and a little suspicious. "How are you doing that? Do you have one of those photographic memories or something?"

It was Logan's turn to shrug. She did, in fact, have a photographic memory, and she'd never been able to tell if that was a demon thing or a regular human thing. She still forgot things, obviously, and her father had messed with her memory so much that she had no real idea what her childhood memories should be like. Maybe the eidetic memory came from her demon lineage, maybe it didn't. "I guess you can call it that," she said, settling for the inadequate answer.

"Cool," Judith nodded. "So you're, like, a detective basically, right?"

"Sure," said Logan, now growing impatient. "Miss Li, do you have any idea which student I'm describing to you?"

"Oh, sorry," said Judith. "Uh, yeah, are you sure she's Latina? We only got like four Latina girls."

"Pretty sure," answered Logan, considering. "Oh—she had— inside her locker, she had a cheerleader outfit. So she's a cheerleader. Do they have practice this time of year?"

"I think they do it all year," Judith answered. "If you're really sure she's Latina, then that's gotta be Bianca Martinez. And she's probably at practice right now, unless she pretended to have her period today or something." She glanced up at the clock on the far wall, then tapped Logan on the arm and pointed her in that direction too. "5:03. Practice has been over for three minutes, so they'll probably all be walking out to their cars pretty soon."

"Good," said Logan darkly, turning toward the parking lot.

Judith's eyes lit up with excitement. "Are we gonna go wait in the parking lot for the monster?"

Logan turned to her sharply and spoke with command in her voice. "I will go wait in the parking lot. You will go home, back to Amy's, where you will be *safe*."

"What?" cried Judith, looking shocked and offended. "Come on! I helped you, can't I stay? I mean—won't I be safer with you anyway?"

Logan almost growled. She hated to admit it, but Li wasn't wrong. "Damn. Fine, but you're going to stay hidden at all times, understood?"

"Absolutely," answered Judith, looking far too pleased by the entire situation.

With a shrug of resignation, Logan turned to the front of the building and started toward the doors. Judith followed close behind as they walked out into the now-fading sunlight.

While the parking lot was by no means full, there were at least fifteen cars left. Apart from the cars, there weren't terribly many places to hide, or even to stand without looking conspicuous. After a moment, she sighed.

"I guess we'll just go stand by my bike," she said, taking a few steps in that direction. "We can pretend to be talking or something."

"Huh," said Judith from a few feet behind her. Logan stopped and turned, noting that her companion had frozen in place, staring back at the door behind them. With some irritation, she went back to Judith.

"What?"

"Oh, sorry, nothing," said Judith, her confused gaze finally breaking away from the unmoving door behind them. "Sorry, I'll follow you. I'm following."

Logan's eyes narrowed involuntarily in suspicion, but she charged forward. They traversed the length of the lot quickly. She felt an illogical sense of relief once she was standing next to her Ninja again: it was like she had escape back in her grasp. With a quick flick, she popped the seat up and pulled out her short battleax and sheath, which she strapped immediately to her back. Then she clicked the seat back down and leaned lightly against it, taking comfort in the solid pressure the bike provided.

"Face me, with your back to the building," she instructed Judith. "I'll tell you when I see her, and then you'll verify her name."

"I *knew* it was a good idea for me to come with you," said Judith smugly as she moved into place.

"You should probably stay quiet for a while."

Judith forced her face back into a serious expression and nodded solemnly. If circumstances had been any different, Logan might have found her earnest reverence amusing. It certainly made her easier to order around.

A few minutes passed in silence.

"Are you sure it was after 5:00 when you looked?"

"Uh, yeah," said Judith nodding. The confusion that had clouded her face as she stared at the entryway door returned. "Is—is no one coming out? Still?"

"Not unless they're invisible. And able to walk through walls."

Judith's face brightened with excitement again. "Is that a thing? Invisible people?"

"Judith. Focus."

"Right, sorry. I'm focusing."

"And you're sure their practice ends at 5:00?"

With that, Judith's excitement evaporated. "Oh. Um, well, it should. It definitely *should*. But…in soccer, we had a two-hour practice last week. So, uh, I guess…they could be doing that."

Logan nodded. "So we may have to wait here an hour."

"Yeah, maybe." Judith looked a little downtrodden, as though she felt she were at fault for this.

Logan nodded again. "It's okay." When Judith's gaze remained downcast, she added, "Well, I guess it's good you came after all. Now I don't have to wait alone."

Judith Li's face broke slowly into a smile so shy it almost seemed to be asking permission. Logan reached out to pat her lightly on the arm, twitching her wrist almost imperceptibly as she pulled it back. Judith didn't notice.

Of course, they didn't have much else to say to each other. And as it turned out, they did have another 37 minutes to wait. Each minute that passed grew progressively more painful. If Logan was being honest, it probably would have been less painful to wait alone. But she would never say it.

Finally, at the very top of minute 38, she spotted movement at the front of the building. As she observed, a few girls spilled out—some in their cheer outfits, some in street clothes. Logan didn't recognize any in the group. Chatting and laughing, they dispersed slowly, trailing into different cars—most of them SUVs.

After a moment, three more girls came out—two were spiritedly clamoring away together, while the third girl trailed quietly behind them. Logan didn't recognize the first two, but she did recognize the third.

"I see her. She's the last one out, wearing a pink shirt and jean shorts. Look quickly."

In a clear attempt to look casual, Judith pulled her face into a bland smile and twisted her head around briefly, then realigned it back to normal.

"Yeah, that's Bianca."

Logan nodded. She watched as Bianca fell a little further behind the other girls. She didn't look nearly as carefree as they did; instead she looked morose and anxious. Somewhere in the parking lot, a car door slammed, and Bianca jumped at the sound, glancing all around her. Then she seemed to try and calm herself, holding a hand to her stomach and taking a slow breath, before walking forward again.

Maybe it was nothing. Or maybe Bianca had a reason to be afraid. Just like Violet had.

"Do you know what Bianca's car looks like?" Logan asked, wondering which direction she might be headed in. She kept walking forward along the sidewalk.

"Uh, I don't think she has a car."

"Then how is she…" Logan let her words trail off as she watched Bianca step into the lot—but head toward the road, instead of the parked cars. Judith turned to see where she was looking.

"Oh yeah, I think she lives nearby. She usually walks home."

Logan took a quick look at the sky to confirm what she already knew—that night was almost on them, and the last of the light was quickly disappearing beneath the tops of the trees. Bianca was walking home through the gathering dark.

She watched as Bianca turned onto the street and kept going. As soon as she reached the low line of bushes that would soon obscure her from view, Logan stood up straight and started after her.

"Wait—what are you doing?" asked Judith in a panicked voice as she struggled to keep up.

"I think that's pretty self-explanatory."

Judith made a few stuttering noises but kept pace as Logan continued to tail the cheerleader.

"But—but—oh no. You know, it's okay. It's fine. Maybe if everyone at school starts talking about how I like to stalk Bianca Martinez, they'll finally stop talking about the stupid flagpole."

"It's good to look on the bright side."

Logan didn't stop to check, but she had a feeling Judith was now shooting her a dirty look. It didn't matter, of course. They had no other choice, unless Judith changed her mind about going home.

As they rounded the corner out of the parking lot, she couldn't immediately locate Bianca in her field of vision, so she picked up the pace precipitously. Odds were that Bianca had simply turned down another street, but she needed to get her back in her sights as soon as possible. The light above was still fading, and it was impossible to say how long they had before the rekal showed up—provided they were right about its next target, of course.

After a few moments, she reached the first cross street and glanced down it, Judith jogging behind her to catch up. She paused at the turn and clocked Bianca about a block down. She breathed a short sigh of relief.

"Act normal," she said, with a quick glance at Judith as she came astride her once more. "Try not to…breathe so heavily."

"You're so fast," said Judith between gasps.

Logan nodded, acknowledging the statement, then took off again. She tried to go a little slower, but Bianca was still so far ahead of them. Yet even with that distance, she had a feeling that Bianca, paranoid as she had seemed in the parking lot, would notice their presence.

Sure enough, as soon as Judith snagged her sweatshirt on an overgrown bush, Bianca startled and made a point-face turn, taking them both in. Seeing them, she straightened her spine and kept walking…quite clearly a little faster than before.

Logan appreciated her impulse to pick up the pace. She just wished that self-protective instinct had kept her from walking home alone in the first place.

In almost no time at all, Bianca was turning another corner. Logan glanced up desperately at the sky, but there was so little light left, it might as well have been none at all. She kept her pace as it was, worried that Bianca might run from them if she realized they were following her.

Within moments, she knew she'd made a mistake. From the next street over, she heard a strange scuffling noise…and a scream.

She broke into a flat-out run, leaving Judith in the dust. Within seconds, she reached the bend where Bianca had disappeared, already fearing the worst. The sight that greeted her was reassuring, but she didn't allow it to slow her down. Bianca must have flung herself sideways to avoid the beast, as she was now scrambling her way up from a prone position in the middle of the street. The monster, meanwhile, had crashed into a nearby tree; the impact had been so hard, the trunk had cracked near the base, and the bulk of the tree had toppled to the ground with the beast on top of it.

Logan wasted no time putting her body between the rekal and the girl. As the rekal began to rise up off the ground, she reached down and pulled one of her short knives out of its sheath on her right calf.

"Run!" she shouted over her shoulder at the girl, who was still struggling to get off the ground.

"I can't," Bianca managed, now crawling away as another attempt to get to her feet failed. "Something's wrong with my leg."

With a grunt of frustration, Logan set her sights back on the rekal, which shook itself as it rose to its full height. Wasting no further time, Logan set off at a run again, crouched as she neared it, and sprang with all her might, launching herself upward.

Her launch point now differed significantly from before, when she'd jumped down from the tree. This time, she landed somewhere around the beast's lower midsection, and thrust her knife into its flesh wildly, hoping only to wound enough to slow it down and buy the girl time. The beast roared and stumbled in response, its movements violent enough to throw her off again.

Fortunately, by now Judith Li had finally caught up to them.

"Get her home!" Logan barked at her, gesturing emphatically at the fallen Bianca.

Behind her, the beast roared again. She turned just in time to see it bearing down on her.

She hadn't gotten a clear look at the thing before. Now that she did, she could make out a sharp snout, pointed ears, and gleaming red eyes. It looked a little like…a wolf. She barely had time to register the information before it swiped furiously at her and its razor-like claws connected with her body. She was thrown sideways.

Ignoring the pain of the hit as well as the pain of the fall, she leapt immediately to her feet again. Before her, the monster hesitated. It looked over at Bianca, limping away from them with her arm slung over Judith's shoulder, then back at Logan as she slipped her second knife out of its sheath, preparing to attack again. She could see the hilt of her first knife still sticking out of its massive form—just underneath where she imagined its ribs should be. She couldn't help but think there was little point attacking it with another small blade, but she didn't have much choice at the moment, especially if it decided to make for Bianca again.

Fortunately, it seemed to decide that she was the better target, and charged.

Just as it overcame her, she dropped into a crouch, avoiding its massive swing and sending it tumbling headfirst into the pavement. She took advantage of the pause to risk a look over her shoulder at Judith and Bianca. They had almost reached the turn in the road.

Her breach in concentration proved to be a mistake. Before she could right herself, she felt a burst of pain as something hooked into her calf—the rekal's long, sharp claw, slicing through her pant leg and into her muscle with ease. As her legs collapsed beneath her, she stifled back any cry of pain, unwilling to give the beast a chance to recognize a sign of weakness and double down its attack. As it dragged her closer, she pulled her left arm above her head and swung it forward, letting loose her blade in a wide arc. With a satisfying swish, it lodged solidly into the beast's shoulder, near the base of the neck—several degrees shy of a decapitating blow.

The demon roared and threw back its head in pain, allowing her just enough leeway to tug her leg painfully free from its grip. It didn't get up again right away; it seemed disoriented now, perhaps even tired. Logan scrambled to stand and crouched low, watching to see how much power the beast had lost before she advanced again. She could already tell she was losing a considerable amount of blood herself.

Just as she decided to ready herself for the attack again, she heard that flute sounding in the distance.

All at once, the beast's concentration came back—and it turned tail and ran.

After the debacle over the weekend, she wasn't about to let this chance slip away from her. She tucked all thoughts of pain aside and took off as fast as she could.

Fortunately for her, the beast took off down an empty road at first, which negated all the advantage it had in the rough terrain around them, allowing her to close in on its lead. When it finally did burst into the trees, she managed to keep up delightfully well, keeping the beast in her sights the whole time.

Finally, after far longer than she would have liked, they careened into an open field, illuminated silver by the first moon rays of the early night. There, on the far end, stood a dark figure in a hooded coat.

Before he lowered his hood, Logan knew without a shadow of a doubt that Kurt Redmond stood before her. Something about him—some uncomfortable, inimitable quality—made anything else impossible.

The beast slowed down when it saw him. She watched as it calmly crossed the expanse, then bowed low before him. Kurt cocked his head to the side, then reached down and tugged Logan's second knife free from its shoulder.

She moved forward but didn't close all the distance between them. She had a feeling that the beast would start healing immediately—which put her at a disadvantage, as her half-human blood still coursed down her leg at an alarming rate.

"Fascinating," she heard Kurt say as he examined her blade. As far as she could tell, he was intrigued by the design of the patterns in the hilt.

So. He'd never seen a knife that had been spelled like hers before. It wasn't anything too complicated—one binding spell to keep the blade sharp so it required less maintenance, and one to strengthen the steel so it was less likely to break mid-battle. She'd carried far more complicated pieces before.

He clicked his gaze upward, narrowing in on her with a certain sharpness. She'd seen looks like that before, and she didn't like them. It had a kind of predatory edge, almost sexual. The suggestion made her more than a little uncomfortable.

"Where'd you get this?" he asked, the greed in his voice clear and unchecked.

"I got it at the magic weapon store, where you get all the

magic weapons," she answered, edging closer still.

"You can stop right there, thank you," he said, scowling at her. "You may have a few fancy knives, but don't forget that I'm the one with the demon." He pointed redundantly at the beast, which still kneeled before him as though it were frozen. "Now, truly, tell me where you got this."

Logan shrugged. "I got it at an army surplus store. Where I got it isn't the point."

"It isn't?" He now held the blade up above him, as though he hoped the glinting moonlight might illuminate its secrets.

"Like I said. I got it at an army surplus store."

"But not like this," he said, holding it out before him. "It looks...*different*. It feels different, too. I can't say how exactly, but I *know* that it feels different from how it should. What did you do to it? Why does it feel this way?"

She shrugged again. He was starting to bore her. "It's been spelled, nothing special. I made it stronger and sharper. You can do that with simple spells, once you have a solid understanding of the basics. But for that, you'd need to be trained somewhere. And I can't imagine you've trained with anyone. Not anyone who knows what they're doing, at least."

Perhaps it was dangerous to antagonize him, but she didn't particularly care. He seemed a shallow threat to her at worst. The beast was the real problem, and the beast couldn't be antagonized with words.

"I am primarily self-taught," he answered haughtily, puffing out his chest as though she might actually be impressed by that. "How can you tell?"

"Because every master I know would have told you never to

summon a rekal," she answered easily, almost lazily. "Even the disreputable masters would have *at least* told you to kill it as soon as it accomplished a single task. You don't keep a rekal long enough for round two."

"You can't scare me," he growled at her. "You may be older than me, but you're still just a girl."

"A girl who's thwarted your big dumb monster twice now."

Kurt turned his gaze on the beast with a mixture of admiration and pride. He was still so pleased with himself for the accomplishment of bringing it forth, completely unaware it was likely the single stupidest thing he'd ever done.

"Don't you like my monster?" he asked, his eyes glinting as he leered at her. He gazed back at the monster, admiration still writ large on his features. "I like my monster just fine. He always does exactly as he's told. Unlike some people."

When he spoke, she only half-heard him. She was preoccupied, replaying the same four words that had haunted her since she'd stepped foot in town.

"Do you worship it?" she asked.

Kurt looked up at her in shock. "Do *I* worship *it*? The beast bows to *me*, not the other way around. *I* have the power."

She sidestepped her first reaction, which was to think that rarely did anyone with true power feel the need to state it. Instead, she cocked her head to the side, wondering what piece of the picture she was still missing.

"Do you worship the wolf?" she asked. The rekal did, indeed, look like a wolf. But she had to admit she was sorely disappointed to think that *the wolf*, whispered to her so fervently by the dreams of the Key, might turn out to be nothing more challenging than this brute demon.

"*The Wolf.*" Kurt's voice betrayed pure shock and confusion. "How do you know that name?"

Name. It's a name. So, proper noun. She left her face impassive, kept her body still. "I just do."

Kurt paused for a moment, then laughed. "But you don't know what it means at all! How else could you think the Wolf could be something so low and simple as this? Well, I'll give you that you're on the right track. After all, I do owe the existence of my special pet to none other than the Wolf, don't I? Mind you, I did all the work myself." He puffed himself up again. "But I never would have thought of it on my own. I'd barely even started with magic when he showed himself to me."

Logan cocked an eyebrow but let nothing else move. "When he showed himself to you?" Her voice was quiet and unobtrusive—almost more a suggestion than anything else. A suggestion that Kurt Redmond saw no reason to ignore.

"Yes, he showed himself to me," he said, his certainty of his own worthiness coating his voice like slime. "When he knew I was ready, he showed himself to me. I earned the privilege, you see. The Wolf won't show himself to just anyone. That's probably why you don't know what he looks like. You may know how to make some cute accessories, but clearly the Wolf doesn't think you're worth his time."

"Clearly," Logan answered, her voice and face still neutral.

"He came to me at the right time, just when I really needed him." Kurt sighed, his hand coming up to his neck, where the flute hung on a thin chain. "I had a problem, you see. A problem with a girl."

"Violet."

"Yes, Violet. Beautiful girl, but not as smart as you would think." He sighed like he had the weight of the world on his shoulders. "She was just good at tricking people, that's why the teachers all loved her so much. Those girls have it so easy. They can trick anyone they want."

Those girls. Maybe he meant pretty girls. Or maybe he meant all of them. It didn't matter.

"Is that why you murdered her?"

Shock flooded his face again. "What? That's not how it happened." He shook his head. "I loved her."

"I doubt that," Logan answered easily. She took another tiny step forward, certain that he would be too distracted to notice. She was correct. "Regardless, you killed her. No doubt about that."

"No!" he nearly shouted. "*I* didn't kill her!" He stomped one of his feet, and the beast actually seemed to inch back from him. Logan wondered idly if it had enough capacity for thought to be as disgusted by its master as she was. "I loved her. If anything, she killed herself—because she couldn't see my love for what it was. She was blind, blind to everything! Just like the rest of them." He got a strange, faraway look in his eye, like the world he saw was something entirely different from the one everyone else saw. "Everyone's always been set against me, my whole life. But they're wrong, every single one of them. They've always been wrong."

Who was he talking about? Logan didn't ask; she was too busy inching steadily forward.

"And she was just like the rest of them, in the end. She had to pay, you know. She had to pay for what she did to me. I couldn't just let it stand."

"Let what stand? Her rejection?"

"My humiliation!" he exclaimed in return. He was easy to rile up. "How could I let her keep on walking around in front of everyone after she'd humiliated me like that?"

She knew from reading her file that Violet could be cruel, but somehow she had a feeling that that wasn't what had happened in this case. Besides, as far as she could tell, the targets of Violet's bullying had all been other girls.

"What did she do to you?" she asked quietly.

His face went blank and his shoulders a little slack. "She couldn't see the truth. She was just a bitch like all the rest of them. All she wanted to do was torture me. You know, she's lucky I did it this way. I could have done something much worse." His face cracked in a smile that didn't reach his eyes. It made her slightly sick to look at. "What if I'd messed up her pretty little face so that no one would ever want her again? She would have been nothing then. She'd *have* to be grateful then. She'd have to beg." As she watched in muted horror, his eyes seemed to drain of light. It was almost as though he'd forgotten she could hear him. "Not that I would stop, if she begged. But I would have liked to hear it."

Logan allowed the silence to fill up between them. She was close enough now, not that he'd noticed. As he'd talked, she'd grown more and more certain that he'd already told her everything he could about the Wolf. He was nothing but a pawn, and whoever the Wolf was, she didn't think he'd had any intention to disclose anything of importance to this whimpering boy.

"I see," she said quietly. "Well, that is amazing."

He turned his empty lamp-like eyes on her. "So now you can see it. My terrible power."

"Oh no, that's not what I meant." With a movement so small he couldn't possibly notice, she unhooked the small button snap at the bottom of her axe's sheath. "I'm amazed at how pathetic you are. And I set my standards pretty low for you the moment I first saw you."

He laughed at her again, but it sounded hollower than before. "Do you really think someone *pathetic* could summon a monster this powerful?"

She didn't laugh. She didn't find any of this funny. "You summoned a monster because you didn't get your way. Yes, that's pathetic."

"Because—because I didn't—get my way?" He was spluttering in outrage. She found it fascinating that he still had the capacity.

"You threw a tantrum, like a small child. Unfortunately for Violet, you had access to magic you were unprepared for and unworthy of, and you used it to kill her."

At that, he stood up straight again, staring with defiance in his eyes. "I didn't kill her."

"You did. You killed her."

"No, no, no!" He even sounded like a child now. "No, see, that's where you're wrong! I didn't kill her—the *beast* killed her."

"The beast was your instrument. You killed her. You are responsible for it."

"I'm not responsible for any of this! She brought this on herself. The rekal answers the plea of *righteous vengeance* only— don't you see? She left me with no other choice! We were meant to be together, and she refused to see it. She refused to see the light. I can't...I'm not responsible. She...she...she didn't understand. She only got what was coming to her."

Logan shook her head slowly. She almost would have pitied him, were it not for his actions. "The rekal came when you called because you did a spell. Its appearance doesn't prove your righteousness; vengeance demons are undiscerning." She sighed heavily, displeased by his continued stupidity. "She didn't want you, Kurt."

"She didn't—she didn't understand—"

"She understood it perfectly. She said no." His face looked like it might crack open any moment. "She said no, and you killed her for it. That's not love. You can't love someone when you don't see them as a person. You didn't love her, and you didn't *deserve* to be with her. You can't *earn* a person. That's not how love works, and that's not how people work. You wanted her to be your little fantasy, and you didn't care what she wanted. That's sick. You had no right to do what you did. It infuriated you that she could say no to you, so you decided to make her pay for it. That's pathetic. You're sick, and you're pathetic. And that's all you are."

"No. No, she didn't get it." His voice was quiet and his eyes were cold as he stared her down. "You don't get it either."

"Was she a robot to you?" A fire was building in her; she let it spread. "Was she a human-sized doll? You say you were meant to be with her, but you didn't listen to her when she spoke, and you wouldn't accept that she was allowed to say no. How could that be love? Are you an idiot?"

His response momentarily failed him. He reminded her of a wind-up toy when it runs into a wall. She felt nothing but contempt for him, though perhaps that was dangerous. Or perhaps not.

"I'll show you." His voice was low. She knew he would do it soon.

"I doubt it."

The next succession of events seemed to happen in slow motion; Logan knew what he was going to do before he did it, and she knew she wouldn't be able to stop him preemptively—but she could interrupt him enough to buy herself a little time.

His fingers, already hovering just over the flute, closed down on it and brought it to his lips. At the same time, she crouched low and launched herself at him, shoving him to the ground just as the first note rang through the air.

She had meant to knock him off balance and prevent him from directing an attack, even if only for a moment. But she hadn't counted his paranoid stupidity into her calculation. If he had simply thrown his arms out to stop his fall, the flute likely would have remained connected to him by the chain on his neck. Instead, he gripped the body tightly, and the force of her hit wrenched his closed fist away from his neck so hard that the chain broke.

And then his body—and his fist—broke hard against the ground. His fingers sprang open, and the flute rolled out of his reach.

Logan felt the change in the air instantaneously. The magic on the beast had broken.

Kurt didn't seem to notice the difference like she did. He scrambled onto his belly and grabbed the flute back in a desperate stab, bringing it immediately to his lips and turning back to see the rekal as he blew.

When he had blown his brief note from the flute just before Logan knocked him to the ground, the rekal had stood at full height, ready to bear down on her, its eyes flashing their dark red. Now it still stood, but the hard set of its intention was gone. For a moment, it stared blankly down at them both, as if it didn't know how to proceed. Kurt blared through the flute again, but the sound reverberated through the clearing to no effect; it was emptied of its magic.

Finally, the rekal's senses seemed to return to itself. It tossed back its head and howled. Logan didn't mistake the sound: it was preparing for the hunt, and it would start with the nearest available prey—the two of them.

"Give me back the knife!" Logan shouted at the boy standing beside her.

He said nothing as he turned to her, terror frozen on his face—his hands empty but for the now-useless flute.

"Just go! Run, now!" She wanted to call him all manner of names, but she didn't have time.

The monster before her still had one hilt sticking out of its side, but apart from that, it was already completely healed. Behind her, she heard Kurt finally starting to run. The beast cocked his head to watch, but stopped before following. She watched in horror as it reached down past its ribs, stuck a claw just under the hilt, and wrenched the first knife free.

Her only advantage lost, Logan saw few other options. With a deep inhale of breath, she brought her arms up across her chest, then thrust them down and out as hard as she could. She felt her spikes shoot out from her skin as she launched herself at the beast once more.

This time, she moved fast. She raked her arms across the beast's skin over and over, aiming to shred its flesh as much as she could before it managed to fling her off. The monster roared with the pain, the sound of its anguish reverberating through the trees around them. Before he could toss her, she jumped to the ground and started running herself.

She'd figured out by now that she was faster than the beast on open ground, so she pressed her speed to her advantage as much as possible, ignoring every branch that scratched her and every twig that snapped in her face. As she ran, she breathed deep through her nose, searching for the sharply unpleasant scent of Kurt's mortal fear. It didn't take her long to locate it.

Either he'd injured himself, or he'd collapsed out of exhaustion. He was slumped behind a tree to her right, perhaps convinced he could hide it out. She jumped over to him.

"I don't care how much you're hurting," she barked. "We have to keep running if you want to live."

He stared up at her, his face stricken with fear.

"How—how—"

"Plant your goddamn feet and push!" she ordered.

"He didn't tell me this—he didn't say it would go like this!"

"Who didn't?"

"Him! The Wolf!"

A wave of disgust came over her. With both their lives in peril, he thought now was the time to stop and complain about something as trivial as his *surprise*?

"Maybe he didn't know, who cares? Just get the fuck up!"

Kurt's eyes turned lamp-like again, fixing her with an empty stare. Almost like he'd forgotten his fear.

"You don't understand, you stupid little girl. He knew everything else, all of it! *He knew you'd come.* He knew you'd show up at the school and try to talk to everyone. He told me to look for a spy—he said you'd be a woman with black hair and cold eyes. He said you would wear long dark pants, even in the summer." Kurt barked out an insane, uncontrolled laugh. "*He told me you were a good runner!*"

Logan didn't have time to react to anything he said. The beast was crashing through the trees behind them—pulling them out by the roots, by the sound of it. With a grunt of displeasure, she bent down, hoisted Kurt up, threw him over her shoulder, and ran.

She couldn't push nearly as fast with the dead weight of a teenage boy slowing her down, but it was better than standing still at least. She streamed forward blindly, moving them away from the beast based on sound alone, ignoring Kurt's ceaseless whining wheeze.

When she was satisfied that she'd put some distance between them, she came to a stop and let Kurt tumble to the ground.

"Will you run now?"

But he was already moving, motivated either by the still-too-close sounds of the monster approaching, or by the threat of her grabbing him again. Whichever one it was, she was glad. She ran after him.

Within moments, they came into another open field. Ten feet into the long grass, she turned to make her stand.

It was on her in a moment, barreling out of the trees, teeth barred. She threw her right arm across her face in her usual defensive posture, and felt the beast's head connect with it. Its jaw bit down, crushing into her arm.

Almost immediately, it let her go again. Black blood dripped from its mouth and onto her jacket. Her bone-like spikes had ripped into the flesh of its gaping mouth. *Good.*

She knew she had to inflict as much damage as possible, so before it recovered from that shock, she leapt onto it again, repeating her method of fast, incisive slashing—shredding all the flesh within her reach.

The beast, still reeling, took longer to buck her this time. But when it finally tossed her to the ground, it did so with wrathful power. She fell hard, her head glancing off the ground as the force of her landing seemed to collapse her chest inward. For a few terrifying moments, she could neither breathe nor see.

Her sight returned to her just in time to see the beast about to pounce—only to change direction at the last moment, its attention diverted by something else. Ever so faintly, she could hear a funny scratching sound.

Slowly, she craned her neck backward to see what she was missing. She was still incapable of forcing her body to move any more than that.

The sound was coming from Kurt. He hadn't kept running, like she'd assumed he would. Instead, he'd reached the end of the clearing...and decided to climb up a tree. He had barely reached the lowest branch.

Why hadn't he run? Dread crept through her body as she lay temporarily paralyzed, unable to affect the scene unfolding before her in any way. *Why hadn't he run?*

The beast advanced on him. Now standing on the first branch, trying to reach up to the second, Kurt scrambled for the flute again, forcing loud, tuneless screams from the pitiful instrument. Far too late, he dropped it entirely and used both hands to grab for the next branch as he jumped for it.

Miraculously, he took hold of the branch above him, but it didn't matter. The beast had already reached him, and with a monstrous claw it grabbed one of his ankles and lifted him clean away from the tree. Logan knew what was coming, but she didn't let herself look away.

For a moment, it held Kurt up high in the air, like it only wanted to listen to him as he screamed. Then it raised him a little higher, swung him violently, and swiped forward with its other claw. A massive torrent of blood sprang from Kurt's chest as the demon claimed his heart. His screams fell silent.

Unbidden, Alexei's voice floated through her thoughts.

Think of it as pest control.

With a strength she wasn't sure she still possessed, Logan leapt to her feet. The rekal seemed to be relishing its kill—after messily consuming his heart, it let Kurt's body drop to the ground before pouncing on top of it. The night around them was completely silent except for the sounds of the demon making its meal. Apparently an unchained rekal didn't limit its feast to the heart only.

Grisly as the scene was, she couldn't have asked for an easier end to her hunt. As the demon gloried in its feed, she slid her axe out of its holster and closed the short distance between them. In one fell swoop, she raised her weapon up high and brought it down with all her strength.

After everything, the end came without a struggle. The rekal was dead.

She felt no triumph in this, though she did feel a certain amount of relief. As she shook her axe free of the corpse, she could feel the natural anesthetic effects of adrenaline beginning to wear off. A sharp bolt of pain shot up her right arm where the rekal had bitten it. Still, the beast was gone; it could kill no one else. If only she'd prevented a second victim…

What would she have done then? Would she have turned him over to the Order? She didn't trust the Order, of course—not the body as a whole nor any individual within it. But it wasn't exactly like she could call the police. And she wasn't inclined to make herself a prison guard any time soon. So what other choice would she have had?

And what other choice did she have now?

After wiping the black blood from her axe on the grass around her, she sheathed it once more and pulled her phone out of a back pocket. This time she didn't dial Knatt.

After exactly one ring, a cold voice spoke on the other end.

"Pass code please."

"Marionberry."

"Proceed."

"This is Henrietta Logan. I have a message for Mr. Atherton."

A brief pause.

"Proceed."

"He can call off his dogs—the job is complete. And I'll need a cleanup at my current coordinates. I'll be sending out a pulse beacon as soon as I end this call."

Another pause.

"Recorded. Please hold."

"Just transmit the message. My job here is done."

With that, she hung up the phone and slipped it back into her pocket. Reaching into her jacket, she tugged open a hidden zipper and pulled out a small pouch.

Inside the pouch were several small round balls of solid stone. She pulled one out and placed it in her palm, then held it up in front of her face.

"*Proiectum*," she whispered.

The stone lifted up off her palm, hovered for just a moment, then shot straight up into the air, disappearing into the night sky. She knew its course long after she couldn't see it anymore. It would fly halfway across the country, eventually coming to land in an old mansion somewhere in Brooklyn—headquarters of the Order of Shadows. Someone there would get it, and they would dispatch a team to follow it back to precisely where she was standing at that very moment.

By which time, she'd be gone. She didn't need to stay here any longer. The Order would clean her mess. She didn't trust them, but she was perfectly willing to use them shamelessly.

As she started walking back in the general direction of town, she remembered the next thing she meant to do. She pulled out her phone again and dialed the number she'd programmed in that morning.

After a moment, Judith Li's puzzled voice sounded in her ear.

"H-hello?"

"Hello, Miss Li."

"How-how are you calling me right now? What phone is this?" She paused for a beat. "Did you *plant* a phone on me?"

Logan sidestepped the question.

"Are you safe? Did you and Bianca get inside somewhere?"

"Yeah, we're at her house. Having a hilariously awkward sleepover. You wanna talk to her?"

"Probably best I don't. You'll be safe now. Danger's passed."

"Really? You killed it?"

"Yeah, killed it. It's dead." She sighed. Her exhaustion would be catching up to her any minute; every step she took revealed a new pain. Her leg was no longer openly bleeding, but it still throbbed when she moved. "Okay, I'm gonna leave you for now. Try to get some sleep."

"Wait! That's not it, is it? I still have so many questions for you."

"I promise I'll find you before I leave town. But I need to go now."

"Okay. Just…please do. Find me. Good night."

"Good night."

She put the phone away just as her right knee gave out momentarily. She righted herself immediately, glad she'd ended the call with Judith before her collapse. Closing her eyes in concentration, she willed her pain to recede to the back again. As she steadied herself, she felt a curious sensation settle over her— it felt, once again, like she was being watched. She turned around slowly, examining the scene around her. But she saw nothing— nothing but the after-effects of violence.

The hour was late by now, and she had miles to go before she slept. She could take the safer route and walk her way back, but she wasn't sure she could stay awake long enough. So instead, she ran.

Looking back on it, she wouldn't be able to say how she managed to run so far after all of that. But somehow she did. She made it back to her motel, and she collapsed into sleep on the bed, never even managing to get her jacket all the way off.

Her sleep that night was completely dreamless. For now, at least, the Key had finished with her.

Chapter 9
After the Storm

When Logan woke up, everything hurt. The Key buzzed with warmth along her spine. Her clothes felt like they'd melted to her skin, and her body was stiff as cement. With a struggle, she sat up and peeled her jacket off, then let it drop on top of her still-sheathed axe, which had ended up near the foot of the bed. Perhaps she should have been grateful she hadn't rolled over onto it in the night. Based on the cold resistance of her muscles, she would guess she'd barely moved at all since she hit the bed.

Eventually, she managed to push herself all the way to standing. Her right elbow was so stiff and painful, she found it better to avoid using that arm entirely. On her way to the bathroom, she pulled the rest of her clothing from her body, dropping it unceremoniously as she went. She turned the shower on as hot as it would go, then stepped delicately inside.

Her calf was caked in dried blood, but the wound itself had mostly healed. A jagged scar had already formed in its place. She stuck her leg under the water first and watched the red-brown stains chip away.

Already yellowing bruises blanketed most of her torso,

marking all the places where she'd slammed hard into the ground—or hard into the beast. Slowly, she pushed the rest of her body under the steady stream of water. Her neck cracked loudly as she rolled it from one side to the other. Sleep had likely healed the worst of her pain, but it had left her with so many other aches she could barely tell the difference. It still hurt too much to move her right elbow at all, so she did all washing with her left arm.

Eventually she felt clean enough of blood and sweat to shut the shower off, however reluctantly. With that done, she had little else to do but start her day.

She toweled herself down loosely before pulling on a new pair of pants and one of the work-ready bras from the clothes rack. Before she could force herself into a work-ready shirt, however, she needed to circulate a little more air into the room, so she went over to throw the window wide.

Now it was time to call Knatt. For once, she had good news for him. She dug her phone out of her jacket and dialed him.

He answered on the second ring.

"You're calling early," he said, by way of greeting.

"Funny—doesn't feel early. Oh, wait, is that why everything sucks right now?" With a slight breeze coming in from the window, she felt just comfortable enough to pull a lightweight blouse on, though she didn't button it up all the way yet. Then she fell heavily back onto the bed, her mending muscles momentarily depleted.

"You have bad news," he guessed.

"Not at all," said Logan. "Well, uh, I guess it depends on your take. But the case is closed. And as a bonus, we don't have to worry about cleanup because I already called the Order. They can make themselves useful for once."

Knatt was silent for a moment. She imagined him standing in the kitchen, drinking tea and giving the coffee machine a judgmental stare.

"Were there further casualties?"

"Yes." An image of Kurt's face flashed before her eyes. "The summoner, a teenage boy who went to school with the victim. The beast was a rekal; the boy was using a flute to control it. I tried to tackle him, and he dropped the flute."

"Ah," said Knatt, drawing out the syllable. "And, control lost, the beast could not be made to heel again. So the boy did not survive?"

She hadn't meant for it to end that way. A sense of shame started to creep its way up Logan's esophagus.

"No, he didn't. I…I tried, but…he didn't run. I told him, but he didn't run."

Knatt gave a heavy sigh. For a moment, Logan braced for his admonition, but when he spoke, his tone was gentle.

"I wouldn't blame yourself for that," he said carefully. "I don't know many who could take on a fully grown rekal and live. Not once it's been unchained." He paused, and when he spoke again, his voice sounded pained and heavy. "Are you decent?"

"Mostly."

"Good. I'll only be a moment."

With that, he hung up. Logan held her phone in front of her face, staring up at it with tired eyes until she heard a sharp knock to her left, followed by a swishing noise.

"Are you hurt?" Knatt's voice sounded from somewhere above her head.

She let her phone drop onto the bed and used her left hand to push herself to a seated position, then stood up entirely, her pride compelling her to downplay what injuries she had left. Only the faintest groan of effort escaped her lips, but her right arm stayed bent and held tight to her side. In front of her stood Hugh Knatt, wearing dark dress pants, a white collared shirt, and a dark grey sweater vest. His gold-rimmed glasses perched on the edge of his nose, and he looked overall so British she could have sworn he smelled like tea and scones.

"Not too damaged. Mostly sore and stiff." She reached her left arm up and back to massage her neck a little. It felt strange, somehow, just seeing him. He looked so comfortable and warm in his nice clean clothes. She felt a stab of embarrassment over her half-buttoned shirt and her messy wet hair. Something about his pristine presentation made her feel unkempt by comparison. But what could she do about it now? "To be honest, I want to sleep for like three more days."

Knatt glanced down at his watch. "You do seem to be up before your usual hour."

"Well, you know. I'm on a school schedule now."

"Ah, yes." He nodded briefly, then pulled his cell phone out of a pocket on his vest. "I need to make your arrangements, don't I? Won't be a moment." He pressed a few buttons, then brought the phone up to his ear. "Yes, hello? May I speak to Mrs. Wendell please? Yes, I'll hold." He closed his eyes serenely and gave Logan a placid smile. "Ah, Mrs. Wendell? It's Mr. Stewart, we've spoken before. I'm from the non-profit that sent Miss Logan to your school for a few days. Yes, that one. Well, I'm sorry to say, we've got a new assignment for Miss Logan, so—well, I'm glad she's worked out so well for you. Yes, unfortunately we need her right away, so she won't be coming in today at all. Certainly, if she comes available again, I'll let you know. Thank you for being so understanding." With that, he hung up.

"You don't like to say *goodbye* on the phone, do you?" said Logan.

Knatt gave her a look that simultaneously conveyed both confusion and a mild irritation.

"Are you sure you don't have any injuries?" With a wave of his hand, he indicated the vague area of her torso.

"You can inspect if you want." She threw her mobile arm up in the air and performed a full-point turn, landing a little suddenly when her left knee gave out unexpectedly. "Uh, well, I guess that's still happening. I'll probably be all better in a day or two."

Knatt grunted in acceptance. "In that case, you should get some more sleep. You may come home now, if you like. The direct way." This time, he indicated the door behind him.

She was almost tempted. He didn't like to let her take the Ninja through the portal, since the easiest way to get it outside after that meant rolling it through the kitchen at the Manor. He was precious about that kitchen. But she knew she wasn't quite done yet.

"I appreciate the offer, but I actually think I'll pass. I have…well, exactly one string to tie up before I can come home. Thanks though."

Knatt grunted again, but this time it sounded more like disapproval. "Very well. I'll take the weapons home, at least. And the clothes of course." He started to move in that direction, but he stopped himself to fix her with a laser stare. "You still ought to spend the day resting. Get a few more hours, at least."

She was a little taken aback. Did she look that bad?

"Yeah," she shrugged, trying not to feel self-conscious. "I got a bed right here. I can't tie up my string until school is over anyway."

"Good." His shoulders seem to slump a little, and he shook his head. "I shouldn't have let you come up here alone. If I'd known you were dealing with a rekal…well, we would have done this differently." He looked at her again, but his gaze had softened. "I'm glad you're all right."

What did that mean? Did he feel guilty?

"Thanks." She shifted uncomfortably. It had been a while since they'd had a moment that wasn't characterized by sarcasm or admonishment. She wasn't sure what to do with it.

Fortunately, Knatt seemed just as uncomfortable with the moment as she did. Even more fortunately, he had the sense to end it.

"I'll be on my way then," he said with a brisk, decisive nod. With that, he pulled open the portal door and left it wide, then started wheeling the clothes rack through. A few moments later, he came back for the armory. He left behind only what could reasonably fit into the hideaway spot on the Ninja.

Once it closed, the door took only a few seconds to dissipate into nothing. She was alone again. She felt an immeasurable relief at the knowledge that she had most of the day to herself once more.

This time, she managed to get her clothes off before she fell into bed. The slight humming warmth of the Key carried with her as she lost herself in sleep.

She hadn't been lying when she'd told Knatt she could have slept for days, but considering her desire to get out of Montana, a few extra hours would do for now. She woke up well into the afternoon. Even though she'd showered in the morning, she already felt sticky again—either from the heat or from continued exposure to the motel bed, she couldn't be sure. So when she finally got up, she rinsed herself off in the shower one more time before finally pulling on clothes. By now, she could at least bend and unbend her elbow, though it still twinged with pain when she did.

There wasn't much in the room to pack up—small weapons, extra underwear, one more pair of pants. The clothes were shoved to the bottom of her satchel, along with one of the knives. She strapped the other two knives to her calves again, hiding them neatly under pant legs. Then she swung the satchel onto her shoulder and walked out of the room for the last time.

The small bag slid to the bottom of the Ninja's hidden compartment. She left the bike behind for a few minutes while she went to the front desk, located in a small room at the center of the long, low building. Its insides were every bit as questionable and grimy as her room had been. She almost quibbled at having to pay for an extra night because she was checking out so late in the day—after all, she'd gone without internet her entire stay—but she was still so tired. While the lackluster girl behind the counter processed her bill with the speed of an indifferent sloth, Logan located a pot of free coffee in the far corner of the room and proceeded to down two cups of its sludge-like contents. Muddy trenches of grounds greeted her at the bottom of each serving.

Finally, the girl was done. Logan took her card back gracefully and waved a friendlier goodbye than she felt. Then she was back outside and on the bike once more.

It might have been her imagination, but this day seemed a little cooler than the few preceding it. Even so, riding in her heavy helmet and leather jacket made her itchy—and it made her long for home, where the weather was always a little bit cooler. A part of her wished she'd taken Knatt up on his offer of immediate transport, but she knew she'd be home soon enough. Besides, she had made a promise. At the center of her shoulder blades, the Key buzzed persistently.

She drove to the high school, which would be letting out any moment now. Forgoing her usual spot in the corner, she parked instead in clear view of the entrance. Everyone leaving would see her as they left—including Judith Li. She threw down the kickstand and hopped off, choosing to lean against the seat until her last task walked out the door.

After a few moments, the laughing, chattering, calamitous crowd swarmed through the front doors, spilling out in every direction. Logan watched the first wave pass, recognizing a few faces here and there. One of them waved at her, and as Logan locked eyes, she placed her immediately—Ashley Carson, the first girl she'd spoken to. She returned the wave and smiled at her warmly.

Perhaps, she thought to herself, *if I were someone else, this would be the moment that I would think I might miss this place after all.* A million images could have come to her then, but the one that swam to the fore was that of Jason Reed's smirking, lizard-brain face. *Nope. I won't miss anything. Well. Maybe the food.*

She was saved any further reminiscing by the appearance of Judith Li. Li carried a backpack that appeared full-to-bursting, along with one large and one small duffel bag. She noticed Logan immediately and tried to wave, but the action almost caused her to lose a bag. Logan rushed forward to help her, grabbing the larger bag off her shoulder and taking it on—even though it was the other one that had nearly fallen. Logan lifted it easily.

"Thanks," said Judith, turning to look Logan face-on. "I was hoping I would see you."

"I did promise." Logan gave her a serenely inscrutable smile.

"So, uh, are you taking off again?"

Before she answered, Logan turned back toward her bike and motioned for Judith to look in that direction. "Why don't you come with me somewhere? I'll buy you a burger. Or something else equally bad for you."

Logan had begun to walk before she was finished asking, and Judith jumped to keep up with her.

"Oh man. Are you taking me for a ride on your motorcycle?" Her voice sounded stunned and awed.

"Only transportation I've got," Logan answered with a shrug. "Hope that's okay."

Judith Li stopped a few feet short of the Ninja, staring at it in reverence. After a long pause, she spoke in a hushed voice.

"This may be the greatest thing that's ever happened to me."

As Logan swung her seat up, she felt a small amount of relief that Knatt had taken the ax with him when he went. She'd carried it with her before, but it usually took up almost the entire compartment. Without it, she was just barely able to squeeze Judith's largest bag inside. She then hefted Li's smaller duffel from her and hooked it to the back of the seat with the attached leather straps. She handed Li the helmet.

"Keep your backpack on and hold on to me as tight as you can."

With that, she swung up onto the Ninja. Judith looked dumbfounded for a moment, then scrambled to catch up to her, clumsily swinging herself onto the seat behind Logan. The girl's arms circled around either side of her, but she hesitated to pull them in, instead leaving them to hover in midair. With a grunt of irritation, Logan grabbed hold of her wrists and forcibly wrapped Li's arms around her torso.

Li's tentative hold tightened to a death grip as soon as the engine roared to life. Logan started at an easy pace, but as she accelerated into her turn out of the lot, Judith gave a small yelp and ducked her head below Logan's shoulder. The action was no small feat given the helmet's heft, and the fact that Judith was by far the taller of the two.

Within a few minutes, they came up on their destination, and Logan pulled up right in front. The diner.

Judith Li removed the helmet and took a few shaky steps away from the bike before turning to Logan with a bemused expression.

"After all that, you wanna go to this place?" She placed the helmet on the back of the seat and looked up at the neon sign that said only *Diner*.

"Yeah. I like it here." Logan didn't quite understand Judith's confusion. "Would you prefer somewhere else?"

"I guess not," Judith shrugged. "I don't know, maybe I thought we'd go somewhere out of town. It's not like there are a lot of good options in Wolf Creek, you know?" Logan felt a small shock when she heard the name; after everything that had happened, she had completely forgotten that particular coincidence. Was it a coincidence? "But yeah, I guess this place is pretty good. Better than my parents' place, anyway."

She gave Logan a cheery smile once more and marched toward the entrance with a bounce in her step. This time, Logan had to jump to catch up.

Once inside, she led them to the table in the far corner, where the sheriff and his deputy had sat before. She liked the symbolism of it: she'd closed their case, so she took their spot. Sherene was with them almost immediately, dropping off menus for both of them and a piping hot coffee for Logan.

"You want coffee?" she asked Judith, her right eyebrow cocked.

"Uh, can I get a strawberry lemonade?" She glanced at Logan, like she was making sure it was okay. Logan gave an almost imperceptible nod.

"Sure, kid."

Judith watched Sherene walk away, waiting until she was out of earshot before turning excitedly back to Logan.

"So, are you gonna tell me what happened?"

"What happened?" Logan poured a little cream in her coffee before bringing it to her lips. Even after the sludge in the motel lobby, she felt like she needed it.

"You know, what happened with the...*monster*." She dropped

her voice to a dramatic whisper on the last word. The act seemed to reinforce for Logan her relatively young age. She realized that the past few days must have been fairly intense to an 18-year-old who barely knew what magic was.

"I killed it," said Logan. Her voice was low but neutral.

Judith scoffed. "Well I know that!" Her eyes widened. "But how? How did you get it? You gotta tell me the whole thing."

Logan nodded, thinking it over. Judith deserved the whole story, but the end was a delicate matter. She gave Judith a summary of their chase, and then a quick overview of her back-and-forth with Kurt. She did, however, sidestep any mention of the Wolf. She didn't know what to make of that yet, and Judith didn't need to be bothered with it. Nor did she think Knatt would appreciate her inclusion on the details.

"Wow," said Judith, after Logan had given her the feel of it. "Sounds like he was a fucked up guy. I mean, I'm not really surprised, honestly. He always kinda freaked me out."

"So, after I all but called him a creepy little weirdo, he did that whole 'I'll show you' bit, and tried to order the beast to attack me. Naturally, I defended myself and tackled him to the ground." She took another deep sip of coffee. "Which is when he dropped his flute and severed his magical connection to the beast. He lost control of it."

"Wait, he dropped his *flute*? What does that mean?"

"Oh, yeah. He was using a flute to control it. A flute with magical properties, obviously."

"Kurt had a *magic flute*? A *magic flute* controlled that giant werewolf monster thing?"

"Yes. A magic flute."

Judith slumped back in her chair. "That's amazing. And kinda stupid."

Logan nodded. "Agreed."

"So what happened after that? After he lost control?"

Logan was about to answer, when Sherene sidled up to them with Judith's massive lemonade in hand. Giant chunks of real strawberries, along with a healthy portion of strawberry syrup, floated up through the bright yellow juice.

"You two know what you're getting?"

Judith snapped to attention and answered immediately. "Yeah—blueberry pecan pancakes with maple whip and a side of bacon."

Logan was impressed, and a little taken aback, by her speed and detail. Then she realized Sherene had turned to her.

"Falafel wrap. And garlic fries for the table."

Sherene nodded briefly and walked off without writing a single thing down. Judith's laser gaze narrowed in on Logan once more.

"So he lost control."

"Yes. I told him to run, then I attacked it with...with another weapon. It kept healing, of course, but I tried to cut it up as much as possible. Then I ran to catch up with Kurt. Actually, I ended up carrying him for a little bit."

"You carried him?"

"Well, he'd stopped running. So, yeah, I carried him. Not for long, he started running again after a minute of that. Then we hit another clearing, so I stopped to fight the monster again." She paused, glancing out into the street through the window so she wouldn't have to meet Judith's eyes for a moment.

Absentmindedly, she reached her left hand over to rub lightly on her right elbow. Pain still throbbed up to greet her if she moved it too fast. "I told Kurt to run again, but he tried to climb up a tree instead. I don't know what he was thinking. Anyway, I attacked the beast again, but this time when it threw me, it almost knocked me out. I couldn't move. And that's when Kurt made a little too much noise trying to get up that damn tree."

Judith's eyes widened ever further as she understood the implication.

"Oh my god. Did—did the demon get him?"

Logan's gaze fell down to the table, to where the little salt and sugar packets were. This particular table carried pretty golden packets of honey, too.

"He didn't make it."

Judith fell silent, too. They both gazed solemnly out the window, as though the gathering twilight outside held some kind of message for them.

Sherene arrived in their silence and placed their plates in front of them without interrupting it. Then she walked off without any further questions.

Logan's guilt threatened to press in on her. What had happened to Kurt was her fault. She was the professional; she should have been able to save him. If she hadn't tackled him like that, he might still be alive. Maybe, on some level, she hadn't cared enough to be careful. Hadn't she told him he disgusted her?

This line of thought did her no good. She shifted her gaze to the fries and forced herself to pick one up and bite into it.

"Eat something," she told Judith. "You'll feel better."

Face still blank, Judith gave a nod and looked down at her plate. After a moment, she seemed to remember herself and set about getting her knife and fork. The pancakes in front of her looked impressive and decadent, piled high with off-white whipped cream—Logan guessed that to be the "maple whip" Judith had specified.

"So," said Judith through a mouthful of sodden pancake, "what happens now? Did you hide his body or something? Because, like, I think *killed by monster* is kind of a legal gray area."

Logan took a healthy bite of her wrap before answering. All at once, she realized she hadn't eaten in almost twenty-four hours.

"Nothing happens now," she said finally. "Well, nothing new. I called some people, they'll take care of it. I imagine they'll make it look like an animal attack. They might even kill a mountain lion or something, and leave it to take the blame. I'm not sure how they normally do it, but they'll clean everything up." She sighed. "Of course, they can't make Kurt not dead. But his parents will have an answer, and so will the town."

"Wow." Judith's eyes were still wider than normal, but she nodded like that answer satisfied her enough. Then she went back to her dessert stack and let herself get carried away with it for a few minutes, pausing only on occasion to wash down with lemonade.

Logan welcomed the moment of silence. In almost no time at all, she'd consumed most of her falafel wrap, and she could feel the satisfaction of it throughout her whole body. Once she'd taken her last bite, she reached over to touch her right elbow experimentally, wondering if the extra fuel might have had any effect on its recovery. It still felt tender to the touch, however.

She did know something that would help, of course. She'd been at this long enough to know the tricks. But the risks were too high, especially now. Every trick had a downside, and she'd long since deemed this one unacceptable.

Letting that thought slip cleanly from her mind, she reached for a few more fries. Forever proving her worth, Sherene came by and replenished her coffee in full. As she mixed in a little more cream and took a sip, she heard Judith drop her knife and fork on her plate and sigh.

"Everything all right?" She took another fry and motioned for Judith to help herself, too.

Judith took a few fries and chewed them thoughtfully. "Yeah. I'm just wondering what I'm gonna do now. I mean, now that the monster's gone, I'm sure you're gonna leave town. And...I don't know, I don't have a lot of friends." She sighed heavily and looked out the window. Logan watched silently as confusion and anxiety washed over her features. Then she cocked an unexpected grin and turned back to Logan. "You totally don't have to worry about Bianca, by the way. She told her parents that she hurt her ankle tripping on some stairs, and she made *me* promise never to tell anyone what happened. So, basically, she's so embarrassed about hanging out with me that she'll never tell anyone what she saw."

Logan smirked at that, completely unsurprised by the arbitrary motivations of teenagers. She was a little surprised to see Judith's quick turn from existential anxiety to lighthearted jokes, but she surmised that it might be easier for the kid to pretend to put a brave face on everything.

An idea had been floating in her head all morning, growing ever more concrete with each passing moment that the Key kept up its insistent tingle at her back. She considered it only a moment longer before she spoke.

"You could come with me."

Like a reassuring hand, the Key pressed warmth into her skin. Judith's expression went blank, momentarily stunned.

"I could—what?"

"Come with me. You could come with me."

"Do you mean like—come live with you?"

"Essentially, yes. You'd have your own space, of course. I suppose we'd need to work a few details out. At the very least, you need somewhere to go after you can't stay with Amy anymore, right? Or were you planning to stay there indefinitely?"

Judith chuckled a little nervously. "Uh, actually, I wasn't totally sure where I was gonna go tonight. I mean, I guess if I really needed to, Amy could…but, well, I've got all my stuff with me. I…I don't know, I was gonna try to…find somewhere else." Her voice trailed off at the end, and her gaze drifted to the window again. Logan got the impression that the façade Judith had used to get herself through the day was breaking down. Given a possible out, she'd finally let herself take a real look at her situation.

"I'm leaving tonight," said Logan. "I'll ride out of town, keep going as long as I can. When it isn't safe for me to ride any longer, I'll find a motel. So, if you come with me, you'll likely be facing a lumpy bed and limp pillows." She glanced outside at the sky, where dark was beginning to gather. "And, well, I can't promise you I won't find a way to get you into trouble somehow.

It doesn't beat much, but it beats nothing at all. Come with me."

Judith's gaze locked back on her. In her eyes, Logan could see hope and doubt in equal measure.

"You're certainly free to stay here, if you like," she said, in the absence of Judith's response. "I would never pressure you into a decision either way. If you come with me, you don't need to think that you're committing to anything. If you want, you can decide you'll just stay with me for a few days until you're up on your feet. Use this as a springboard to a whole new life, far away from this little town in the middle of nowhere." She drummed her fingers on the table. She didn't want to be mean. "Or you can stay here. There's no pressure either way. After all, you said Amy would let you stay a bit longer. And maybe you like it here; I'm sure some people do." Judith's expression soured, perhaps involuntarily. "Of course, there is something I can offer you that you won't find here."

Judith seemed to straighten a little. "What's that?"

"If you come with me...you could learn from me. About magic, I mean. I'm not a great teacher, but I know a lot more about magic than you do. I have a library full of information you'll never get on the internet, not without knowing the right people. And if you don't like libraries, then I can introduce you to all those people. And I can train you. Spell work, fighting—that sort of thing. If you want to, that is. Like I said, no pressure." She performed a nonchalant shrug. "Maybe magic isn't your thing. I understand."

For a moment, Judith gaped at her, her mouth moving without making any noise. Finally, her voice returned.

"I want—I want to go with you! I want the whole thing. I

want to go, and I want to learn." She paused, and the look on her face seemed to say that she was still waiting for the catch—the reason why none of this was real. "I can't pay you."

"I wouldn't expect you to," said Logan. "Think of me like a patron."

Judith's face melted into a wide smile, and she nodded in comprehension. "Yes! You'll be my patron! Heh, that's so old-timey. That's, like, Renaissance old."

"Well, call me old-fashioned."

At first, Judith nodded blandly, but after a moment, another thought dawned over her features and she looked at Logan with suspicion. "Wait, you're not, like, secretly five hundred years old, right? Like you never met Michelangelo or anything, right?"

Amused, Logan supplied her with a laugh that was just a touch too loud, followed by a sly grin. "Don't be ridiculous. Of course I've never met Michelangelo."

Judith laughed too, but she stopped it short. "That doesn't actually answer both questions."

"Good point. You know, I was thinking about ordering more fries. Do you think you could eat any more?"

"Always," answered Judith sincerely. She looked like she wanted to speak again, but Sherene was walking in their direction, so Logan flagged her over.

"Another order of fries, please. Thank you." She smiled pleasantly as Sherene walked off again. Then she turned back to Judith. "There's just one more thing before we consider this a done deal."

"What's that?"

Logan sighed heavily and gave Judith a heavy stare, hoping to impart her dire seriousness as she spoke. "It's a warning. My life is dangerous. Any life that entangles itself with magic is dangerous, but mine is especially so. I take on the tasks that other people don't want to take. Generally speaking, that's how I make my living. It can be messy, and it can be violent. I'll do my best to protect you, but odds are you will get hurt from time to time. You may die. Is that a risk you're willing to take?"

For a moment, Judith was quiet, staring down at the chrome table between them. Then she looked up and met Logan's gaze with equal solemnity.

"Yes. Absolutely."

"Okay then. We've got a deal." She offered her hand across the table, and Judith shook it with an easy grin. "Well. Are you sure you've got everything you had at Amy's?"

"Yeah," Judith nodded.

"Do you want to stop by there at all, to say goodbye maybe? We could also drop by your parents' house, if you think there's anything else there you want. It might be months before you come back here again."

Judith shook her head resolutely. "There's nothing I want from them. Besides, I'm not even sure I could get in and out of the house safely."

"I would keep you safe."

She shrugged sheepishly. "Thanks, but that's okay. I don't need to go there. I probably don't need to go to Amy's either. But, uh, I should give her a call, I guess." She pushed herself out of the booth. "I'm just gonna step outside for a minute and call her. I'll be right back."

She turned and walked back out the way they had come. Logan

watched her pull out her phone and bring it up to her face as it rang.

As she settled back in her chair, she noticed a change: the Key had finally gone quiet. No warmth, no insistence. Finally, it was satisfied. Logan had concluded its final task. For the moment, anyway.

By the time Judith got back inside, Sherene had already brought the second round of fries. They both dug into them, munching away in an easy silence.

Of course, Logan still had to figure out how to tell Knatt about this part. He wasn't likely to welcome the idea of a permanent houseguest. But she would just have to cross that bridge when she came to it.

A few minutes later, they left the diner together. Logan placed a final hearty tip on the table behind her, and felt a slight pang of loss as she passed the counter one last time, noticing the giant cinnamon bun still lay encased in glass for anyone to see. But it was best not to dwell.

So she set her mind to the road ahead, instead. She couldn't tell if it was a front or not, but Judith looked happy to be getting back on the bike, despite how it had gone for her before. She lurched when the bike moved again, but she didn't duck her head down. By the time they stopped at their first stoplight, Logan could feel that her fear had started to ebb. And that was just as well. They might need to ride a good long while.

As they crossed the border out of town, Logan felt an uncomfortably familiar tingle in her spine. She'd felt it more than once these past two weeks, but it was stronger now. There was no more denying it.

Someone was watching her.

If you would like to get access to free content and be notified when Tess Adair's next novel is released, please sign up for her mailing list by going to her website at: https://www.tessadair.com/

Authors live and die by the power of the word; if you enjoyed the book, please consider putting a few words into a review wherever you purchased it. The author thanks you!

About the Author

Tess Adair has lived in the Midwest and the Northeast, and currently resides in the Pacific Northwest. She enjoys discovering new cafes, making friends with cats, and not hiking. Follow her on her blog at: https://www.tessadair.com/thebodypolitic/